P9-BYX-111

DEEP DOWN

Also by Deborah Coates

Wide Open

What Makes a River (e-original)

DEEP DOWN

DEBORAH COATES

A TOM DOHERTY ASSOCIATES BOOK TOR® NEW YORK

This is a work of fiction. All of the characters, organizations, and events portrayed in this novel are either products of the author's imagination or are used fictitiously.

DEEP DOWN

Edited by Stacy Hill

A Tor Book
Published by Tom Doherty Associates, LLC
175 Fifth Avenue
New York, NY 10010

www.tor-forge.com

ISBN 978-0-7653-2900-4 (hardcover)
ISBN 978-1-4299-4284-3 (e-book)

First Edition: March 2013

Printed in the United States of America

0 9 8 7 6 5 4 3 2 1

To my own black dogs—you're the best

ACKNOWLEDGMENTS

Novels don't get written by one person, at least mine don't. It turns out they require lots of generous, smart people to provide expertise and support and feedback.

First, belated thanks to two people I neglected to mention in *Wide Open*—Paul Melko, who not only gave me feedback on that book but also read an early version of *Deep Down,* and Mike Mauton, my go-to guy for questions about guns and ammunition and hunting. All mistakes are mine, but if it sounds knowledgeable, I owe it to him.

To my editor, Stacy Hill, thanks for your insight and encouragement. You always make me feel as if it's all going to work, even when there's more work to do.

To my agent, Caitlin Blasdell, who "gets" my books and who does a terrific job of explaining what I'm trying to do and doing so in a way that helps me figure out how to actually do it.

To Marco Palmieri, Eliani Torres, Irene Gallo, and the Tor production team, thank you for keeping me on track, finding my mistakes, and producing a beautiful book.

To Alexis Nixon, thank you. When I see people talking about my book in new and unexpected places, I know your efforts helped them find it.

To the writers at Starry Heaven and Blue Heaven, you are supportive and smart, and this book is far better for your thoughtful analysis and feedback. Thank you. In particular, thanks to Robert Levy, Kris Dikeman, Cassie Alexander, and Paul Melko for reading early drafts of *Deep Down* and helping to uncover the story.

To Sarah Prineas, Greg Van Eekhout, and Jenn Reese, thank you for being all-around awesome and insightful and honest, for reading countless drafts and portions of drafts, for giving me those all-important reality checks, and, most important, for convincing me that this would all be worth it in the end.

As always, thank you to my family, who gave me the background and support to reach this point.

I am grateful every day that I get to write about things I care deeply about—flyover country, rural towns and people, magic, power, and things that might be or could be or are.

DEEP DOWN

1

Hallie Michaels had been up since six, running big round bales of hay out to the cattle and her father's small herd of bison in the far southwest pasture. She was heading back in, thinking about breakfast—toast and scrambled eggs and half a dozen slices of bacon—when a shadow so dark, it felt as if a curtain had been drawn, passed by on her right. She looked up—but there was nothing, not a cloud in the sky—looked back down, and she could see the shadow still, like a black patch on the ground, heading due south.

She stopped the tractor, a brand-new Kubota her father had bought after the old one burned with the equipment shed and everything else in September. Where the shadow—or whatever it was—had passed, the grass looked flat, like it had lain for a month under heavy winter snow. But it was early November and unseasonably warm—there hadn't been a killing frost. She was a quarter mile from the house; the field she was in stretched long toward the horizon. She could see flattened grass all the way out, like something huge had just passed by.

Hallie set the brake on the tractor and hopped down. She looked at the grass, looked at the rest of the field. It was different—wasn't it? She crouched and put her hand out. Her fingers brushed the flattened grass and she was hit by a stab of pain through her skull so fierce, it knocked her over.

Shit.

She said it several more times, only louder and more annoyed. Shit. Shit. Shit.

She hadn't seen a ghost in two months, hadn't had a blinding headache in a week and a half. All that was gone.

Right?

Goddamnit.

She sat for a long moment on the cold, hard ground, sat until the world didn't look like it was rainbow-tinted, until her head felt less likely to split in two.

She imagined herself ignoring it, imagined herself pretending it had never happened. Which, yeah, never actually worked.

As she struggled to her feet, her phone beeped.

Voice mail from her father.

"Hey, you on your way back?" Like this was a regular conversation and she was going to answer him. "Don Pabahar called. Says he hasn't heard from his mom in a couple of days. Asked if one of us could stop over there and check on her. I'm heading into Rapid City. Be gone all morning, looks like. Figured you could do it. Okay? Yeah, talk to you later."

Great.

She checked for other messages as she climbed back on the tractor and started toward the ranch house again. Nothing. Boyd had been back three weeks. They'd been to dinner once, to breakfast twice. This was his first week back in a patrol car since he'd been shot in September. She didn't have any reason to think he would call. She'd picked a fight with him Friday night when he asked her to go to Rapid City with him for dinner, with the idea that maybe they'd stay the night. And she wanted that, she did. But what she wanted was a night, and what Boyd wanted, she was pretty sure, was more.

Right now she didn't have more.

She'd applied for a job running dispatch for a trucking firm in Rapid City, something she could probably do in her sleep after the army, and another job as an apprentice line worker in eastern Minnesota. Neither one of them were quite "it," what she was looking for, but they'd be something. Most days she missed the army so much, it felt like she could taste it. Soldiers griped about the food and the days on watch and the boredom and stupid orders that made no sense, but Hallie'd known who she was when she'd been a soldier. Now she had to figure that out all over again.

She pulled the tractor into the lee of the horse barn, where it sat next to the second tractor, a grain wagon, two ATVs, and an auger, all of which would normally be housed in the big equipment shed, if they had a big equipment shed instead of a concrete slab and stacked lumber for the framing. There was still a slight smell of burnt wood and metal in the air, even though the old shed had burned more than two months ago, burnt to the ground in what her father insisted must have been a freak lightning storm—came out of nowhere, he'd tell anyone who asked. Hallie'd tried to explain about Martin Weber, about the things he'd done. Not that it did any good. Hallie's father was pretty much a master at not hearing what he didn't want to hear.

It started to snow as she walked up to the house, light dry flakes that scattered across the ground like dust from an old ghost town—first snow of the season, even though it was already mid-November, grass still green, which Hallie couldn't help but think was fallout from Martin Weber messing with the weather.

She knocked her boots on the doorjamb before she walked into the kitchen, where she was greeted by the smell of fresh coffee and a note that said, *Stuff in the oven.* Which, when she looked, proved to be scrambled eggs and bacon.

Before she sat down to eat, she called Boyd, then hung up without leaving a message. She wanted to talk to him about the shadow she'd seen, wanted to talk to him, just . . . wanted him. And all that was good, was fine, really. The problem was, she didn't want it to hold her here, didn't want him to expect that it would. And it wasn't fair—to him or her—to be calling him every five minutes.

She dialed Brett Fowker, her oldest friend from high school. "Want to come into town tonight?" she said when Brett answered. "We could meet at Cleary's for dinner, head out to the Bob for a drink after."

"I—well—" Brett fumbled for words. Hallie frowned because that wasn't like her. "I've got a date. In the City. Tonight. I've got a date tonight is what I mean."

"Okay," Hallie said, half a question. "Another time."

She hadn't seen a lot of Brett since September. Hallie liked to think it was because she'd been busy, though she hadn't. Maybe it was Brett who'd been busy, because she was getting a master's in psychology somewhere in Rapid City and, though Hallie didn't really pay attention, she figured there were classes and exams and other things involved. Brett talked about going to the University of Chicago next year for a PhD, but Hallie couldn't picture Brett anywhere but in the West River, training cutting horses with her father and, well, being there.

Things changed, though. That's what she told herself. Hell, Hallie'd never expected to die in Afghanistan, never expected to come back, never expected ghosts. Life was mostly what you didn't expect; that's what Hallie'd been learning lately.

She finished her breakfast and an hour later had washed and changed and was in her pickup headed down the long drive from the ranch house to the county blacktop. Delores Pabahar, known to all and sundry as Pabby, was her father's closest neighbor to the south. Pabby was . . . well, Pabby. Hallie hadn't seen her in years, except briefly—the way you did see people—at Dell's funeral.

At the end of the long driveway, her cell phone rang. Hallie looked at the number before she answered. Not Boyd.

"Hallie? Well, goddamn! Don't you ever answer your email?"

It was Kate Matousek, whom Hallie'd first met at Fort Leonard Wood at the end of basic training and then again at a forward base outside Kabul. Kate had been a medic. She was also a hiker and a mountain climber who would take her leave anywhere there were hills to climb, who'd wanted the war in Afghanistan to end so she could hike the Hindu Kush.

"There'll be land mines and bandits and probably rebel soldiers," Hallie'd told her.

"I don't know," Kate had said. "It might be worth it."

She was supposed to have been with Hallie's platoon on that trail the day Hallie had died, but she switched at the last minute with another medic, the one who'd brought Hallie back from the dead, and she rotated out before Hallie'd been released from the hospital.

"What's up?" Hallie asked. She was never one for wasting time on small talk.

"Heard you were out," Kate said. "Thought you might be looking for work."

"I might be," Hallie said cautiously, because if Kate wanted her to climb mountains in the Hindu Kush, she could look for someone else. She didn't mind heights, kind of liked them, actually, but she could think of easier ways of getting killed than going back to Afghanistan.

"Look," Kate said, "I'm starting a business with my brother. Well, he's been doing this for a while, but he's finally going out on his own and I'm going in with him. Painting water towers. He's got all the equipment, got a bunch of references—the guy he worked for is retiring—but we need a job estimator. Figured you might be looking for something."

"Wait. What?"

"You're not afraid of heights, right?"

"No." Because she might not be as crazy as Kate, but she wasn't afraid to climb a water tower.

"We need someone who can get up to speed quick," Kate said. "There's a lot of travel, a little danger, plenty of variety, and better pay than you ever saw in the army. What do you say?"

Hallie'd thought she'd leap right in, both feet, when an offer came, but she didn't. "Think about it," Kate said when the silence stretched a half second too long. She hung up without saying good-bye.

Hallie called Boyd again, like her first thought was to tell him, which pissed her off a little, but not enough to disconnect. "Hey," she said when his voice mail picked up. "I'll be in town later. Can you get free? Call me."

She put the truck in gear again and turned right onto the highway. Just past the drive, Jake Javinovich's big old Buick sat by the side of the road with the hood up. Hallie slowed, but she didn't see Jake, who was a mechanic over at Big Dog's Auto. She figured he must have gotten a ride from someone or he'd walked up to the house before she got back, and her father had taken him into town.

Ten minutes later, she turned onto the rough lane up to Pabby's ranch house. Halfway up the lane, there was a low spot that washed out every spring. Hallie dropped into second, and the tail end of her pickup slid sideways along old ruts and morning-frosted grass. Then the tires caught, the engine revved up half a note, and she moved on.

She drove around the final shallow curve and stopped with the front of her pickup pointing toward the main ranch house. A skinny black dog slunk across the drive in front of her. It stopped when it reached the far side just short of a trio of scrub trees. A second dog, as skinny and lank as the first, settled next to it, tongue lolling and sharp teeth gleaming.

Hallie studied them, the truck idling almost silently. As far as she knew, Pabby didn't have a dog, hadn't had one since her old collie died ten years ago. "They just die in the end," she'd told a thirteen-year-old Hallie. "What's the point?" Which was a weird thing to tell a kid who'd lost her mother two years before. Not that Pabby worried about things like that. Which had always been the part of her Hallie liked.

But maybe things had changed—Hallie'd been gone, after all. Maybe these were Pabby's new dogs. Maybe these dogs were why Don didn't come out and check on his mother himself. The thought of that, of Don sitting in his car while dogs loped around it in a large circle and barked at him, made Hallie grin. She put the truck back in gear, pulled past the dogs, and on up into the yard.

She was barely out of the truck when Pabby appeared on the front porch with a rifle in her hands. "Do you see 'em?" she demanded. No, How the hell are you? Or, Been a long time, there. Or even, Who are you and what are you doing here? But then, Hallie wasn't much for that herself.

"What?" she asked.

"Those damn dogs," Pabby said, stepping off the porch. Pabby was about seventy-five by Hallie's reckoning, though she looked younger. Her hair, originally a glorious red gold, hadn't so much grayed as faded. She wore a denim shirt starched and ironed within an inch of its life over a red T-shirt, blue jeans, and a broken-down pair of boots. "There's a couple more of 'em around back," Pabby said as she approached Hallie.

"They're not yours?" Hallie asked, walking half-backwards to keep an eye on the dogs as she crossed the yard. The two dogs from the drive were now at the edge of the yard, one of them standing with its head dropped, like a border collie watching a flock of sheep, the other flopped on the ground, its tongue hanging out, as if it had just run a hard race.

Pabby leaned in close. "You can see 'em?"

"Well . . . yeah."

"Pfft!" Pabby blew breath out her nose and lowered her rifle. "Don says he can't see 'em. I can't tell anymore if he's trying to drive me crazy or he's the one who's nuts."

Hallie looked at the dogs again. "He can't see them? How long have they been here?"

"Come on up to the house," Pabby said by way of an answer. "We should talk." She didn't say more until they were sitting on the porch on rusting patio chairs with steaming mugs of coffee set on an incongruous white iron and glass table. Despite the early-morning frost on the ground, it was warm for November. The wind had a penetrating bite, though, and Hallie was grateful for the warmth of her barn coat. It was a little cold to be sitting outside on the front porch, but Hallie was okay with it. She wanted to keep an eye on those dogs; she figured Pabby was thinking the same.

"I saw the first one three weeks ago," Pabby said. "I thought it was after the chickens. Slinking around like it was looking for something. I fired over its head and it just sat down and looked at me. Like it couldn't care less. I knew something was up right then. Because that ain't normal." Pabby glared across the yard where the two dogs remained, watching them. "The next week there were two more of them."

"Have they attacked you?" Hallie asked.

"Damn things," Pabby said. Hallie wasn't sure if that meant yes or no.

"And Don can't see them?"

Jesus.

"So he says." She paused, squinted like she was staring into the sun. "I expect he's talking to doctors all over the City. Maybe even Chicago. Who the hell knows with Don. Thinks I'm senile. He's wanted me off the ranch for years."

"To sell it?"

"Hell, there's no market for this place. It's too damn small and it's got water problems. Maybe your daddy would buy it, but not unless he got a damn good deal. No, he wants me to come live in Rapid City with him and Gloria and the kids. Drive me crazy. I've lived on this ranch nearly my whole life."

Hallie'd always thought Don Pabahar was a bore and more than a little self-righteous. It didn't surprise her at all that he wanted to order Pabby's life the same way he ordered everything else. It did surprise her that he thought it would work.

"He send you out here to check on me, did he?"

Hallie grinned. "You think he's waiting for me to come back and tell him you're crazy?"

"You know, he would hate it if I actually lived with him. He never thinks ahead about things like that."

Hallie took a long swallow of the scalding hot coffee. It was bitter and strong, like it had been brewing for days. A muscle twitched along her jawline when she swallowed. She stood and stepped off the porch.

"You want the rifle?" Pabby asked.

Hallie shook her head. They didn't act like feral dogs, out to grab a few chickens. They didn't crowd the house and hadn't come toward Hallie when she stepped out of the pickup. They acted like they were waiting for something.

The dogs didn't move as she approached, though she spotted a third one slinking around the corner of the old horse barn. Grass rustled in its wake. That meant it was solid, right? That it wasn't a ghost. But if it were a real dog—a feral dog, say—why couldn't Don see them? Why could she and Pabby?

2

When Hallie was within ten yards of the two black dogs, she stopped. The third dog crept across the farthest edge of the yard. Hallie took a step back and watched. It didn't try to circle behind her, though she was completely in the open. As it fetched up beside the other two, a fourth dog came out of the grass to her right and lay down with its head on the ground, watching her. A few inches in front of its nose, a strip of faded plaid cloth tied to a few strands of prairie grass fluttered in the breeze.

"What do you want?" Hallie asked. Not because she thought the dogs would answer, more that she didn't know what else to do.

"So."

Sibilant, like a snake, the word startled her so much—not least because it was directly inside her head—that she stumbled backwards a couple of steps. Stopped herself and raised a hand quick before Pabby came off the porch with her rifle.

"You see us." Again, in her head, soft and the *s*'s hissing, like a sharp blade through butter.

"Well . . . yeah," Hallie said. Its voice was like an itch she couldn't scratch. Not scary, really, more mildly unpleasant. "What are you?"

"Harbingers." The word dragged out like a midnight breath of wind.

"Harbingers of what?"

"Death."

Hallie backed up a step. Death. It was all about death these days, had been since that single moment on that mountain in Afghanistan. Sometimes it hit her like this, like all death since then, even Dell—even—was her fault. That she was alive and other people paid.

She cleared her throat. "Seriously?" she said. She guessed that would be why she could see them, like ghosts. "So you, what? You came to kill Pabby? She looks plenty healthy to me."

The dogs were silent. Or maybe they were talking to one another, because the one she thought had been talking to her turned to the dog next to it and cocked its head, ears pricked, like it was listening to something. It turned back to Hallie.

"Can't," it finally said. It pawed the ground. "Can't get past."

"This isn't how we die," she said. She should know.

The dog rose to its feet and stretched, head low and back arched. It stretched one back leg and then the other; then it sank to the ground once more. "We're not for everyone," it said. "We're sent for." It drew out the world "sent" like a caress.

The dogs were a combination of eerie stillness and movement, one of them always in motion, the others like statues. Sometimes only their eyes moved. And their eyes . . . they flashed red when they caught the sunlight just right. Mostly they were a gray blue, like winter skies.

"How do I make you go away?" Hallie asked.

The dog made a sound that she finally decided was a laugh, echoing, like all of them joined in. "We never go away," it said. "We become more."

"If it's not her time, then you can't take her," Hallie said.

"Who says?"

"I do."

More huffing laughter.

Okay, it was true she had no idea how to do it. She hadn't even known they existed until ten minutes ago. It didn't mean she wouldn't try.

She watched them as they slipped into the prairie grass. The one who'd been talking to her turned at the last moment and looked at her, like it was studying her. Because she could see them. Because she was going to stop them.

She turned away and walked back up to the porch, sat down heavily at the patio table, and took a gulp of cold coffee.

"Well?" Pabby demanded.

"Huh," Hallie said. "Have you talked to them?"

"Talked to them? No. They're dogs."

Hallie leaned back in her chair. "I think you know they're not."

A long silence. Pabby laid her rifle up against the side of the house, gathered the mugs, and went inside. Hallie waited. Five minutes passed. Finally Pabby reemerged, set a fresh cup of coffee in front of Hallie, and sat down again.

"Someone told me you died. Over there."

"What?" That wasn't what Hallie'd been expecting at all.

"Yup. They said you died and came back and you see things now. Things other people don't see."

"*Who* said?" Because it wasn't like she told anyone. Ever. Except Boyd. And maybe Brett.

Pabby made a vague gesture. The sleeves on her denim shirt were rolled up, and there was a gauze bandage on her left arm just above the wrist. "I hear things," she said.

"You don't just hear things like that. My whole life I never heard something like that. About anyone. Ever."

"I been around a bit longer than you have."

Which was hard to argue with, seeing how Pabby was seventy-five or so and Hallie was twenty-three, but still . . . "Do you say shit like that to Don? Because it's no wonder he thinks you're crazy."

Pabby burst out laughing, coughed harshly into her hand, then sobered. "I was sorry about your sister," she said, which was so out of nowhere, Hallie startled like a horse at a dropped tree limb. Pabby laid a hand on hers. "People used to talk about the two of you in town. Did you know that? Because you were always a little different. Not," she added, "like what we're talking about here, like those dogs or like dying and coming back. Not like that. Like girls without a mother. Like you were a little wild. Like they wished they could be you, but they weren't."

After a moment, she went on. "Dell was the brightest thing I ever saw," she said. "Not bright like smart. Like the sun."

"Yeah." Hallie wasn't really surprised at how much talking about Dell still hurt, but not being surprised didn't make it hurt less.

"Because you were always the smart one."

"What?"

"You're going to help me with this problem, aren't you?" Pabby asked, like that had been the subject all along.

"What exactly is the problem?"

Pabby scratched a thoughtful hand across her chin. She put both hands on her coffee mug and looked across the yard past the old barn, across the prairie toward the far horizon.

"My mother had the sight. Or said she did. Said it was pretty worthless except for one thing. She knew when anyone was going to die." She looked intently at Hallie, like she was gauging what Hallie thought of that. Hallie just looked back. It wasn't like she hadn't heard weirder things recently. "She used to write things down on cards and then seal them in envelopes and put them on the top shelf in the kitchen. Then sometimes, when we got the paper, or a letter from a relative, she'd get down one of those envelopes and open it up and show me the card inside."

She paused, took a sip from her coffee. She set the mug down carefully before continuing. "I always thought it was the other kind of magic. Like magicians. Like pulling a rabbit out of a hat. That somehow she'd changed that card in that envelope when I wasn't looking. 'Cept she never laughed. Never acted like it was any kind of funny at all."

"She told you when you were going to die?" Whose mother would do that?

"I asked her."

"Jesus. You did?"

Pabby smiled, a quick grin that Hallie remembered from when she was a kid. She'd been a little afraid of Pabby when she was five or six, and she'd felt funny about it, because Hallie hadn't been a kid who was afraid of things. She'd climbed trees and launched herself out of haylofts and tried to ride the biggest horse in the corral. But she never wanted to be around Pabby, though Pabby hadn't done anything except give her peppermint candies and lemonade.

"She put it in an envelope. Told me it was up to me what I did with it, but she'd recommend I burn it. I forgot about it for a long time. But then, I turned sixty-five. Addie'd died ten years before. I'd lost Don—oh hell, I'd lost Don when he was ten years old and took off down the drive with his suitcase because he wanted to go live in Chicago with the Bears. I figured I didn't have anything to lose. And I could make plans."

"And what?" Hallie asked. One of the black dogs had reemerged from the tall grass. It sat, head up, staring at the house. Hallie felt its gaze like an itch along her jawline.

Pabby shrugged, like she was embarrassed. "Ninety," she said.

Hallie looked at her for a minute because sometimes she couldn't believe the conversations she'd had in the last couple of months. "And she was always right? Your mother?"

Pabby fiddled with the handle of her coffee mug. "Sometimes magic works," she said. She shrugged. "And sometimes it don't. Magic is small. I don't think you understand how small it is. When it affects people like my mother, it's one thing—one small thing—and it's easy to say, well, that's just weird. That's not magic. People shrug and move on."

Hallie didn't think Pabby had any idea about magic. About how big it could be if someone was willing to cross the line, willing to spill blood. Magic was not to be messed with. The supernatural, though, like ghosts and, she guessed, black dogs, the supernatural came whether you wanted it to or not. At least that was Hallie's experience.

"Okay," Hallie said, not because she was agreeing with anything, especially not that she had to learn this stuff, but more to say that she understood what Pabby was saying. "But then why are the dogs here?"

"I believe they have been misinformed." Pabby looked straight ahead when she said it, like she was speaking directly to the dogs.

"Seriously? Who do you think they want instead of you?" Because it better not be her father or—

"They don't kill," Pabby said unexpectedly. "They're—"

"Yeah, I know, harbingers."

Pabby rose abruptly and went into the house again. Hallie put her head in her hand because this whole thing wasn't anything she'd expected. Seeing ghosts—she'd mostly gotten used to that. She could figure out their unfinished business, send them on their way. But if she was going to be seeing harbingers of death . . . And what did that mean, anyway? Because they didn't come for everyone. If they did, she'd have seen them. Too bad too. It sure would have been handy in September. She'd have worried a lot less about Martin if there'd been black dogs following him around.

She didn't raise her head when Pabby came back out on the porch, when she refilled her mug with another round of steaming dark coffee. The smell, thick and pungent, tickled at Hallie's nose. Finally, she rubbed an eye and picked up the mug again.

"What do you want from me?" she asked.

"I want you to make them go away. They can't touch me right now, but I can't leave either. And there's another one every couple of days. It's only a matter of time."

Hallie grabbed on to one statement, like if that made sense, everything else would too. "Why can't they touch you?" The dog had said it too, Can't get past.

"I told you my mother was a little . . . 'off' in her last years. After Daddy died—and she knew *when,* you understand—well, after that she got convinced she'd be able to cheat death herself."

"But that's not—" Hallie was going to say it wasn't possible, but wasn't she proof you could?

"Addie and I were living in Sioux City back then. Only been married about a year. My mother was just fifty or so at the time, but like I said, she'd gotten . . . strange."

Hallie raised an eyebrow. "Is there a point to this?" she asked, because Pabby and this story could take all day.

Pabby stared at her. "Did the army make you rude?"

"Sorry." Which she wasn't. "But I've always been rude." Hallie stood, walked to the edge of the porch, and scanned the fields. Only one dog still watched the house, but she knew the others were out there.

Pabby made a sound that might have been a laugh. "I tried to convince Momma to live with us or move to town. Instead she sold all the cattle and used the money to bury an iron hex all around the yard, the close-in corral, the house, and the barn."

"What?" Now Hallie was interested.

"She was all excited that year when we came home for Thanksgiving. Didn't tell us why, but she said she'd figured it all out and everything was going to be fine." Pabby leaned forward. "She thought she could cheat death, you see. Because they won't cross iron. Never knew who 'they' were, back then, thought it was just crazy. But—" She gestured at the spot where the dogs had been a few minutes before. "—you can see." She took a long swallow of coffee. "She hired folks—we found this out later, you understand—to weld iron rails and bury them. There's a great big hex circle under the whole yard, the near corral, and a bit of the pasture out back. Those dogs can't cross it."

Hallie resumed her seat at the table. "But she's dead, right?" she asked. "Your mother's been dead for years." Because Hallie didn't even remember her, so she must have died before Hallie's mother, before they used to come and visit—buy eggs and sit on the wide front porch.

Pabby scraped her thumbnail across the curve of her mug's handle. "We didn't know about the hex—Addie and I. And I'm not sure we'd have believed it if we had. Your daddy, of course, was young at the time, but he got in on the deal—she hired seven people to cut and weld and bury all that iron. And she thought she'd done it—cheated death. Her day—the day she'd seen herself die, clear and true as any of them—that day came and went and she was still alive.

"Of course, she couldn't go into town or come visit us in Sioux City or anything. It wore on her."

"What happened?"

"Near as I can tell, one day she just walked outside the lines."

Hallie rubbed a hand across her face. She wasn't confused. The story was clear and she'd seen enough that she could believe it. Or believe it was possible. Still . . .

"I'm not sure what you're asking." Though she was. Knew exactly what she was asking: Solve this for me.

"Solve this for me." Because Pabby wasn't any better than Hallie at beating around the bush.

"What makes you think I'll be any better at it than you?"

Pabby looked at her with narrowed eyes. "Because I care about staying alive and getting those dogs away from me. You care about stopping bad things."

"I could be leaving at any time," Hallie pointed out. Because she had plans. She had a job offer.

Pabby made that sound that wasn't quite a laugh again. "All right," she said. "But as you're still around right now, how about it?"

Hallie frowned. She had a life to figure out. And yet, she did want to stop bad things—in this case, to stop Pabby from dying before she should. Because it wasn't fair. She knew too many people who'd died too early. And, anyway, who wouldn't? If a bad thing crossed your path, shouldn't you stop it? If you could? It wasn't like she went looking for trouble.

"I have no idea where to start," she finally said.

"You will," Pabby told her.

3

Back in her pickup, Hallie pulled out her cell phone and dialed from the history; Kate answered on the second ring. "How long?" she asked, didn't bother with hello.

"Before I need an answer?" Kate asked, not even faintly confused about who was calling or what she was asking. "Sooner, the better," she said. "Here's the deal: I won't offer it to anyone else for a week. After that . . . well, it's a business, not charity for ex-soldiers."

"Thanks," Hallie said, and disconnected. She could see herself in that job, climbing water towers in Colorado or Minnesota or southern Missouri, gauging wind and weather. It would fit her. But she'd take the week. Fix this thing for Pabby. Get out clean. Or get out, anyway. It might already be too late to get out clean.

She was halfway down the drive, thinking at least black dogs were better than ghosts, when something dark and fast hurtled toward the truck from her right. She slammed on the brakes. The truck slewed sideways. She twisted, arms raised, and braced for impact.

A sudden flurry, sound like a sharp rush of wind, hot breath on her face, and a dog sat on the seat next to her.

What the hell?

Because it had just jumped into her truck through the window. The closed window.

The dog looked at her, panting a little, like it was just an ordinary dog, like it was just enjoying the ride.

"Don't you have to be invited in or something?" Hallie asked, ignoring the painful thump of her heart against her breastbone, the taste of adrenaline on her tongue.

The dog laughed, like a breathy whisper. "Want to watch," it said. Then it circled three times and lay down on the seat, curled up with its nose touching its tail.

Hallie lowered her arms. The dog looked like it was already asleep, like it spent its life riding in trucks with girls. After a minute, she shrugged and put the truck in gear and headed down the drive. This was obviously the way things were now. And what else was she going to do?

It was almost noon when she got back to the ranch, the sky full of low gray clouds that hinted at a winter that had not yet come. The air was damp when she got out of the pickup, and though it felt a dozen degrees colder than the forty-three the thermometer showed, it was still unseasonably warm.

The dog slipped out the truck door while she was closing it and followed her up to the house.

"Jesus," she said, irritated. "Why are you here?"

"Told you," the dog responded. "Watching."

"Don't you have someplace you need to be?"

The dog looked at her. "No."

She entered the house on a rush of warmer air, the kitchen smelling like hand cleaner and straw. The dog didn't follow.

Her father was in the dining room with a set of blueprints spread out in front of him, making notes along the edges.

"You want lunch?" she asked.

"I could eat," he said.

Hallie pulled out bread, milk, sliced roast beef, some chips from on top of the refrigerator, and lettuce that was not quite too old. With the silence of long habit, they stood side by side at the counter and made sandwiches. Her father took his plate back to the dining room table and the blueprints he'd been working on. Hallie followed, sitting down across from him.

After a couple of bites of sandwich and a few more penciled notes, her father set his pencil aside and looked at her, which, for him, was a question: Yeah, do you want something?

"Do you remember Pabby's mother?" Hallie asked.

Her father took a long swallow of milk, set the glass down, and tilted his head back, like it would make it easier to remember. "Oh, hell," he said, "she died—I don't know—it must be forty years ago now."

"Did you know about the iron rails?" she asked.

Her father had started to lean back in his chair, but he stopped at Hallie's question and leaned forward again. "The hex?"

"That's what Pabby calls it," Hallie agreed. "How come I never heard anything about it?"

Her father shrugged and this time he did lean back, plucked a potato chip from his plate, and chewed on it before answering. "Not that much to tell," he said. "She was always a little—different, I'd guess you'd say, Pabby's mother. Kind of—" He paused, like he was searching for the right words. "—I mean, she was always a nice lady. Gracious. You don't see that much around here." He stared at the framed pictures above the dining room sideboard. "Well, I mean there's no call for it. Gracious doesn't get the calves out of the rain, does it?"

Hallie unbuttoned her shirt cuffs and rolled up the sleeves, stuck her elbows on the table, and leaned forward. "Did you help build it?" she asked.

"Oh, yeah." Her father drained his milk, then set the glass down with a thump on the table. "Was a hell of a thing. Montifall—her husband, you know. That was Pabby's name before she got married—Montifall. Anyway, he'd died the year before, and everyone thought she'd move to town. Then one day she came driving over and asked Davey and me if we wanted to earn some extra money." He looked toward the kitchen as if he were looking at something much farther away. "Well, hell—we did, you know. I was only sixteen. Davey was, let's see, twenty—getting ready to go in the army come fall and not enough here to keep both of us and your granddad busy."

"So you buried a bunch of iron rails in her yard."

"Didn't hurt anybody." He sniffed. "She paid good and she was easy to work for. It wasn't iron, though. Not exactly," he added. "You can't put pure iron in the ground like that and expect it to last. Steel rails with a high iron content. But basically steel."

"Did she ever tell you why?"

"Said it was a hex. Keep things out. Hell, I don't know. People can do what they want, as far as I'm concerned."

He looked at Hallie. "What's Pabby want, telling you that old story?" he asked. "I haven't heard anyone even mention those rails in twenty years."

"I don't know," Hallie said, because what was she going to tell him? That there were black dogs circling Pabby's yard? "You know she likes to talk."

Her father looked at her close for several long seconds, then hitched one shoulder up and settled back in his chair. "Yeah," he said finally. "She's a talker."

They were still sitting at the table when the phone rang. Hallie didn't even wait for her father, just got up and answered it. She wondered how often he'd just let it ring when he was alone, after she and Dell had both left.

"This is Buehl over to the Templeton ag supply. Bearing kit for that Big Bear Vance bought off Cal Littlejohn come in. You can come pick it up anytime today or tomorrow."

"Thanks," Hallie said.

Having said what he'd called to say, Forest Buehl hung up without saying good-bye. He hadn't said hello either; figured, like half the men Hallie knew, that the two were just wasted words tacked on to conversations to make them longer.

"Buehl says those parts are in," she told her father, who was deep in analyzing the blueprints again when she went back into the dining room.

"Yeah, okay. Thanks," he said. Like she had already told him she would pick them up.

"I could pick them up," she said. Because he could ask. It wasn't so impossible.

He looked up from his papers and grinned. He looked young, just-starting-out young, not-a-care-in-the-world young, like he hadn't been in years. "If you have time to pick those parts up, that'd be real helpful," he said.

Hallie tapped the blueprints. "It's just a pole barn," she said, "not the Empire State Building."

"Might as well add a few improvements," he said, tapping his pencil on the paper in front of him.

She was halfway out of the room again when she stopped and turned back, shoved her hands in the pockets of her jeans, and leaned against the doorjamb. "Got a job offer today," she said.

Her father put his pencil down. "Yeah?" He waited.

"Not around here," she said.

"Yeah," he said, like that was only to be expected. "Does it pay good?"

"Pretty good," she said.

"You should take it."

"Yeah. I could leave it till spring," she said, though she wasn't actually sure that was true. "If you want help for the winter." She gestured at the blueprints. "To rebuild."

Her father looked at her with something that almost resembled a scowl. "I'll survive," he said. He put his hands on the table, preparatory to rising. "You want to stay, stay. But this ranch isn't going to get any bigger." He went into the kitchen. Hallie could hear him grab a hat and jacket off the pegs by the door, heard the kitchen door open and close and the muted slap of the storm door.

Yeah, she thought, okay.

She went upstairs thinking about what she'd get if she stayed: cold sandwiches for lunch, picking up parts in town, and a ranch too small to support either one of them, let alone both.

At the top of the stairs, something cold brushed the back of her neck—arctic-ice cold, blizzard-winter cold—she knew it was a ghost, but when she turned, there was nothing there.

She grabbed her keys and a jacket, shoved her cell phone in her pocket, and realized on her way back down the stairs that Boyd had never called her back.

Damn him.

4

A half-hour drive to Templeton and it took her five minutes to pick up the parts. No sign of the dog when she'd come back outside to her truck or on the drive over. Maybe it had decided she wasn't all that interesting after all.

Forest Buehl, who was maybe three years older than she was, claimed they'd never met, which wasn't true. He'd worked in the ag supply since he was fourteen, and she'd been there plenty of times before she left home.

"Nah," he said, "I'd remember."

"Think back," Hallie said, waiting for him to hand her the last box.

After a minute, as if he'd actually tried to think back, he shrugged and handed her the box. He wasn't bad-looking—broad shouldered and tall—but maybe not the sharpest pin in the cushion.

"Say," he said, leaning against the side of her truck so she'd have to go around him to get to the driver's door, not stopping her on purpose, just that he couldn't imagine she wouldn't take the time to visit a little, now that she was here. "We do a bowling and beer thing here most Saturday nights. Softball in the summer, of course. It's great to get new folks, if you want to come."

"Okay," Hallie said. He'd finally moved back two steps and her hand was already on the door. "Sounds good." Though she wouldn't actually do it.

It wasn't that she didn't want to do those things or might not enjoy them; it was that everything, every new person she met and liked, every task she took on was like another nail in what wasn't a coffin, but sure felt like a trap. And she wasn't staying.

She wasn't. Maybe she hadn't given Kate an answer yet, but it wasn't because she didn't know what the answer would be. What it had to be.

Still, she had a week before Kate needed an answer. A week to work on Pabby's problem. To work on other things, like what she'd leave behind and what that meant. Maybe it would be simple, the thing with Pabby. Right. Maybe all of it would just be as easy as pie.

On the main street out of Templeton headed south, she noticed a faded sign. She'd seen it a hundred times before, but never stopped:

BEYOND THE VEIL.

FUTURES. FORTUNES. GLIMPSES OF THE AFTERLIFE.

10–5 EVERY DAY. EXCEPT FRIDAY AFTERNOONS.

ALL DAY SATURDAY. AND TUESDAY MORNINGS.

Past the sign, set back at the edge of a large gravel parking lot was a 1940s ranch house with a shiny new blue tin roof and a front porch that slanted forward, like it was trying to separate itself from the house. Half the parking lot and a side yard of mowed weeds and three old oak trees were surrounded by a four-foot chain-link fence with a sign that read DANGER: PIT BULL next to the gate. There were three outbuildings behind the house, an equipment shed and a couple of grain-storage buildings, as well as some old automobiles, a school bus painted lime green, and an old red and yellow Case tricycle tractor with one front wheel off.

She pulled in near the house and parked. Her truck was the only vehicle in the lot. As she walked up the dusty cracked sidewalk, a small white and tan terrier with a patch of black fur around one eye charged the fence and barked at her. The only other dog Hallie could see lay next to one of the oak trees. It wagged its tail without lifting its head. It wasn't a pit bull either.

COME ON IN, the sign at the door said. So Hallie did. She wasn't entirely sure why she'd stopped or what use it would be. But the information she needed wasn't the sort of thing that could be found on the Internet. She'd learned that in September. And maybe someone who claimed to see "Glimpses of the Afterlife" knew something that could help.

The front door led straight into the living room, which was furnished with a love seat, two chairs, and a battered oak coffee table all on one side of the room. On the other side, on a brown sisal rug with purple stars stenciled in a border along the edge, sat a wooden card table and three folding chairs. Underneath the windows was an old metal lateral filing cabinet that looked like it had been freshly painted. The doorway to the rest of the house was covered by a thin red curtain that didn't quite hang to the floor.

She heard movement behind the curtain, and a man emerged. He was tall and thin, maybe in his forties, dressed in old jeans, battered work boots, and a dark brown work shirt. His hair was flat against his head, and though his face was mostly tan, his forehead was pale.

"Fortune read?" he said.

"What?"

"Are you here to have your fortune read?" he repeated.

"I just have some questions," Hallie said.

The man gestured her toward the card table. "Have a seat," he said, and sat opposite her.

Hallie looked at him. He wasn't what she'd expected—not old or a woman or wearing an armful of bracelets and a shawl. Plus, he looked familiar. "Aren't you Laddie Kennedy?" she asked.

"Yup," he said. "That's me."

"And you read fortunes?"

Laddie shrugged. "It's a sideline."

The Kennedys had lived ten miles north of the Michaelses until their ranch went under six years ago. Laddie and his brother Tom sold up to someone from out of state just ahead of the bank, and Hallie thought they'd both left for Rapid City or Kansas City or someplace there were jobs.

"Can you actually read fortunes or do you just make things up?" she asked.

Laddie, who'd picked up a deck of cards and started shuffling them, stopped midshuffle and looked at her. "I don't know," he said.

"You don't know?"

He was quiet for a minute, not like no one had ever asked him that question before, though Hallie would have bet that no one had. More like, he was getting the words straight in his head, like that was just the way he did things.

"I make things up," he finally said. "But then, some of it happens. So"—he flipped four cards out in front of him—"I don't know, you tell me. Am I just that lucky or is it something else?"

Hallie had just that morning learned that Pabby's mother knew when people were going to die; Boyd had dreams that turned out to be about the future, so she wasn't going to say one way or the other, because in her experience either one was possible. "And glimpses of the afterlife?" she asked. "Fake or real?"

Laddie picked up the cards in front of him and put them back in the deck, cut it, and left one half on the table. He shuffled the other half and laid out four more cards. "I heard you see ghosts," he said.

Hallie scowled. You didn't even have to tell people things anymore. "I've seen a couple." Which was almost not exactly a lie.

Laddie gathered up the cards he'd laid out, put them on the stack on the table, then joined the whole set to the cards in his hand.

"Do you know anything about black dogs?" Hallie asked.

Laddie stopped shuffling. "Harbingers?"

"Yeah, those."

He looked out the window, like he thought there might be a bunch outside. "Never seen one," he said. "But I've heard that if you can see them, then the reapers are coming."

Hallie felt a sharp pain, like a skewer through her right eye. She rubbed her hand hard across her face.

"You all right?" Laddie asked.

"Fine," she said. "Is there a way to make them go away?"

"What? The reapers?"

"Well, black dogs, for now," Hallie said. "Just black dogs." She hoped.

Laddie shrugged. "I can ask," he said.

"You can ask?"

Laddie turned away from the window. Hallie could see something that looked like desperation in his eyes. "Sometimes dead people talk to me."

"What, like ghosts?" Because they never talked to her.

"Not ghosts. People on the other side," he said. "Dead people."

"The other side of what?" How had she never known that people could predict death and talk to the dead and whatever else was possible? How could all that be right here and she hadn't known? But then, maybe she just hadn't looked and wouldn't have believed it anyway.

"The line between life and death," Laddie said.

Hallie sighed, like she'd stepped on soft ground and was still sinking. "Okay," she said. "That'd be great. If you would ask."

He told her it might take a couple days and he would call. She gave him her cell number and got his in return. She paid him twenty dollars, which would be a bargain if he actually found some answers. "I'm on the Internet too," he said. "You can email."

She was at the front door when he said, "Hallie Michaels."

She turned.

He seemed to be studying the name and number she'd written down for him. He looked up. "You should take that job," he said.

A couple miles outside Templeton, Hallie turned onto SR54, then a mile later onto old CR 7.

You should take that job.

Hallie was and wasn't skeptical of the things she'd seen in the last several months. She'd gone her whole life not believing in ghosts or harbingers of death or blood magic. But when she saw them right in front of her, she didn't spend much time denying them. What was the point? They were right there, cold or talking or trying to kill her. Accepting them was actually the easy route.

But what Laddie did—or claimed he did—all she could see was him, not the dead people, all she heard was what he told her. It didn't prove anything. It couldn't.

And yet, he knew about the offer from Kate, or knew something. It was like it had been when she stopped there in the first place, a chance, the chance that he actually did know what he was talking about. And she was taking it.

There was a whine in the engine of the ten-year-old pickup, and she entertained herself for several minutes, trying to figure out what it was and when it was audible, more pleased than she should have been to have something concrete to tackle. She'd about decided it was the fan belt when she saw something in the intersection a mile up the road.

She slowed, then stopped, pulled over onto gravel at the side of the road, but left the engine running. It looked as if a grain truck had T-boned a car, the side of the car buckled in and half under the front of the truck. A heavy one-ton truck and a small two-door red coupe. It never stood a chance—the coupe—but they should have seen each other. It was fall, everything gone brown, crops not tall enough to obscure the intersection—wouldn't happen at this intersection anyway, county road to county road, wide shoulders all around.

It was quiet everywhere, except for the low rumble of Hallie's own pickup engine. Hallie approached the car first. There was no one inside. Which was odd because the way the car was shoved tight up underneath the grain truck, the dashboard crumpled downward and the steering wheel smashed, there was no way a driver could have gotten out.

But there was no driver. No blood. No sign that anyone had been inside when the truck hit it. And maybe that was it. Maybe they'd seen it coming. But if that was the case, where were they?

Hallie crossed to the grain truck, hopped up on the runner. The driver's-side window was open, a half-eaten sandwich perched on the passenger seat and a take-out cup of coffee in the cup holder. She jumped down, looked around. There was nothing here. The closest house was at least a mile and a half away—not even visible from where Hallie was standing. She looked in the car again, like she'd missed the driver earlier.

Jesus.

She called it in.

The dispatcher said it would take twenty minutes for a car to get there. Hallie turned off her pickup, pocketed the keys, and walked around the car and truck again. There were no tire marks, as if neither the truck nor the car had tried to stop. They sat in the center of the intersection, which seemed weird to Hallie. The truck was two or three times heavier than the car; she'd have expected the wreckage to be on the opposite side of the intersection. But no, dead center.

There were still no other cars, which was unusual but not unprecedented. It was empty out here, not much traffic on an ordinary day. She leaned against a telephone pole for a while, noticed something on the opposite side of the road, and shoved herself off to investigate. Two small evergreen trees growing in the ditch had died, the needles dry and still falling in the wake of a brisk westerly breeze.

The grass around them was dead too. Hallie bent and brushed her fingers through the dry bristly stalks. All dead underneath, even the newest growth. She hopped the old fence into the adjacent field. Dead grass out to nearly twenty paces; past that, there was dry grass, sure, but green underneath, small cedar trees in good shape and one largish stand of goldenrod still in flower despite the season.

She circled the accident—field, cross the road, field, road and back, everything dead out to thirty yards. She found two dead birds next to a north-leaning fence post and the corpse of a rabbit in the far ditch.

No ghosts. But something wrong, all the same.

She leaned against the utility pole and studied the accident scene through narrowed eyes. What the hell had happened here?

"Ask him about his wife."

Hallie startled so hard, she could feel her muscles snap. She jerked away from the utility pole. A man stood in the middle of the road, halfway between her and the wreckage. He looked older than Hallie, maybe thirty-five or forty, wearing lightweight wool dress pants, polished leather shoes, and a navy V-necked sweater. He had an odd half smile on his face, and his hands were shoved into the pockets of his trousers.

"Who the hell are you?" Hallie asked, though what she meant was, *Where did you come from?*

He took half a dozen casual steps toward her. Everything about him was clearly designed to seem casual, relaxed, and easy.

Everything about him was a lie.

He stopped a judicious ten yards from where Hallie was standing. "Sometimes you think you know a person," he said. "You've, say, been through hard times, one of you has been shot or, I don't know—" He shrugged. "—died.

"But do you ever really know anyone?"

"I don't see a car," Hallie said. She shoved her hands in her pockets and leaned back against the utility pole because she could see what he wanted—his entire purpose, maybe—was to shake her up. And Hallie never liked giving people what they wanted. "And you weren't here when I got here. I'd have seen you." She paused. "You're not a ghost."

The man laughed. "Does it really matter who or what I am?"

Hallie could hear a car. Maybe a mile away, maybe ten—hard to tell sometimes out on the prairie. "Oh yeah," she said. "It matters."

"What matters," the man said, and his voice was suddenly significantly less easy, "is what I *want* to matter."

"Yeah," Hallie said. "No."

"Ask him."

"Who?"

"You know who."

"Boyd." Because she did know. But she didn't play games. And this guy? This guy—or whatever—was all about the games. "Why?" Hallie asked. "Because you want to drive a wedge?" She was two paces from him, and he was so . . . off, it wasn't funny. "You want me to mistrust him? Why should I care what you say? I don't know you."

"You don't know him." He laughed at her, like the whole thing was a joke . . . the cars, Boyd's past, his own presence in the middle of the empty road.

Fuck you, Hallie thought. She grabbed the front of his shirt. He was solid, real in that respect, but he wasn't alive in the human sense. She could tell by the stab of pain through her head, like she'd been skewered. Not cold, like the ghosts, but unreal all the same.

"I know him," she said. The car she'd heard was definitely closer.

"You only think you do," he said.

Then he was gone so quickly, she thought she must have blinked, though she hadn't. Cold wind ruffled her hair, like a quick blast from an arctic clime.

5

The wind whipped dry grass and a few scattered leaves down the edge of the road as Hallie waited for the sheriff's car, which she could see approaching, though it was still a half mile down the road. A quick eddy of twigs and gravel right in front of the little red car's bumper, then the wind died, abrupt, like it had hit an impenetrable wall.

She looked up and the car was there, all white and gold and shiny, like it had just been through a car wash. And though it should have been impossible—all the Taylor County patrol cars were exactly the same, she recognized this one, whether by the way he drove or by how neat as a pin and shiny it was—Boyd.

And that was good. It was.

The car stopped on the other side of the intersection. It didn't pull to the shoulder. It just . . . stopped, right in the middle of the lane.

A small bird—a sparrow, maybe—flew quick, like it was panicked, across the road, almost hitting Hallie in the head. She stepped back.

Boyd opened his door and got out of the car.

He looked like he always did—like he'd just stepped out of the barbershop, his hair perfectly neat and precisely trimmed. His white shirt and his creased khaki pants looked as if they'd only that moment been slipped from a plastic bag, everything completely smooth, completely under control.

He didn't say a word, walked right past her with barely a sideways glance. He walked around the car, around the truck. For a long minute while he was on the other side of the truck, Hallie couldn't see him. Then, he reemerged, notebook in hand, writing down the license plate of the truck, like this was just another accident, like he was just another cop, though Hallie could tell from the way he moved and the tension in his muscles that neither of those things was true.

A ghost drifted around the truck behind him. Hallie sucked in her breath. She had seen that ghost before. Twice. It was a girl, maybe seventeen or eighteen, with short hair dyed blond, dark roots showing through. She wore a long skirt, engineering boots, and a leather wrist cuff. When she reached out and touched Boyd on the shoulder, he flinched.

Hallie said, "Boyd—"

He looked at her. His face was . . . blank, like he was in shock, like Boyd would naturally look if he were in shock, like he was trying so hard to control everything both inside and out that there wasn't room for anything to show. Hallie could hear him breathing, and it was weird because he didn't seem to be breathing particularly quickly. Just that she could hear him, like the entire rest of the world had gone silent.

His cell phone rang. He reached down and turned it off without looking at it.

"What the hell is going on with you?" Hallie asked him.

She saw movement out of the corner of her eye and turned to see the black dog flopped down in the gravel by the side of the road.

She wanted to ask if it, the black dog, had anything to do with the two wrecked vehicles or with the man who had been here earlier and who had disappeared. Because black dogs were all about death, and there was a lot of death right here—grass and birds and trees, not to mention whatever had happened to the people in the vehicles.

Boyd still hadn't said anything, but Hallie could see that he was angry, really bone-deep pissed off in a way she'd never seen before. It didn't show in his face, but she could tell, in the rigid set of his shoulders and the wire-tight line of his jaw.

"What are you doing here?" he asked.

Hallie blinked. "I called it in."

"Goddamnit," he said, and it was almost under his breath, almost not directed at her. "I mean," and now he was addressing her, "why? Why does this kind of thing happen around you?"

"What are you *talking* about?" She'd closed the gap between them, and now they were standing almost toe to toe. "This is an *accident*." Even though it wasn't, even though there was the thirty-yard zone of death around the intersection, even though there had been a man who appeared out of nowhere and disappeared the same way. Even though . . .

"Does this have something to do with your wife?"

Boyd jerked back, like she'd hit him. And he looked hurt, like she'd gone down a path she wasn't supposed to go down, or even know about, and ripped open a door she was never supposed to enter.

"Boyd—," she began again.

"Leave it alone, Hallie," he said. He stepped even closer to her, nearly vibrating with what she'd been thinking was anger, but maybe also was fear. Or desperation. "Get in your truck and drive away."

Hallie stepped back, like they were dancing, only not with each other. "No."

"I can make you leave."

"No, you can't."

He stepped back too, but only so he could put his hand on her arm. She almost shook it off. Almost.

"I can ask you, then. I'm asking you, Hallie." And it might have sounded better if he weren't gripping her elbow so hard it hurt, and if he weren't so pissed off and trying so hard to hide it. "This is an accident. Two vehicles in the middle of an intersection. I'm here now. I can take care of it. You don't have to sign anything, you don't have to stand out here in the wind.

"Just get in your truck and go."

She let him finish because he wasn't listening to her anyway. Let him finish even though by now she was vibrating with anger herself. Because he should know better than this. He should know. In September, with Martin and Pete and calling the weather, had he told her to get in her truck then? Had he asked her to leave it to him? Well, he had, actually—at least once, but they got better. They were better than this.

There was a brisk cold wind running straight down the county road from the north. The sky was a thin bright blue directly above them, but along the western horizon a band of clouds sat like a stark gray wall. "Look," Hallie said, "I get that you're pissed. I don't know why, but I get it. But you need to stop being pissed for a minute and *listen to me*."

She watched his right hand clench slowly into a fist so tight, it turned his knuckles white; watched as he visibly willed himself to stop, to think. She wanted desperately to know what was going on, what this accident meant to him, meant something she couldn't see from looking at it, meant something about the wife she hadn't known he had. And it felt so strange to be the calm one, to be the one who waited, to be the reasonable center. She didn't really want to do it, wanted to stand toe to toe with him and feed his anger right back to him word for word, unfairness for unfairness.

But she did it. Because he would do it for her.

A minute passed.

The ghost touched Boyd on the shoulder, and Hallie saw something stop in him.

Just stop.

She laid a hand on his arm and he shuddered; his arm felt rigid as steel underneath his shirt.

She closed her eyes and took a breath. She had to be careful, so careful, and careful wasn't what she was good at. She said, "I don't know what this is. I need you to tell me."

He looked at her, but she was pretty sure he still didn't see her. The wind had shifted, straight out of the west, and the thick bank of clouds moved slowly in their direction, fading out the sun so that the day wasn't dark, exactly, but gray.

"Really. You should leave," he said, though she could tell his heart wasn't in the words, or he'd finally remembered that asking her to leave was practically the same as demanding that she stay.

She grasped, finally, that he wanted her safe, out of there, away from cars without drivers and men who appeared and disappeared and thirty-yard dead zones. Which wasn't going to happen. It wasn't. If someone wanted to plunk an accident down in front of her, they were going to have to deal with the consequences.

"Tell me what's going on," she said.

He didn't respond immediately except to let out his breath, like he'd been holding it. He closed his notebook, put it in his shirt pocket, and buttoned the flap, each movement precise and deliberate. He started to walk, circling the wreckage, like there was some angle he hadn't seen yet. When he spoke, it was like he'd rehearsed it—concise and smooth and all in one breath.

"I was married," he said. "She died. She died in an accident like this one. *Exactly* like this one."

Not one of those words was a surprise to Hallie, and still, they felt like it, like hammers that hit her square in the chest. Because none of those words were ones she'd expected to hear at the beginning of the day. Yet, here they were.

"I was nineteen," Boyd continued after a moment. "I was a sophomore at Iowa State. Majoring in Animal Science."

Another surprise, because Hallie would have guessed he'd always been a cop.

"I was going back to the farm," he said, as if Hallie had actually asked. He wasn't wearing a jacket, and Hallie wondered if he was cold. She wondered if he would know he was cold even if he was. He'd stopped walking, was standing three feet away from her, and it felt farther, like he'd pulled himself away, like if she wouldn't leave, if physical distance couldn't keep her safe, maybe emotional distance would.

But he would tell her the truth anyway. Because he was Boyd.

"Her name was Lily. Lil." He swallowed. "We met at a party. Some guys were harassing her. I walked her home."

So simple. A girl and a boy and a party. But also the most complicated thing in the world.

"She's here," Hallie said. Wasn't sure why she said it. Not right then, though she'd have told him sooner or later.

"Really?" She could see him swallow hard.

"Pretty sure. She's been following you for a while."

Boyd didn't turn around, didn't try to see, which he couldn't and he knew it. "There was this guy," he said.

"At the party."

"No," he said. "Those were just guys. But there was this other guy."

He leaned against his car, facing the wreckage, like he had to keep it in sight, like everything depended on it. Hallie could see his anger in the tight corners of his mouth, the tension of the skin across his cheekbones, in the way his left index finger tapped against his right thumb.

"At first I thought it was a coincidence," he continued. "Lily and I would meet at the union after class and I'd see him in the hall on my way into the food court. I'd run into her in the library studying and he'd be at the main desk talking to a librarian. I'd pass him on central campus or sitting on the steps at Curtiss. And it was nothing. You see people like that all the time.

"But he never had books or even a briefcase. And there didn't seem to be anything regular about where he'd be, like he was going to class or to his office. Only Lily." He took a breath and continued. "She was from south central Iowa, originally. There are some good farms down there, but a lot of it's scrabble land, empty and rough to make a living on. Her stepfather got into debt to this guy he'd grown up with. Thought he was a friend, but then he got mean or desperate or just greedy. I don't really know. And her stepfather cried—she said he cried. Because all he had was the farm. He didn't even have—it was all he had. But the guy, this guy her stepfather owed money to, wanted to marry Lily." He shook his head. "I don't know. It sounds like a barter—marry me or your stepfather loses the farm. But she didn't say no. She just said she wanted college first. Her stepfather and this guy, they agreed."

He's not a guy, Hallie wanted to say, but she held her tongue. Let him finish. Because she sensed that right now he needed to finish, to lay it all out.

"I don't know if she was really going to do it—marry him. I don't know if she even knew herself, but it was there and she'd have to deal with it sooner or later."

"We weren't dating then, not really, but I liked her. I liked her a lot. She was smart and funny, but not—she didn't know a lot about the way the world worked. She kept trying to figure out how to get a job that paid real money, how to get her stepfather out of debt. She switched majors a lot, looking for the one that would be her ticket to fortune. She bought lottery tickets every Monday afternoon."

"So you married her."

"Her stepfather died," he said. He seemed to be staring hard at something in the middle distance. Hallie hoped he was seeing her,

Lily. Hoped they'd had some good times, not just stalkers and getting married too young. She wondered if she was supposed to be jealous. She didn't think she was. Nineteen was a different world.

"It was the end of her freshman year. Heart attack or something. The farm got sold. She didn't have to marry anyone she didn't want to. But sophomore year, there he was. On campus. Pushing at her. Really pushing. He had a contract, he said. There were debts. And that's when we got married."

He shrugged, like, yeah, what had seemed simple and right at nineteen was somehow harder to explain at twenty-six. "It seemed like a good idea. We could share expenses. I could—yeah, I know it sounds stupid, but I thought I could protect her. I wanted to protect her. I wanted to be the one to fix things for her." He paused, like he was thinking about what he wanted to say. "Maybe it never made sense. But he was at least forty. She'd just turned eighteen. And why should she have to marry him? Because he was pushy? Because he wanted to? And I could help her. At least I could help her."

"Did you dream about her?" Is that where all this had come from?

"No." He looked at the ground. "I hadn't had any dreams since I was sixteen. I thought that was over, done. And it was a problem because I wasn't—I never dreamed about her dying."

After a minute, he said, "I thought that I was saving her. I married her to save her. But in the end she saved me."

"I don't understand," she said.

Boyd rubbed a hand across the back of his neck. "Sorry. I don't talk about it much."

Hallie figured if they had a list of all the things Boyd didn't talk about, it would stretch from Rapid City to Pierre.

"This is the accident she died in," he said, pointing at the car and the grain truck. "This car and this truck. Exactly. Exactly like this." As if that couldn't be said too many times, as if that were the fundamental wrongness, which in some ways it was. Because Boyd was right—who would do this? Or, more to the point, why? Because Hallie had a feeling she already knew who. Or, rather, what.

"This is a threat," he said. "And it's my problem. Not yours. Not the sheriff's department. Mine. And I won't let this hurt you. Or anyone else. I won't." His voice was flat and hard.

You don't get to choose, Hallie thought, what I get involved in and what I don't. But she didn't say it. Bit her tongue so hard, she almost drew blood, because this wasn't about arguing. For once. Or, right now. This was about figuring out what was going on.

Boyd walked over to the wreckage one more time, then back, like he couldn't actually believe it was there, for which Hallie didn't blame him.

She said, "Okay. Okay. But if this was the accident—"

"It was."

"How was this to save you?" Hallie hated this conversation in so many ways. Hated it because she was holding back, which was wrong; she knew it was wrong and yet she also knew, right now, she couldn't talk about this on her terms. Right now, right this minute, she had to talk about it on his. And that was hard. Way harder than fighting with him. And not because she cared that Boyd had been married before, though she did care a little because it changed how she knew him, what she knew about him. She hated it because she couldn't figure out what it was supposed to mean. How had a dead man re-created this accident in the middle of nowhere in the middle of South Dakota? Why? Why here? Why now?

"After we got married," Boyd said, looking at the vehicles rather than at Hallie, "he didn't follow Lily anymore. He started following me. And that was all right with me. I figured I could handle him." He turned to Hallie, his gaze steady. "I had no idea."

6

Boyd, this guy . . . this guy is dead, right?"

Boyd looked at her. The black dog rose from where it had been lying next to the wreckage, stretched, and trotted across the road to them. Hallie moved so she was standing between the dog and Boyd. Don't you touch him, she thought. Don't you even think about touching him.

"He's dead. I saw him die. Or, I saw him . . . dead." He swallowed. "Lily was in her car—that red car there, or one just like it. Hollowell—that was his name, Travis Hollowell—he was in the grain truck. She'd have just gotten off work. And I think she was coming to meet me because it was raining. She must have recognized Hollowell or saw the truck headed for me. But it's not something I know. That I can ever know. Not now." And Hallie knew how that was, that something could never be understood, that you just had to live with not knowing. She didn't like it, but she understood it.

"There'd been some weird incidents the week before she died," Boyd continued after a moment. "A broken step, an out-of-control motorcycle, some dog that tried to attack me in an alley near downtown. But I never saw him—Hollowell. I didn't understand what was happening. Maybe if I had—" He cut himself off, like he'd been down that path a hundred times. Nothing ever changed, but he still thought about it, Hallie figured. Still wanted to rewind that day or week or year, still wanted it to turn out different.

"What happened that day?" Hallie asked. It wasn't going to be less painful this time, thinking about the things he should have done or could have done, but she needed to know. Until she knew, she couldn't tell what parts were important. And parts *were* important. That was clear just from the fact that they were here and the vehicles were here.

"That day," Boyd said, "I was walking. We had an apartment south of campus and I'd just gotten off the bus. It had been raining, drizzling, and the road was slick—or at least that's what they said, after. It was dusk and there wasn't really a sidewalk, not right there, not then."

Hallie felt as if she was holding her breath, or the world was, like time itself had stopped. If there was wind or birds or the sound of tires on pavement, she didn't hear them.

"I don't even remember what I was thinking about, probably biochem or feed formulations. Or maybe running out to the farm for the weekend. My parents liked Lily. They didn't like that we'd gotten married, but they liked her. So, I don't know. I was paying attention, but not *paying attention*. Not like I would have been if I'd know what was going to happen. Not like I should have been. The first I knew anything was happening was when I heard tires squealing. I looked up in time to see Lily accelerate into the intersection and right underneath that—that truck."

Hallie put her hand on his arm. Lily's ghost hovered off his left shoulder. When Boyd spoke again, his voice was harsh. "She was already dead when I reached the car. I don't know *anything*." As if that were part of the problem, that he couldn't know each detail, what was thought and why it was done. "Nothing. Except she saved my life."

"I'm sorry," Hallie said.

Boyd turned away from the wreck once more and looked at her, his expression bleak. "It was seven years ago," he said.

Hallie's mother had died thirteen years ago and it didn't matter. Sometimes things were fine. And sometimes—like maybe when you saw a wreck exactly like—it slammed right through you like yesterday.

Hallie looked at the wreck herself, looked at the little red car shoved under the heavy front end of the grain truck. "Hollowell was driving the truck?" she asked.

Boyd nodded.

"But—" She didn't understand. "I mean, did he go through the windshield? It was a big truck."

"It was weird," Boyd said. He'd turned away from the wreck now, was staring across the open field to the west. "Although they said it happens like that sometimes. He got out of the truck. He was walking around, telling everyone she just drove right in front of him, that he couldn't stop. I remember wanting to kill him. I've never wanted to kill anyone, but I wanted to kill him. But I didn't want to leave her. She was dead. I could tell she was, but I didn't want to leave her alone."

He raised a hand, like he was going to point to something, then let it drop. "Then he just . . . died. A heart attack, I guess, or some sort of latent injury. I never asked. Never cared. For a while I thought maybe I just wanted it enough, for him to die. For a while, I hoped that was it."

Hallie waited, but when he didn't say anything more, she said, "So, this guy. He's in his forties, right?"

"He was," Boyd conceded.

"Dark brown hair cut fairly short. Not as short as yours, but precise, good barber, I bet. He's got some gray hair, like you said, though not much, just a little at the temples. He wears nice clothes, dress pants, a navy sweater. Not as tall as you. Taller than me. His eyes are really light colored. Like—" She had to think. "—like old snow."

Hallie hadn't thought Boyd could look any paler, but she'd been wrong. "Not the eyes," he said, "but the rest. Yes. How do you know?"

"He was here," she said.

"His ghost?"

"No," she said. "He appeared, right here, while I was waiting for you. Out of nowhere. Like a ghost. Only he wasn't. He was solid. I touched him."

"He's dead," Boyd said, his voice like ground stone, like repeating it would make the car wreck and the conversation, and maybe even Lily's death seven years ago, go away. They were standing on the edge of the highway, asphalt crumpling slightly just underneath their feet. Behind them was the wreck like a giant grotesque memorial. Hallie didn't even have to turn her head, and she could still see it. The red car's hood was nearly swallowed by the front of the grain truck, the car itself twisted sideways, like it hadn't hit straight on, but almost, its back wheels six inches off the ground, the right one bent almost in half. Such a small car and such a big truck. No question Hollowell had meant to kill Boyd. No one hit by that truck could have survived.

"Maybe he was something else back then," Hallie said. She thought of the black dogs—not everything that wasn't alive was a ghost. "Maybe he was never human."

"He was a real guy."

"Are you sure? Because he's solid. He could have fooled you."

"Yeah," he said. "I'm sure. Not," he added, "that he couldn't have fooled me. Because I didn't know anything, not back then. I thought the world was . . . well, the way you think the world is."

"You had dreams," Hallie pointed out.

"But I thought that was just me," he told her. He stepped away, like the conversation was finished, then he turned back. "People knew him, Hallie," he said. "Lily's stepfather knew him. He had to be real."

You hope he was real, Hallie thought. But he'd also said that Hollowell's eyes were different, and maybe that meant something. Maybe it meant he'd been alive then, that he'd died, that he was something else now. One more thing that Hallie didn't know anything about.

Hallie heard another vehicle, really close, like it had probably been audible for several minutes and she and Boyd just hadn't noticed. It wasn't long before a tow truck—Big Dog's Auto in Prairie City—pulled up, the engine rumbling. Tom Hauser stepped out, and Hallie and Boyd crossed the short distance back to where he'd stopped, just behind Boyd's patrol car.

"What's going on?" Tom asked.

"Wreck." Hallie stepped in front of Boyd, because she thought he might need a moment.

"Yeah," Tom said dryly, "I got that."

"Can you get them out of here?" Boyd said from behind Hallie, sounding so normal that Hallie almost whipped her head around to look at him, like he'd swapped himself out for someone else, which in a way he probably had.

"They go to the hospital already?" Tom said. He approached the wreckage and ducked his head to look inside the car.

"Yeah," Hallie said, "there isn't anybody."

Tom straightened. "Well, there had to be somebody."

"Just tow them," Boyd said, apparently no longer trying for "normal." He opened the door of his patrol car with a movement so violent, the door almost bounced back at him. He got in, shut the door, and reached for the radio.

"What bug flew up his butt?" Tom asked.

"It's fine," Hallie said.

Tom looked at her, like he could see things clearer than either Hallie or Boyd might have wanted him to. "There aren't any tire marks," he finally said.

"Yeah," Hallie said. "You should just move them."

Tom shrugged. "Sure."

He went back to his truck and started to maneuver it into position. Hallie walked over to Boyd's patrol car and tapped on the window. Boyd had been staring out the windshield at the wreckage, but he didn't jump when Hallie tapped the window, like he was aware of everything—Hallie, the tow truck, the pattern of the wind across the dried stalks of grass at the side of the road.

"Look," Hallie said when Boyd stepped out of the car, "there's something else you need to see."

"I called in the plates," he said.

"Why?" She looked at him.

"These vehicles," and she could see that he was trying to put himself back together, to be calm, precise, and organized. It wasn't quite working, but she could see that he was trying as hard as he knew how. "These vehicles have to belong to someone. They had to get here somehow. If I can trace them back to their owners, maybe I can find out what's going on. Maybe it really is just someone's elaborate and sick idea of a joke."

"And that explains the guy I saw, how?" Hallie asked.

"Maybe you were wrong." He said each word separately and distinctly, like providing the right emphasis would be the same as being right.

"Yeah," Hallie said, matching his tone, "let me show you something."

Tom had by this time towed the red car to the side of the road. Boyd looked at it hard, and for a minute Hallie didn't think he'd heard her, but then he said, "Sure, show me."

The wind rose as they crossed the road. It was still out of the west, but sharper now, heavy with the promise of winter, finally, as if the sky and the earth had been waiting until just this exact moment for the season to change. Into the wide ditch and back out. The field on this side of the road hadn't been cultivated or grazed for years, all low grass and occasional brambles.

Hallie walked Boyd straight through the field to the perimeter of the circle of death, then along that perimeter across field and road and field again with several side trips to show him the dead trees and birds and rabbits. He didn't seem terribly interested, kept looking back at the intersection and tapping his radio mike, like he wondered if it had stopped working.

"It's November," he finally said.

"And we haven't had a killing frost. Look." She straddled the line between dead and not-dead, bent down and showed him—green grass on one side, admittedly buried amongst dried late fall stalks, but there, nonetheless. On the dead side—nothing. "What about the dead trees, the rabbits?"

"Okay," Boyd said, but she could see that he wasn't going to spend time on it. The accident was weird and disturbing, but it could be investigated. He could call in license plates and check VIN numbers and registrations. He could interview people up and down the road. It was an empty stretch of highway, but maybe there was someone. And maybe they'd seen something. Someone towing vehicles or driving too fast. Those were concrete things—making phone calls, interviewing people. Dead grass and birds and trees? What was he supposed to do with that?

As they returned to the intersection, Tom trotted over. The little red car sat on the side of the road, its hood crumpled and its front tires splayed left and right. Tom had the grain truck hooked for towing, ready to drive it back to town.

"Need you to sign these, Deputy," he said to Boyd.

Boyd signed them without looking, his signature a slanted scrawl. Tom studied it, then looked at Hallie, like, What's going on?

Hallie shrugged, then walked with him across the road to his truck.

"Thanks," she said as Tom pulled the door open.

Tom jerked a thumb back at Boyd. "He okay?"

"I don't know," Hallie said honestly.

Tom looked at her close, then nodded, like he understood at least half of what she wasn't saying. He turned to climb into the truck.

"Did Jake get his car?" Hallie asked.

Tom turned back. "Jake?"

"I saw it on the road this morning." She gestured with her hand. "Over by the ranch."

"It's his day off," Tom said. "So I haven't seen him, but that car's been leaving him by the side of the road all over the county. Needs the engine rebuilt. Keeps saying he doesn't have time. I think he just likes tinkering with it, you know? Told him last time I had to tow it, he could get someone else next time it crapped out on him." He laughed. "Guess he thought I meant it."

Hallie stepped back as he climbed up into the cab of his tow truck, then walked back across the road as Tom pulled out, towing the big grain truck behind.

She was just approaching Boyd's car when his radio crackled to life.

"Those plates you wanted run?" Hallie recognized Patty Littlejohn, who'd been a friend of her mother's way back and was the daytime dispatcher for the sheriff.

Boyd said, "Go ahead."

"Well, they *exist,*" Patty said.

Boyd frowned. "What does that mean?"

"They're Iowa plates, right? That's what you said?"

"Yes." Boyd's voice had that tight undercurrent again, not quite anger—though that was there too—more like he was afraid he was starting to unravel.

"Iowa claims," Patty said, her tone implying that as it was Iowa, any information could not be completely relied upon. "Well, they claim that the plates aren't assigned to anyone."

"That's a mistake," Boyd said flatly.

"You would think so," Patty said. "Unless you made a mistake on the numbers, transposed them or something?"

"No."

"Okay," Patty said after a pause. "The thing is, they checked. They physically have the plates. In Iowa. Right now."

Boyd rubbed a hand across his forehead as if his head hurt.

"Ask her if they've ever been assigned to anyone," Hallie said.

Boyd looked at her, then nodded and passed the question along to Patty.

"I can ask," Patty said doubtfully. "Do you want the whole history, then?"

"Yes," Boyd said.

"All righty." A short pause. "Oh, and by the way, is your phone off? Someone's been trying to call you. Didn't know her, but I said I'd tell you to listen to your messages."

Boyd's hand reached automatically for his phone. He'd turned it off right after he first got there, which Hallie was sure was something he never did.

Lily, which Hallie now knew was the ghost's name, though she tended to think of her as "Boyd's dead wife," drifted over. She'd followed them into the dead zone, paused at the edge, like she could tell the difference, then drifted back to the center of the intersection. Hallie'd thought maybe she'd disappear once the vehicles were moved, but ghosts never did the logical thing. And besides, her car was still here.

With the red car by the side of the road and the grain truck on its way to Prairie City, the intersection looked huge, though it wasn't. It was just an ordinary intersection—a couple of two-lane old asphalt roads come together in the flat, big-horizon middle of nowhere. There was a smell in the air of approaching rain and dry leaves. The wind ruffled grass against a single old fence post on the north side of the road. Hallie and Boyd stood across the road from the red car so that it was right there, like a red slash across the landscape.

Boyd had turned his phone back on and was scrolling for messages when his radio crackled again.

"Are you finished out there?" Patty asked.

Boyd looked around as if he had no idea. "Yeah," he finally said. "Pretty much."

"Tell her you're taking the rest of the day off," Hallie said.

"What have you got?" Boyd asked, ignoring Hallie. His voice sounded almost normal.

"Since you're out that way," Patty said, "you want to run by the old Packer place? Sigurdson claims someone's running cattle out there. Says he's got the only lease, from the bank, and there shouldn't be anyone else on it. I'm sure he's been out there with his hands a half dozen times before it occurred to him to call it in. In any case, I said we'd check on it."

"Sure," Boyd said. "I'll take care of it."

"You can't just go back to work," Hallie said.

"What's your better idea?" he said.

"What's my *better idea*? My better idea is to do something about this." She flung her arm wide, to encompass the intersection and the dead circle and the whole damn prairie if it came to that.

"I don't want you to touch this."

"Seriously? You're seriously telling me to stay out of this? No."

Something shifted in him as he looked at her, from angry to tired, like all this coming up from seven years ago and not making any sense had made him weary in his bones. "What, Hallie?" he asked. "What are you going to do? What do you know about it? About any of it?"

"Boyd," Hallie said, like saying his name would make this stop. "This is a problem. It's in my backyard. Hollowell knew me. I don't know what's going on, but neither do you. I'm sure as hell going to do something."

"I thought you were leaving."

And there it was. That she was leaving. And he was not. "I'm not leaving today," she said.

"This is commitment, Hallie," Boyd said. "You're committing to something."

"This is solving a problem."

"There are always problems."

"Not like this one."

"Look," he said. He looked at the cloud-covered sky, like looking at Hallie was just too hard. "I am going to finish my shift. Then I'm going to run these VIN numbers and track down where Travis Hollowell is buried. I'm going to return my phone calls and put together a list of what I know and what I need to do and who I should call, because that's what I do. If you want me to call you after that, I can call."

Hallie's right hand squeezed into a fist, which she shoved into her jacket pocket. "Yes, Boyd," and was pleased that her voice was so calm and even. "I want you to call me after that."

"Fine."

He turned away and walked the ten feet back to his car, then paused with his hand on the car door. "Be careful, Hallie. I mean it.

Whatever he is now, whatever he wants, he's gone to a lot of trouble. This was a damned elaborate setup in order to give me a message."

Hallie looked over at the intersection where the two vehicles had sat, each tangled in the other before Tom had separated them; she looked at her pickup truck still sitting at the other side of the intersection. "He didn't just give it to you," she said. "He gave it to me too."

7

"Damn it," Hallie said to no one in particular as she watched Boyd drive away a few minutes later. She walked back to her truck.

The black dog was already there when she opened the driver's door, curled up on the seat as if it had never left. Lily's ghost was there too, floating in the space between Hallie and the dog. It surprised her that the ghost was there. She'd thought, for some reason, that it would stick with Boyd.

But no, it was clearly her ghost now. And that was all right. She was prepared—or as prepared as someone could be—for that. It meant that no matter what Boyd said or thought, this was her problem too.

Like Pabby was her problem.

"Ghosts," the dog said when Hallie opened the door, hissing on the final *s*. Hallie couldn't tell if it was annoyed or pleased.

"Yeah," she said. "You can always leave."

The dog put its paw forward on the seat. Lily's ghost looked down as if, unlike every other ghost Hallie had seen, it was aware. Or maybe it was because it was a black dog, because weren't they sort of on the same plane, ghosts and black dogs? Both of them dead or nearly dead or left over after death. The ghost touched the dog's paw and the dog huffed out that sound that was almost a laugh.

Jesus, thought Hallie, this is my life.

She started up the truck and pulled back out onto the road. She caught up with Tom easily, waved out the window as she went by and watched him disappear in the rearview mirror. She thought about Travis Hollowell—wasn't that what Boyd had said the disappearing man's name was?—most of the half hour it took to get to West Prairie City. Three things stood out: He was dead, he had a history with Boyd, and whatever was going on, it wasn't just about Boyd, no matter how much Boyd wanted it to be. Hollowell could have set that accident up so only Boyd would see it—however he'd set it up, which didn't particularly worry Hallie, the how, though it probably should. But he hadn't. He hadn't popped in to talk to Boyd either. He'd talked to her.

She glanced down at the dog on the seat. "What do you know about that back there?" Hallie asked it. If it was going to hang around, it might as well be useful.

The dog cocked an ear at her. "Ask the ghost," it said, hissing all the *s*'s.

"Ghosts don't talk," Hallie said.

"Too bad," said the dog. Lily floated against the dash as if neither of them were anything to her.

A few minutes later, Hallie pulled into the parking lot of the single grocery store in West PC. Lily disappeared when she parked. Just—poof—gone, warm air rushing in to replace the cold. The black dog rose and stretched, then jumped through the closed passenger-side window, disappearing just before it touched the ground. Hallie shook her head and exited the truck herself, the normal way, through the open door.

Everything she picked up for the ranch, she picked up a duplicate for Pabby—milk, eggs, vegetables, and bread. She figured Pabby had beef in her big freezer, but she tossed a couple of pounds of bacon, some flour, and two sacks of sugar into the cart.

The sun was setting by the time she got to Pabby's and dropped off the supplies. Tiny bits of cloth tied to scattered clumps of prairie grass, to an old fencepost, to a tree branch fluttered in the raw evening breeze. They'd always been there, in the yard, along the corral. Hallie'd never paid attention, just something that made the place Pabby's. But now she knew—the boundary of a hex ring.

"Did you get anywhere yet?" Pabby asked when she opened the door to Hallie.

Hallie stared at her. "I've been busy."

"Well, I haven't got forever."

"You owe me for the groceries," Hallie told her. Pabby looked at her. "And I'll get on it," Hallie said. "I will." She was pretty sure Pabby wouldn't be impressed by Laddie Kennedy or the afternoon she'd spent by the side of the road.

Pabby paid her with six five-dollar bills, fourteen ones, and seven dollars in dimes and quarters. She invited Hallie for dinner, but Hallie told her she had more groceries in the truck, which was true. Besides, she felt like she'd been sitting all day even though she hadn't.

Jake's car still sat by the side of the road when Hallie finally drove back home. It was not quite dark, the sky fading out like an old fluorescent light. She slowed going by—an old car with the hood up. Maybe he was waiting on a part.

If it was still there in the morning, she'd call him. Offer to get a tractor and chain, at least tow it up the drive until he could fix it.

The house was empty. She put groceries away, then put on a warmer jacket and gloves and went down to check that the horses near the barns had enough hay and water.

The black dog joined her—Hallie was getting used to it by now—and the horses, who'd been approaching the fence, wheeled as one and raced to the other end of the pasture, clods of dirt flung back as they passed.

"It's like you make friends wherever you go," Hallie said to the dog.

"Like you," the dog said.

Hallie blinked.

Sometimes at night since she'd been back from the army, Hallie wandered the house looking for things to do. She'd never been much for sitting; her interests in high school had been horses and cars. She was on the softball team in eighth grade, but it had been too hard to get to practice and especially to the games. She'd been a good hitter, a mediocre fielder, and a lousy team player.

Once they were old enough, she'd had Dell to drag her places, Dell to make her do things like—once Dell had her license and, okay, maybe a year or two before, they'd ride into town in the summers to the Silver Dove for ice cream. There were always kids who knew Dell, who wanted to do something. There'd be a drag race or a bunch of kids down by the tracks or some place to hang out. Hallie didn't go with her all the time, but Dell was how she learned where to go, how to find people. Dell would toss books at her and say, Hey, read this. Dell would sign them up for 4-H projects, for the county fair, for a Christmas pageant at a church they never went to the rest of the year.

But all of that was gone now—no Dell, no 4-H, no hanging on corners on hot summer nights. Everything was blown to hell and gone, and Hallie hadn't figured out yet what to do about it or how to stop missing Dell.

She walked down to the horse barn, turned on the strung lights, and rooted out all the tack that needed cleaning. She'd been there maybe an hour, had shed her jacket and was wearing a Carhartt vest and a flannel shirt with the sleeves rolled up, when she heard a car heading up the drive.

She didn't bother to look out. If it was someone she didn't know, the dog would bark. If it was someone she knew—and, frankly, she was pretty sure it would be Boyd—they'd find her.

"Hallie."

There was something about the way he said her name, about the way he entered a space, whether she was looking at him or not, like the air changed, like he figured she would always know that it was him. And maybe she would. Like a dance without music. Like they almost knew each other.

She laid aside the cloth and saddle soap and turned, setting her hip against the old tack box she'd been using as a workbench. She waited for Boyd to speak. He was still pissed, she could tell, but he'd bitten it back down, fit it back into the way he liked to keep himself, though it came through in the tension across his shoulders and the hard light in his eyes. She didn't think he was pissed at her, except in a general way that he wouldn't admit to. It didn't matter if he was. Hallie could handle that. What mattered was that he was here.

As she waited for him to speak, Lily's ghost drifted through the side wall of the barn and floated a few inches away from Hallie's left elbow. It was like sitting too close to an old window in February. The cold made Hallie roll the cuffs of her flannel shirt back down and button the buttons. The black dog, which had been sitting on the tack box watching her, jumped down, sniffed at Boyd as it walked past, and settled in the shadows underneath the old hayloft.

Boyd stuck a hand in the pocket of his jeans and leaned against a pole a few feet from Hallie. He rubbed his other hand across the bridge of his nose. The imperfect light cast a shadow across the right side of his face and made it look more angular than usual, which, in turn, made him look older.

"I have to go out of town for a couple of days," he said.

"Like, leaving?" Hallie said, which was, probably, exactly the wrong thing to say.

Boyd's eyes narrowed, but all he said was, "For a couple of days."

He paused, like he was figuring out what to say next, a problem they both had, not just because they didn't know who or what they were to each other, but because the subject of their conversations kept being things neither of them had ever heard of or knew anything about.

Hallie drew in her breath and held it. Stop it, she told herself. Just . . . stop.

"Can I help?" she asked instead.

When he spoke, it was almost like he'd changed the subject. "There are things that you should know," he said. "Things that might help. I mean, I don't know that they'll help, but I don't want something to happen while I'm gone because you didn't know something you needed to know."

Hallie raised an eyebrow, though Boyd probably couldn't see it in the indifferent light. "Okay," she said.

He continued. "Travis Hollowell. He was . . . not anyone special. I spent some time researching him after," a trace of bitterness in his voice, like he wished he'd done something sooner or smarter or different. "He was a systems analyst for some company in Cedar Rapids. He drove a five-year-old Toyota. He was thirty-nine years old. He didn't have a criminal record. He had an ex-girlfriend who said nice things about him. He and Lily's stepfather both grew up in Steamboat Rock, that was how they knew each other. He had liver cancer. He wouldn't have lived another year."

"He was *dying*?"

Boyd nodded. "Yeah."

"Wait. He was dying and he was spending his time stalking your wife?"

"Yes."

"That doesn't make any sense."

"Things like that, they don't always," Boyd said.

"No, I know," Hallie said. "But he came back from the dead." Which, even with everything she'd seen, felt so odd to say, like it changed the world just by saying it, like she'd accepted her own death and Martin and black dogs, but this was a whole new scale. *She'd* been dead seven minutes after all, not seven years.

"Maybe it wasn't him," Boyd said.

"Even if we pretend for a minute that it wasn't him, that someone for some inexplicable reason was impersonating him, how do you explain the wreckage? Even Martin couldn't have done that, and Martin had a lot of power. It's him. You and I both know it's him. We just haven't figured out how."

"There's something else," Boyd said.

Hallie'd assumed there was. She was pretty sure he wasn't leaving town because Travis Hollowell had been dying before he died. "Lily's sister called," he said. "That's who was trying to reach me when we were out on—when we were at the accident." He paused, shifted his weight from one leg to the other. "She was pretty upset. She was crying. She's just eighteen. She's working her way through college. Her mother died a couple of years ago, and her stepfather . . ." He shrugged. "I don't know. She calls me sometimes because I'm sort of the only family she has."

Wind swept in around the corner of the open barn door and stirred the loose straw under the hayloft. It was a cold wind, as cold as it had been so far all fall, promising that a killing frost would come soon, maybe even tonight.

"Today she called to tell me that on her way to class she came across an accident in the middle of an intersection." He looked straight at Hallie. "An accident involving a red car and a grain truck. An accident with no drivers, no skid marks. An accident just like the one that killed her sister."

"Jesus," Hallie said. "Are you kidding me?"

Boyd shook his head. "I don't know," he said. "It can't be a joke." Like he wished it were a joke, cruel and possibly evil, but at least if it was a joke, they could figure out what to do.

"I told her I would come," Boyd said.

"Yeah, but, Boyd—"

"I have to go," he said, his voice quiet and firm.

"No, I understand that," Hallie said. "But what if it's a trap?"

"What?"

"A trap. Like he wants to lure you to Iowa."

He frowned. "Why would that be a trap and not the one here this morning?"

"He wants something, Boyd. This kind of thing doesn't happen for no reason."

"I know. But I have to go."

"Yeah," Hallie said. Because he did. Of course. Because someone needed him. "I should come with you."

"No." His response was unequivocal.

Hallie's hackles rose.

"The next time you leave South Dakota," Boyd said, "something is going to happen."

Hallie just looked at him. *Really?*

He stumbled over his words. "I mean . . . I don't mean you should never leave. I'm not trying to tell you what you should do or not do. Or, I guess I am. Huh." He took a breath and started over. "I don't mean you shouldn't ever leave South Dakota. Because I would never tell you that. Even if I wanted to tell you that. Which I—I don't know, Hallie, why is this so complicated?"

And suddenly they weren't talking about ghosts or disappearing men or Boyd's dreams anymore. "It's not complicated," she said. "That's what I've been telling you."

"It is for me," he said.

"Yeah," Hallie said. "Everything's complicated for you."

He almost laughed, like the sound the black dog made when it talked to Hallie.

8

Some of Boyd's anger had dissipated since he walked into the barn, but there was still a tension in him, in the way he moved. And who could blame him? Even if it had been partly about rescuing her, he must have loved Lily. He'd married her. And she'd died. Died saving him in some way Hallie wasn't completely clear on—in some way Boyd wasn't even completely clear on. Hallie would be down at the courthouse breaking windows if it had happened to her.

"Come over here," she said.

He closed the distance between them.

"Look over there." She pointed in the direction of the black dog. Boyd turned and leaned against the tack box, bracing himself with an arm behind her back. His face was right next to hers; she could feel the warmth of his skin almost, but not quite, touching her own.

The spot she pointed at was just to the right of the open door where the black dog was lying. "What do you see?" she asked. She pretty much expected that he wouldn't see it, but she had to ask.

"There?" Boyd pointed too.

Hallie moved his hand an inch to the right. "There," she said.

"Loose straw? A crack in that windowpane?"

"You can see a crack in the windowpane from here?" Hallie asked, because it was thirty feet away and in shadow.

Boyd turned and put his hand on her knee. His eyes were dark in the dimly lit barn. "What do you see?" he asked.

"A black dog," Hallie said.

"What?" He was looking at her profile, not at the spot where the dog was, like he could see what she was seeing by looking at her face.

"It says it's a harbinger."

"Of death?"

"Well, I guess," Hallie said.

His hand tightened on her knee. His face was less than three inches from hers.

"Not of my death," she said. "Or yours either," she added after a moment in case that wasn't clear. "And I don't think it has anything to do with the thing out on old CR7. The accident."

"You don't?" He sounded skeptical, and who could blame him? Today had been death all around.

"Pretty sure," she said. She didn't offer him the details of her morning visit to Pabby's. He had enough on his mind already. It would keep for now, what with Pabby safe behind the hex ring.

"What does it want, then?" Boyd asked.

"I have no idea."

Boyd looked where Hallie had pointed again, but the dog was up now and moving toward them. It leaped onto the tack box and settled beside her on the side opposite Boyd.

"Interesting," it said, its voice like the sighing of the wind.

"Is it a problem?" Boyd asked.

"Yeah, I'm still trying to figure that out," Hallie said. "Do you know anything about black dogs? Had any dreams about them?" She turned toward him on the tack box, raised a knee, and rested her chin on it.

It was a long moment before he answered, and Hallie had almost decided that maybe he *had* been dreaming about black dogs. He put a hand on her other knee and she didn't move, like moving would make this moment disappear forever. "I dream about you."

She couldn't help it: she laughed. "Is that like a line? Are you giving me a line?" She looked at him and he was smiling, but he shook his head.

"I dreamt about you and a dog, and you were alone on the big open prairie. There was a shallow ditch. It didn't look any different on one side or the other, but I knew, in the dream, that if you crossed that ditch, everything changed."

"So you're saying don't leave?"

He drew back a little. "I told you," he said. "I will never say that."

She wanted to call him a bastard for that, but it probably wasn't a trick. He probably meant it.

He moved his hand up her leg just along the inside of her thigh. "You're not like anyone I've ever known," he said.

Was that a line too? But she didn't ask. She knew that it wasn't.

And it wasn't like Hallie hadn't kissed boys, because she had. More than one. But this mattered and she knew it mattered. Even if she took Kate Matousek's job, this, right here, would matter.

She slid off the tack box. He put a hand around her waist and drew her close. When he kissed her, his lips tasted like summer, like the kind of summer she hadn't seen in years. She put her hand on the back of his neck, felt the rough bristles of his short hair, like a soldier's. His hand slid down the vee of her shirt and paused at the first button. He unbuttoned it without fumbling, like he'd done it a hundred times before. Slid down to the next one and it felt right, felt like coming home in a way that actually coming home had never felt.

She dropped her hands to his waist and pulled the tail of his shirt out of his jeans. Slid her hand along his waist and when she touched his spine he shivered, but his skin felt so warm to her, like he held all the warmth in the universe, like he always had. She kept her hand there, in the hollow of his back, and pulled him close.

He'd unbuttoned her shirt to the waist, but then he stopped, stymied by the thermal shirt she was wearing and the top button on her jeans. She pushed him away, pulled both shirts out of the waistband and finished unbuttoning the flannel one. She reached for his belt, looked at him, like a question. He responded with a smile.

Warmth rushed through her, anticipation and also nerves because she wanted this, wanted him, wanted everything about this moment, but it was the wanting that scared her. Because these were the moments that held a person in place, held them until twenty years had passed and nothing had happened. Except this. Then, he kissed her again and his hand slid along her hip and she didn't think about any of that, of before or after, just fumbled with his belt buckle, which seemed to be much more complicated than it looked.

And oh hell, what did it matter, she would get it later. She put her arms around his neck and he lifted her onto the tack box like she weighed nothing.

She wished that time would stop, that they would stay here forever, that the world outside would leave them—

She felt cold like ice against her spine.

Not a ghost. Not now. She wanted to lose herself. And why not? Didn't she, didn't they, deserve even one brief moment outside the world?

The cold intensified, all along her left side, walk-in-freezer cold. Hallie realized whose ghost it was.

Crap.

Crap crap crap crap. She jumped off the tack box and was halfway across the barn and buttoning her shirt while Boyd stood and looked at her, like she'd gone nuts.

"Jesus," she said. How was this fair?

"What?" Boyd sounded irritated, and who could blame him?

"Your wife. Jesus Christ, it's—it's your *wife*." Hallie hadn't actually imagined ever saying a line like that, but if she had imagined it, she would have expected a flesh-and-blood wife. Not this. And it wasn't fair, of her to say it or of it to be that way, not fair to Lily or Boyd or Hallie, not to any of them. But it was that way all the same.

"My wife?"

Hallie crossed the barn again, grabbed him by the front of his shirt, pulled him close to her, and kissed him hard, because it wasn't going to end with her halfway across the floor. It wasn't, sadly, going to end with anything else either.

"I've done a lot of things," she said, still holding his shirtfront in a tight fist. "Some of them were . . . crazy." Because when she was in Germany she'd done it at three thirty in the morning in a public fountain. "And I've never been shy. But I can't do this. I'm sorry. I know you can't see her. I know it's been seven years and she's gone. I know all that. But—no."

Boyd brushed a stray hair off her face and Hallie could see that he wanted to be amused, because, frankly, it was amusing, or would be in some future they had yet to reach, but he couldn't do it. Because Lily wasn't just a ghost to him.

She stared at her hand gripping his shirt, wanted to grip it tighter, wanted to hold on forever and never let go. Boyd covered her hand with his and squeezed. "I wrinkled your shirt," she said.

"It doesn't matter," he told her.

But it did. That was the problem. All of it mattered. She just hadn't yet figured out how it mattered or what it meant.

After a long minute or two, she stepped away, unwound her hand, and tried to smooth out the creases in the front of his once-crisp shirt. She cleared her throat. "How long will you be gone?"

"Three days, I guess. I'll be back by Thursday at the latest." He kissed her, like a promise, which made her feel as if she were all edges and angles. She didn't want promises; she wanted him.

"I'll call you," he said.

"Good plan," Hallie told him.

She stood in the open barn door and watched Boyd walk back to his Jeep Cherokee. He'd driven down the lane almost to the horse barn before he parked and she wondered how he'd known she was there. The big equipment shed didn't exist anymore except as a new concrete slab and stacks of timber, and she couldn't see any lights in the house, though her father must be home because she could see his truck on the edge of the circle cast by the yard light.

She waited until the taillights of Boyd's Jeep disappeared into the shallow dip halfway down the long drive, then stood another few minutes with her head against the rough wood of the door framing. She hadn't told him about Kate Matousek's job offer.

Crap.

Because she'd meant to tell him. She might feel a powerful need to move and keep moving, but she never meant to lie to him or to pretend it wasn't his business or that he wouldn't care. She thought about calling him, but thought that would look like she couldn't or wouldn't tell him to his face. But Hallie would tell anyone anything face-to-face. She liked it that way. Everything in the open.

She went back into the barn, put away the tack she'd been cleaning, and turned out the lights. Outside, she slid the door along its track with a deep satisfying rumble. Just before it slid completely closed it jumped the track, as it was prone to do, and Hallie grabbed the handle and the rough edge of the door and gave the whole thing a hard heave upward to jump it back on. It probably needed a new track and she figured she'd look at it tomorrow. Or, as she ticked off all the things already on her list—Pabby and Boyd and the shadow she'd seen so long ago, it almost felt like a lifetime—the day after.

As she walked up the lane to the house, her cell phone rang. Thinking it was Boyd, she answered, saying, "Look, I should tell you—"

At the same time, Laddie Kennedy said, "It's Laddie."

And because Hallie was thinking about Boyd and Lily and Travis Hollowell rather than Pabby and hex rings and black dogs, she said without preamble, "What kind of person comes back from the dead?"

There was a brief pause. "Is that a new question?" Laddie asked.

Hallie guessed it was. "Yes," she said.

"You know, I gotta make a living," Laddie told her.

"Yeah. Okay." Because he did. Everyone did. "Another twenty dollars, then?" Hallie asked. This was going to get expensive. And it wasn't like Pabby was paying her. Or Lily. Or even Boyd. Not that she would ask him. Or any one of them. But Hallie didn't have much money either, hadn't talked to her dad about money for working the ranch. That was just something she did. Because she was here. And his daughter. She had some savings from the army, but that was it.

"If money's an issue," Laddie said quick, like he'd already been thinking about it, "we could trade. I got a few head of cattle. I need a place to run them. It's not much," he added. "Someday I'll have my own place again. But, well . . . not yet."

"I can ask," Hallie said. She'd almost said, sure, fine; then she'd remembered—this wasn't her ranch, her grazing, her resources.

Laddie was quiet. "Vance don't like me much," he said.

Hallie didn't remember her father ever mentioning Laddie or any of the Kennedys, except once, when their ranch had gone to the bank. "It won't be a problem," Hallie said. If her father didn't like it, she'd ask Brett. Brett and her father weren't running cattle anymore, a lot of acres over there that weren't being grazed at all.

"Thanks," Laddie said, his voice flat as if he didn't want to be grateful for something he wouldn't have to do if the fates had been kinder, if he hadn't lost his land, and Hallie knew how that felt. It was the way the world worked. "I'll give you a question for every week they graze," he said.

They haggled a bit about winter feed, then got back to the business at hand.

"I've never heard of the dead coming back," Laddie said. "Except ghosts, which are different. But I can ask."

"Yeah," Hallie said. "Ask. Thanks. Did you find anything out about the dogs?"

"I . . . had a conversation," Laddie began. "Don't know how useful it'll be." He drew in a breath and let it out, like a sigh. "The dead, you know, they're, well, they're dead."

"Okay," Hallie said. Because—really?

"They don't think like we do," he said.

"Where *are* they?"

"What?"

"The dead. Where do they—I don't know—hang out? Are they in heaven? Hell?"

"I don't actually know," Laddie said, like it was a revelation. "They're just . . . someplace else."

"How do you know they're dead?" She was standing in the shadow of the yard light. A breeze so soft, she felt it only against the exposed back of her neck and the tip of her nose, drifted up the drive from the east.

"They tell me." He sounded surprised like, what else would they be?

"Okay, fine." Because clearly he believed it. "But the black dogs, did they tell you how to get rid of them?"

"You don't."

"You don't?" What kind of an answer was that?

"They're not alive. They can't be killed."

"They exist, don't they? If they exist, then they can . . . not exist." She just needed to know how.

"Look," Laddie said, "it's not the dogs you need to worry about. They don't hurt anything. It's the reapers."

"Don't the dogs bring the reapers?" It seemed simple to Hallie. No dogs. No reapers. No dead Pabby.

Hallie walked out onto the concrete slab, which would eventually be the new equipment shed. She stepped over some framing two-by-fours and paced across the open expanse. Her boots made a hollow sound on the smooth hard surface. The breeze had grown colder, a clear hint of frost in the air. She turned up the collar on her jacket.

"The dogs are just to find you," Laddie said. "Reapers don't always need them."

"Wouldn't they always know?" Wasn't that their job?

"When there's a lot of death, they know," Laddie said. "Like a battlefield or an earthquake or something. But one person? I guess they send out scouts."

"How do you know this?" Hallie asked.

"People know how they die," Laddie said.

Hallie didn't and she wondered briefly if that was the difference. If remembering how she died would be the last thing that happened before she really was dead.

"How do I stop a reaper, then? What if there's a mistake?"

"You can't stop a reaper," Laddie said, his voice ticking up a notch like the conversation had suddenly tipped over into real from theory. "If a reaper touches you, you're dead."

"Just . . . touches you?"

"That's their job."

"If it's your time to die," Hallie said.

"If you get in their way," Laddie said.

"Seriously?"

"This is death we're talking about," he said. "And I'll tell you this for free." His voice got flat and serious. "Death always wins."

9

Hallie woke the next morning, watered and fed and checked on cattle and horses and bison, ate breakfast and showered. She'd thought about what Laddie told her for a good long while the night before. He had to be wrong. There had to be a way to save Pabby. Death didn't always win. Wasn't she proof?

She found her father pacing off measurements on the equipment shed slab and marking numbers directly on the concrete with a pencil.

"Won't that come off when it snows?" she asked.

"I'll measure it a couple more times," he said. "To make sure."

She asked him about Laddie Kennedy running his cattle in with theirs.

He looked at her. "He's unlucky," he finally said.

"Because he lost his ranch? It happens." Their ranch had almost gone under after Hallie's mother died. Cattle prices had been way down and her father hadn't really cared. He'd had to sell six hundred acres to Tel Sigurdson and work two winters in Rapid City for an appraiser to get enough actual cash to put things back in some kind of order.

Her father ticked items off on his fingers. "He lost his ranch. His wife left him a year later for some fella over in St. Paul. His truck burned up right in front of the West PC fire station last January. They won't even let him into the Viking over to Box Elder anymore because he breaks a chair every time he sits down. And he's not a big guy, you've seen him." He took his tape measure, snapped it out, looked at the notebook in his hand, checked the tape measure again, and wrote three numbers and a couple of words Hallie couldn't read on the pristine concrete. Then, he said, "But, hell, yeah, let him run his cattle." He squinted at her. "You're not thinking he can actually tell the future, are you?"

"No," Hallie said. She'd tried to explain to her father what happened in September, tried to explain Martin Weber and ghosts and Boyd's dreams and how all that had worked together. He'd sat and listened, even asked her a couple of questions. Then he said, "So he thought he could control the weather?"

"He *could* control the weather," Hallie said.

"That's pretty strange, thinking he could do something like that," her father said.

"Yeah," Hallie said. "Strange."

So all she said now was, "He's going to do some research for me."

Her father nodded. He went back to his notebook and pencil and measurements.

Hallie had to admire it, the stubborn insistence that the world worked as Vance Michaels expected it to work. And it worked, not despite evidence to the contrary, but with—in his mind—no evidence to the contrary at all. Any actual evidence, particularly right before his eyes, was dismissed as inconclusive or not actually there.

She reached out impulsively and touched his arm. He stopped measuring, straightened, and looked at her. "If I take this job," she said, "how's that going to work for you?"

He tapped his pencil against the back of his wrist and looked past the unbuilt equipment shed, across the open field, maybe all the way to the far horizon. "People leave here all the time," he said. "That's just the kind of place this is."

"Yeah," she said, "I know." She'd already been gone for four years in the army. "But stuff changes. People—things happen."

"When Dell came home," her father said, his voice rough, "that was good. That was fine. But I don't expect it, for you to come back or to stay. You gotta have something more than a ranch that can't support you or a part-time job with lousy pay and worse hours. You don't stay because you don't have anything better. You stay because it's where you want to be."

"Why do you stay?" Hallie asked.

"Because it's open," he replied without hesitating. "All laid out so you can see it. And everything I need, or needed, or want to remember, it's all right here. I belong right here."

He laughed, one quick hard *ha*. "Can you see me in Chicago or Los Angeles?" He pronounced the latter with a long *e* on the end. "Wearing flip-flops?"

"Shorts?" Hallie'd never seen him in anything but blue jeans and the occasional dress pants.

He smiled. "Before you were born, or Dell either, your mom and I went to Florida for a couple of weeks. We did all the things you're supposed to do—snorkeling, parasailing, took a boat ride through the Everglades. And it was fun—different as hell—but that was part of it. We flew back into Rapid City at night and it was starting to snow as we headed back here. Snowed harder and the wind came up and it was pretty much a whiteout by the time we hit the end of the drive. We made it up to the house, practically sideways the whole way. We didn't have boots, coats, nothing. Snow over our shoes and we're bent against the wind crossing the yard.

"Then it stopped. Snow still falling, but straight down and the moon came out. Your mom and me, we stood there in the cold like idiots looking out across the fields all clean and still and home. That's the thing, we knew we were home."

He looked at her finally. "It's not prettier or better than other places and it sure as hell isn't an easy place, but I know how to live here. And that counts." He laughed again, that low almost not-sound. "You move away, you can come back whenever you want. I'll come see you once in a while. And that'll be fine.

"But I ain't wearing any damn flip-flops."

"I'll keep that in mind," Hallie said, her smile quick and sharp. "And thanks for letting Laddie run his cattle here."

"Yeah, well, I'm a soft touch," her father said, turning back to his measurements and calculations. "But he better not bring that bad luck with him."

Hallie called Laddie before heading into town.

"Here's another question," she said after she'd told him he could bring his cattle out whenever he wanted. "What can kill everything in a thirty-yard radius?"

"Like people?"

"Like everything. I don't know about people, because there weren't any people."

"Could be herbicide," Laddie pointed out.

"Yeah," Hallie said. "It's not. I'm asking you and not the chemical rep because I'm pretty sure it has to do with—" She paused because what was she pretty sure of? That Hollowell was a dead man. That Laddie talked to the dead. "Well, with what I asked you last night. Can the dead come back?" she asked.

"Do you have any idea what you're stirring up here?" Laddie asked.

"No," Hallie said. "I don't. If I did, I wouldn't be asking. Do you?"

Hallie could picture Laddie shuffling cards and laying them out. "Not . . . exactly," he admitted. "But I bet it ain't anything good."

"Will you ask?"

"Yeah." Laddie drew the word out, like a sigh.

"Thanks," Hallie said. "I appreciate it."

It was just after eight o'clock when she crossed SR54, turned right, and continued on old West Prairie Road. A mile farther on, where a gravel road crossed the old asphalt, she saw the shadow—or *a* shadow, because she had no idea if it was the same one she'd seen before or another one—right in the middle of the intersection.

Hallie slowed.

Should she drive through it? She remembered that feeling when she'd touched the grass where the shadow had passed—pain fierce enough to knock her back. She pulled to the side of the road and left the truck running.

The shadow was irregularly shaped, six feet or so in diameter. It was inky black and looked like it would absorb light, though the day was cloudy and cold so it was impossible to tell for sure. It had no thickness, in that respect like a real shadow, though it was darker than a shadow, more like a black hole, like if you stepped on it, you'd disappear forever. It had no smell. Hallie couldn't feel anything emanating from it, not cold or heat. She put out her hand, hovered inches above it. She wanted to touch it even though it was probably dangerous, wanted to know what it was and what it was doing.

She heard a car a long way off and stood. She couldn't figure out afterwards if she hadn't been watching where she stood or if the shadow moved, but when she stood back up, her right foot came down on top of it.

Flash flash flash.

Image after image. A thousand images in a second, a minute, forever.

Sky as black as velvet, cold pinpoints for stars, desert camo—a leg, an arm, strapped-on packs, stark sunlight on bright mountain snow, dusty Humvee tires, new-planted wheat, old hay, Earth from space, shattered windows, soft wood exploded like shrapnel, cell phones, airplanes, mile-high storm clouds, lightning bright as phosphorous, mountain lions with twitching tails, and timber wolves.

She came back to herself, the shadow was gone, and she was on her ass on the ground. She felt like she'd run a mile, was breathing hard and fast.

She heard an engine, high-pitched, like an angry bee, and scrambled to her feet, dusting off the seat of her jeans with her hands. She was out of the intersection and back at her truck when a late-model cream and tan pickup entered the intersection from the crossroad. The driver slowed when he saw Hallie. There was a smooth hum as the passenger-side window powered down.

"Everything all right, there?" Tel Sigurdson leaned toward the window. He had to raise his voice because he was a good thirty feet away from her, but Tel had a voice that carried even with the brisk north wind.

"It's good," Hallie called, resisting the urge to put a hand above her eyes to block the suddenly too-bright sun. "Thought I had a tire going soft, but it's fine."

"You sure? I could follow you into town," Tel said.

Hallie waved her hand. "It's all good," she said.

Tel powered his window back up and drove on. As he crossed the asphalt back onto gravel, dust kicked up along the wheel wells of his truck. Hallie could see him looking back at her as if he was still wondering if he should turn and come back.

Her hands were shaking when she got back in the truck, which pissed her off. Even when she'd first gone to Afghanistan, even when she'd first been under fire, even when her heart beat like a locomotive, she hadn't been the kind of person whose hands shook. She wasn't going to be that person now.

She put the truck in gear and got back on the road. She resolutely put the shadow, what it was, and what it wanted to the back of her mind. She had more immediate concerns. In another fifteen minutes, she'd reached her destination.

The building still looked brand-new when Hallie pulled into the empty parking lot. A few weeds along the edge of the asphalt, the narrow strip of lawn between the building and the prairie a bit ragged, but those were the only signs that this wasn't any other corporate building on a lazy weekend. Hallie sat in her truck for a minute before switching off the ignition.

Uku-Weber.

This was the place. The place her sister had worked before she'd been killed. The place that had killed her sister. Hallie'd never talked to Dell after she came back to South Dakota, after she started working with Martin, so she didn't know—would never know—what Dell had thought Uku-Weber was, whether she'd genuinely thought it was about alternative energy sources. Which, in a way, it had been, except Martin's ability to control the weather had come from blood sacrifice and magic. Not from high-efficiency wind turbines or solar power.

But Martin was dead now, she thought as she got out of the pickup and shut the door, the distinctive sound of metal against frame loud and thin in the empty lot. And this was the only place Hallie knew where there was magic. Or had been magic. And what Hollowell had done—as she'd told Boyd—was more powerful than anything Martin had been able to do. And Martin had been able to do a lot. Maybe there was something here that could tell her more about what Hollowell was, how he could do what he'd done, and how she could stop him.

She assumed there was security, because why not? Then again, who would pay for it? Martin had owned the land and the building outright. No bank. He had no living relatives—at least none anyone could find. He hadn't left a will. The power'd been turned off, all that. But the building was just sitting, might sit there forever for all anyone knew. Because that happened all the time with buildings on the prairie. They stayed until the weather took them down.

Lily's ghost was beside her as she crossed the parking lot, cold like February when it had been winter too long to believe in spring. She was tucked in close to Hallie like they were walking arm in arm. Hallie stepped sideways, but Lily stuck like glue. So she gritted her teeth to keep them from chattering and kept walking. The black dog was nowhere in sight.

The double glass doors into the two-story atrium were locked and chained. Hallie stepped back, planning to circle around to the side entrance, but then stopped to study the fountain where she'd once seen Sarah Hale's ghost. The fountain was dry, but she ran her fingers along the barely visible symbols etched into the stone basin—lightning bolts and hammers, mythic dogs, deer, and ravens.

Lily drifted past her, hovering in the spot where Hallie had first seen the ghost in the fountain.

"She's buried here," Hallie said. "Sarah Hale. Can you tell?" Not that she expected an answer. Ghosts never answered.

Hallie had wanted the authorities to dig up Sarah Hale's body, though she was the only one certain that Sarah was buried under the fountain. She'd been persistent enough that they'd agreed to look. But every time they brought equipment in to break up the concrete and stone and dig underneath, something happened—equipment wouldn't run, a generator broke, a hail storm moved in unexpectedly. There was still magic here, something that didn't want the fountain or the ground around it or anything on the property, maybe, to be touched. Hallie hoped that meant she would find something here that would help her figure out what was happening with the black dogs or with Hollowell, something that would tell her why and what to do about it.

In the center of the fountain was a stone and steel pillar with twisting branches carved all along its length. Hallie hadn't really noticed it before because there'd been water coming from holes all up and down the pillar so the pillar itself had been blurred, and besides, there'd been a dead girl's ghost in the fountain, which had taken most of her attention at the time. But now, with the water turned off, she could see that it had been carved all along its length, impossible to tell more than that from where she stood. She stepped into the empty fountain, careful of her footing because the stone comprising the basin was smooth as glass beneath her boots. She felt an odd snap when she stepped over the low edge, like the jab of a needle, or a spark of static electricity.

Lily drifted back, past Hallie then away, clear over to the front of the building where she stared at the blank glass as if it held important secrets. Hallie examined the pillar, but she had no idea what she was looking for. She ran a hand along the carved stone. Something was definitely etched there, but so thinly that it was impossible to make out what.

It was a cloudy day, though the air was dry. A bitter wind, like the thin edge of a razor, blew out of the west and Hallie shrugged up the collar of her jacket. She traced a finger along the etched stone, but still couldn't tell what the carvings were. Maybe it was nothing. Maybe this was all a waste of time. Maybe she should have gone to Iowa with Boyd despite his reservations or waited for Laddie to talk to his dead friends who might or might not know what he was asking or give him answers that were useful.

She walked back out of the fountain and realized only when she'd crossed the rim again that the static electricity feeling, like the hairs on the back of her neck were standing up, had been persistent while she was in the fountain, gone now that she was outside again. She looked back at the fountain. It looked innocent enough.

But she was pretty sure nothing Martin Weber had touched was ever innocent.

She returned to the truck and dug in the glove box for a small spiral notebook and a pencil that had been sharpened almost to a nub. Back at the fountain, she laid one of the notebook pages on the stone and rubbed it lightly with the pencil.

It took a moment to realize that the thin lines formed letters. She moved the paper slightly, took another rubbing, moved it again.

The sun emerged briefly from the broken clouds overhead. She looked at the paper.

DEATH

She stepped back.

Martin's magic had had a lot to do with death. And maybe death was always part of magic, despite what she'd been told. Martin had told her that people called what he did perversion magic, a perversion of small cultural magics that, he told her, could be practiced without blood, without death. But maybe that was denial, the idea that any magic could be practiced without involving sacrifice and blood. Maybe everything was death. Maybe it always had been.

She flipped to another page and moved down the pillar.

Rook. Owl. Raven. Crow. Dog. Banshee. Reaper. Ghost. Hell. Devil. Angel. Death.

Death.

Harbingers and afterlives and taking up souls. Death. All of it.

Near the bottom of the pillar a pair of words were carved, just three-quarters of an inch high but deep and thick and infused with black and gold. Set so low, they would have been obscured by water when the fountain was turned on. Visible now only because she was squatting and had tilted her head at an awkward angle. They weren't meant to be seen, but it must have been important for them to be there.

EMBRACE DEATH

Hallie touched her hand to the carved words. Her arm jerked like she'd grabbed a live electric wire. Every muscle spasmed. She tried to jerk her hand away, but it was as if she'd been welded to the stone. She tried harder, used all the will she had, like she had to instruct each specific nerve between her brain and the fingers on her right hand. Let. Go. Her hand finally released and the momentum knocked her on her ass with a thump.

Okay. That was something. Definitely magic, though what kind and what it actually was supposed to do, she didn't know. Not yet.

She wanted to touch the words again. Wanted to see if the same thing happened or if it had been a weird combination of wind and temperature and the way she'd been standing. Even after everything that had happened in September, she found it hard to believe that this . . . this . . . whatever had just happened, that there was still power here even after Martin had died. Then she thought, Hollowell came back from the dead. Somehow. Would Martin? *Could* he?

10

Souls."

The voice, in her head and instantly recognizable, was so unexpected that Hallie leaped back and knocked her elbow hard into the fountain's central pillar, numbing her forearm. The black dog sat on the sidewalk next to a large pot filled with dried stalks of something unidentifiable.

"What?" Hallie said, though what she wanted to say was, Don't sneak up on me.

"Wanted to steal souls from reapers," the dog said after a pause so long, Hallie had decided it wasn't going to answer. As she'd come to expect, on the word "reaper," a flash of pain erupted in her right temple, piercing and hot and gone so quick, she might have thought she'd imagined it.

Reaper.

Even thinking the word gave her a twinge, like a muscle spasm. So she repeated it like a mantra until it almost didn't actually bother her anymore.

It seemed like reapers—or at least talk of them—were coming up all over.

"What does that mean?" she finally said. "Stealing souls from reapers. How would he do it? Why?"

The dog rose and paced around the fountain, one slow deliberate circle. "Power," it said.

"More power than blood magic?" Hallie didn't like that the dog went out of sight on the back side of the fountain. She walked carefully across the base and stepped over the low edge.

"Different."

"But you can do it? Steal souls from reapers?" Which wasn't even the right question because what were reapers? Why did they exist? What did they do with a soul and what did it mean if Martin were able to steal it?

The wind had shifted to the north, almost northeast, and Hallie smelled salt and big water, like they were no longer on the prairie, but somewhere on the coast. The dog walked up to the base of the fountain and sniffed. There was a snap, like static electricity; the dog jumped back.

"Maybe," it said.

"But I still—I don't understand," Hallie said. "Are you saying that this fountain is—that it holds power in some way? Is it—"

A gust of wind so fierce, it almost knocked her back a step whipped her jacket against her spine and blew a half-empty clay planter off a ledge so that it shattered on the concrete, scattering dirt and shards. The black dog disappeared and Hallie wasn't sure she'd seen it go, though she'd been looking right at it the whole time.

Something had changed with that rush of wind, but she couldn't tell what. The way things smelled, the sunlight overhead, static electricity in the air. Something.

Hallie walked back down the sidewalk, her senses on high alert, feeling like she was back in Afghanistan, in a place where anything could happen and probably would. Her fingers curled like she could will a gun into her hands. And a squad to watch her back. There was a shotgun in her pickup, which was clear across the parking lot. A pair of birds warbled back and forth to each other somewhere nearby. She could smell dry grass and wet leaves. It all seemed perfectly normal.

She rounded the last pillar and thumped back hard against it, stopped cold.

Across the parking lot in the waist-high prairie grass, dry as old straw and smashed flat, sat a late-model Ford Focus with rental-car plates and a tall, impossible Ponderosa pine. The car had rammed headlong into the tree, windshield shattered, engine shoved back a half foot, tires flat, and the front wheels splayed out like a spavined mule.

Hallie swallowed hard against a sudden lump in her throat.

This was Dell's accident. This was how Dell had died. Hallie didn't know what kind of car Dell had been driving, had never actually seen this, the wreckage. But she'd seen that tree, had gone to Seven Mile Creek and stood right in front of it, seen the savage and vivid scar sliced out of its bark. That tree.

Jesus Christ.

Hallie blinked and swallowed hard a second time. She scanned her immediate surroundings. Nothing moved in any direction. She crossed the parking lot on the diagonal, opened the driver's door on the fly, grabbed her shotgun from behind the seat, shoved her hand into the shell box next to it, knocked the door shut with her hip, and edged along the truck, her back against the smooth cold metal as she loaded three rounds and shoved the two remaining shells into her jacket pocket. One more scan in all directions and she left the cover of the truck and walked out into the open prairie.

She stumbled as she approached the driver's side of the car even though she was sure—pretty sure—there would be no one inside.

"I can show you anyone's death."

She jerked, like a twitch, though she'd been expecting him, and turned, leveling her shotgun. As soon as she saw the car and the tree, she'd known he would come.

"I hear you died," she said.

Hollowell stood on the edge of the parking lot maybe fifteen feet away from her. He wore the same clothes he'd worn yesterday, like clothes weren't that important to him, though it was obvious from the style and the cut of the cloth that they were. Hallie walked out from under the shadow of the Ponderosa pine. The stalk-dry dead prairie grass rustled like old paper. She stopped when she stood ten feet from him, her shotgun pointed steady at his chest. She didn't know that a shotgun would do any good. In fact, she was reasonably sure it wouldn't. She'd shot Martin in the chest—twice. It hadn't stopped him. And this guy was already dead.

Hollowell didn't appear to be particularly worried about the shotgun in any case. He watched her, relaxed and apparently calm, the faint hint of a smile on his face.

"Did he tell you?" he asked Hallie.

"He told me you were dead," Hallie said.

"Did you ask about his wife?"

"I didn't fight with him, if that's what you're asking." Hallie's hands felt like they were shaking, but they couldn't be, because the gun was rock steady in her hands.

She could feel the accident behind her, even with her back turned, even though she couldn't see it. Like an ocean wave that grew and grew until it was taller than houses, than old-growth forest, than towers. Until it had to break. Would break. Like she, standing there, was all that held it back. Hollowell had no business showing her this, showing her Dell's death. The fact that he could do it was not half so infuriating as the fact that he thought doing it would stop her. Hell, that? That was an encouragement.

Hollowell smiled. Not like he was amused, more like he thought it was something he ought to do. His light eyes looked hard as carbon steel.

"I want what's mine," he said.

"Leave Boyd alone," she said.

"Oh, no," he replied. "He's instrumental." He tilted his head and looked at her sideways. "But . . . you are too. You have the stink of death on you, you know. I could smell it a thousand miles away."

"So?" she said.

"I thought," he continued, as if she hadn't spoken, "that it would be a problem. But now I think it will work out fine."

"It's not going to work out at all," Hallie said.

Hollowell continued to smile.

Hallie really wanted to shoot him. Instead, she said, "Martin Weber. Is he coming back too?"

"Who?"

"Martin Weber. He owned this building. He used magic. Like you do."

"No, not like I do." Hollowell looked amused, which irritated Hallie.

"He used magic," Hallie persisted. "Now he's dead. I want to know if he's coming back."

Hollowell shrugged. "If he's dead, he's dead."

"And yet, here you are."

"I may be dead, but I don't deserve to be dead, and I particularly don't deserve—" He stopped, took a step back, his face dark where before he'd been smug, and looked at her with narrowed eyes as if things hadn't gone as he expected.

He closed his eyes, and when he opened them, he was relaxed and smug again.

"Davies is going to get me what I want," he said.

"No, he's not," Hallie said. "If you think he is, you don't actually know him very well."

"I think he will," Hollowell said. "I think he'll do it for you." He moved impossibly fast, between one blink and the next, knocking the shotgun out of Hallie's hands. He grabbed her by the front of her jacket and flung her back six feet, where she hit hard against the rear bumper of Dell's car.

Hallie scrambled to her feet. Hollowell did something with his hands, palms forward like he was pushing something. She felt a light thump in her chest, but that was all. Hollowell's eyes widened slightly; then he laughed. Hallie closed the distance between them and punched him low, beneath the ribs, a hard, stabbing action that should have doubled him over.

Hollowell didn't seem to feel a thing. He grabbed her again, hands like Vise-Grips around her upper arms. "At the risk of being melodramatic," he said, "you're coming with me." Like she was today's prize. Hallie reached up to grab his arm, then stopped. Over Hollowell's shoulder, the sky all along the horizon was black, not gradually turning from gray to black like storm clouds or approaching night, but instant one-minute-to-the-next black, black like India ink, like the end of time, like the shadow she'd seen at the crossroads this morning—black. And it was moving toward them, flowing over the prairie like a wave, like swallowing the world.

"Holy shit."

Hollowell turned his head.

Hallie took the opportunity to kick him square in the knee. She reached up with her left hand, grabbed his right arm above the wrist, and pushed down hard on the opposite elbow, breaking his grip on her before he actually realized what was happening. She flung herself wildly to her left and scrambled for her shotgun, hoping it would at least slow him down.

Her arms where he'd held her protested as she swung to face Hollowell.

She was too late. The black had arrived.

It rolled over them like a wave, casting day into night. The world spun. Branches whipped past her, followed by a large planter, a sign, a signpost, and a rabbit, looking strangely unconcerned. She could barely see Hollowell, and she felt as if she were straining to hold herself upright though she felt no rush of wind.

A roar filled her ears, like a stadium or a freight train, the black surrounded everything—Hollowell and Hallie, the parking lot, and possibly the entire prairie.

Hollowell "pushed," palms forward, as he'd pushed at Hallie.

Something—something Hallie couldn't see—pushed back. Hollowell flew past Hallie, his body arced toward the ground, and he disappeared.

The black lifted.

Everything was gone—Hollowell, the car Dell had died in, the giant pine tree that had killed her—all of it. Hallie collapsed to the ground, knocked back by the rush of, well . . . nothing, surrounded by dead grass in a circle that went farther than she could see. She'd lost her grip on her shotgun again, and it took her a moment to find it, six feet away. She grabbed it and rose, stumbling as a wave of dizziness swept over her.

The Uku-Weber building and everything else outside the hundred-yard circle of dead grass was untouched.

11

Hallie walked slowly out of the field. Her head ached and she was seeing flashes, like oil-slicked rainbows at the periphery of her vision.

She leaned heavily against the passenger door of the pickup, then straightened. Her back was scraped and sore from hitting the car and the ground. Her right knee ached and she couldn't see well enough to drive yet. She wasn't sure what had happened to Hollowell, whether he'd banished the black or the black had banished him. She walked to the back of the truck, dropped the tailgate, and sat down before she fell down. She lay the shotgun on the truck bed beside her.

"He's bad."

The black dog sat on the pavement just in front of her.

"*You're* bad," Hallie told it. "You're a harbinger of fucking death."

The dog licked its tongue over its nose, but it didn't say anything.

"He's a reaper, isn't he?" Hallie said, feeling again that familiar spike of pain that she'd felt each time Hollowell touched her, that she felt each time she heard that word—"reaper."

The dog looked at her, like it was waiting.

"Yeah," Hallie said. "That's what he is. So, he—what? Takes people's souls?" She winced as she moved her left arm back and forth.

"He kills people." Not even a question because that's what Laddie had told her. So why hadn't he killed her? He'd grabbed her by the front of her jacket, grabbed her by the arms. But he'd never touched her, skin on skin. Was that the reason? It had to be. So, he didn't want to kill her. At least not yet.

The dog rose. It circled Hallie and then the truck, trotted over to the edge of the parking lot, sniffed the dead grass, and snorted, like it smelled something rotten. The sun drifted behind a cloud, and Hallie could see Lily's ghost floating across the parking lot toward them.

Her cell phone rang. It took her a minute to dig it out of her pocket.

"Are you okay?" It was Boyd.

"Yes," she said, drawing the word out slow, like a question, like, Why are you calling me? Because he couldn't know what had just happened. She looked at the time, just after ten, the sun still thin, not generating much warmth. "Where are you?"

"I had a dream," he said instead of answering her question. "I dreamed you drowned."

"In South Dakota?" She tried to make it a joke, but realized she couldn't quite pull it off.

"Something's happened," he said.

"Well, I didn't drown." Not exactly.

He waited. And Boyd could wait all day. Hallie would have to pace or scrub floors or go out to the barn and sling feed bags. But Boyd would wait.

"It's fine," she finally said. "I'm fine." She took a breath and slid off the tailgate; she could think better, talk better on her feet. "I saw Hollowell."

"What?" His voice held a steely undercurrent.

"Yeah," Hallie said. "I think he's a reaper."

Another moment of silence. "I don't know what that is," Boyd said, like he should, like either of them had known anything about this side of existence—other than Boyd's dreams—before September.

"I don't entirely know either," she said.

"Hallie," he began, then stopped. "Can't you—? I don't know . . . is there somewhere you can be safe?"

"I'll be safe," she said.

"That's not—" Silence again. "I know that you're capable," he finally said. "You're smart, you're practical, and though I think you rush into things, you also think on your feet, and that works for you. It does. I know it does. But, Hallie, it's not that I want to *keep* you safe. I want you to be safe. If anything happens to you—I don't want anything to happen to you. And—" He stopped.

I want the same for you, Hallie thought, but didn't say. She wanted him with her right now, in fact, wanted to reach out and just . . . just touch him, like a talisman. Or, more than that, because if she could put her hand on his face, if she could smell that—he always smelled clean and . . . like home, like things would work out, like—

She rubbed her arm where Hollowell had grabbed her. "How are things going for you?" she asked him. "In Iowa?"

"I can't find where he's buried."

"Hollowell?" Because hadn't he gone there for Lily's sister?

"Yeah, I decided—things are weird here, Hallie."

"Things are always weird," Hallie said. "Wouldn't it have been in the papers?"

"There are three local papers and I've searched all of them for the week after the accident. The accident's in every single one of them—big news. So, I know I'm right about the date. Lily—" He paused so briefly, it was barely noticeable. "—Lily's obituary is in two of the three papers. I put it in one." Hallie blinked, because he'd been nineteen, nineteen and sending obituaries to the newspapers, which people did, she guessed, if they had to. She just hadn't actually thought of him doing it. "I think her mother must have sent the other one. Both of them, though, they both name the funeral home and the service. It would be easy to know where she's buried. But, there's nothing—no obituary—for Hollowell."

"Wouldn't the police know? Or the medical examiner? Someone would know, right?"

"I'm trying to track someone down, but it's been a few years. And I can't find any family. It's getting really complicated," he said.

"It wasn't complicated before?"

"Yeah." She could imagine his expression, half rueful and half concentrated on the problem at hand. "The VIN numbers and the license plates from the accident? They were exactly the same as the numbers on the vehicles down here."

"The other accident?"

"The one Lily's sister called about, yes. The state police are interested. Cars with the same VIN number don't happen."

They didn't *have* to happen, Hallie thought. Because Hollowell had made them—somehow. And she wasn't even sure the "somehow" mattered as much as that he could and that he did.

"Did you find her? Lily's sister?"

"Beth?

"Is that her name?"

"Beth Hannah." He paused. "She's seen him too."

"Jesus. Hollowell?"

"Yeah."

"Wow. He gets around. What does he want?" Something from Boyd, Hallie knew. Or something Boyd could get. But what?

"Let's figure that out," Boyd said, his voice flat with that implacable undertone he got when something was poking at him, at his idea of how the world should work.

They talked another minute or so about logistics and general nothing. Boyd was taking Beth out to his parents' farm, which apparently was only an hour or so from Cedar Rapids. He thought Hollowell wouldn't look there for her, and after he hung up, Hallie began to wonder how Hollowell had found her, Hallie, today. He'd said he could smell her—smell her from a thousand miles away.

Because she'd died.

She sat on the tailgate again. The dog jumped up beside her, startling her because she hadn't heard it. For a minute, a long minute for Hallie, she sat there, studied the dog, turned her head and looked at the broad expanse of dead and flattened prairie grass. She shifted on the hard, cold tailgate. She'd talked to Boyd like things were still normal, as normal as things had been the last two months. But Hollowell had just jumped the stakes up a notch or two. If he came after her once, he'd come again. And she needed to figure out what to do about it.

She felt as if her skin were stretched tight across her cheekbones, like wind had stripped her to wire and bone. She stood, started to walk back out onto the prairie, and stopped—reluctant, she realized, to leave the solid steel bulk of the pickup truck, which pissed her off. Hollowell had tried to grab her, to take her with him, to use her to get to Boyd. And she didn't know what had stopped him.

She turned. The dog was right behind her.

"What happened?" she asked it.

The dog sat. "You know," it said. "Reaper."

"I couldn't have stopped him," she said, hating to admit it, but smart enough not to kid herself. "But something stopped him. What was it?"

The dog looked around, like whatever it was might be lurking behind them. But the black was gone. Completely gone. The day was cold with a northwest wind that knifed straight through Hallie's jacket, but the sky was clear, nothing more than a few thin clouds along the horizon.

"Things change," the dog finally said. Then it paused, panting. It swiped at its face with one front paw and said, "He doesn't have the power to do what he wants. Not yet."

"What power?"

But the dog was gone again, its departure so quick, between blinks, that it was as if it hadn't been there at all.

Hallie walked back to the Uku-Weber building, shotgun in hand, inspected the fountain, and circled the building itself. Not because she expected to find anything, but if there was something to find, she didn't want to miss it.

Finally, she got back in the truck. Even if he was a reaper. Even if he could kill with a touch, there was a way to protect herself from Travis Hollowell. There had to be. Otherwise, she might as well give up right now.

She drove from Uku-Weber to West Prairie City, ticking off on her fingers what she did and didn't know. It didn't take long. She was pretty sure she *didn't* know more things than she did. She knew who Travis Hollowell was. She knew what he was—a reaper. She knew that he wanted something he thought Boyd could give him and he wanted to use her as leverage to get it from him. But why? What? What the hell did he actually want?

He'd stalked and ultimately killed Boyd's wife—been responsible for her death anyway. And he hadn't been a reaper then. He'd been human. He'd died. And now he was back. A reaper. Who could kill anyone just by touching them.

Besides that, he could create solid objects out of—what? All that death he left behind—grass and trees and birds. But, according to the dog, he didn't have as much power as he thought he had? As he expected to have? How much more power could he draw? How would she stop him then?

She thought she'd learned a lot back in September—ghosts and blood sacrifice and big magic that could control the weather. But this was all new, like starting over, except this time she was prepared, right? Or . . . if not prepared, at least willing to dive in and figure out what it all meant.

When Hallie hit the outskirts of West Prairie City, the black dog reappeared. It didn't say anything, like where it had gone, just curled up into a ball that seemed too small for its bulk, with one paw covering its nose and went to sleep—or at least appeared to.

Hallie pulled into the parking lot of the hardware store on the west end of Main. Small broadleaf weeds grew in cracks in the concrete, and the storefront, once a bright red, had faded to something that might, perhaps, be described as pink. The glass door was propped open with a shiny black anvil and when Hallie crossed the threshold, she could smell seed corn, though it was the wrong time of year, and linseed oil.

If the hex ring kept things out, then iron, she figured, could be a weapon. At least she hoped it could be. Hoped she'd have the chance to find out.

"Like cabinet hardware?" the clerk said.

"Is it made of iron?" Hallie asked.

He scratched his head as if he wanted her to ask different questions, questions he had answers to. "Iron cabinet hardware? Nothing we have in the store right now," he said. "But I can order something for you."

"What else do you have?" she asked.

"Maybe if you tell me what you're planning to do, I can suggest something suitable," he said.

"I just need iron," she said. "Or maybe steel." Because hadn't her father said that the rails were high-iron steel? Not pure iron. But if that were the case, if anything with a little iron in it worked . . . "Excuse me," she said to the bewildered clerk, left the store, and went back outside.

"How are you here?" she asked the dog, who was still curled up on the seat as if it hadn't moved so much as an ear while she was in the store.

It raised its head. "Told you," it said. "You're interesting." It drew out the "in" in "interesting" and hissed slightly on the *s,* like a long sigh.

"I don't mean why," Hallie said. "I mean, how. How are you in this truck? How did you jump through that window? This truck is made of steel, right? Iron. Or from iron. Like the hex ring out at Pabby's ranch."

"Not the same," the dog said.

"*How* is it not the same?" Hallie asked. "You can't cross iron, right? You can't cross the hex ring."

The dog stretched its neck so that its nose touched the steering wheel. Standing out here in the open made the back of Hallie's neck itch. Because Hollowell could appear anywhere. At any time. As far as she knew. Which wasn't very goddamned far. "Wrong question," the dog finally said.

"Wrong question?" This was maddening. "What the hell does that mean?"

The dog rose, turned around three times, and lay back down.

Hallie waited.

Finally, it said, "Can't cross pure iron. Yeah. Impure. Call it steel? This truck. Can cross."

"Then why can't you cross Pabby's hex ring?"

"Sacrament," it said, hissing the *s*. "And dead man's blood."

"Really? Dead man's blood?" Where the hell was she going to get that?

"Ha," the dog said, like a quick puff of breath.

Hallie took a deep breath and thought about hitting something.

Then, as if afternoon sun had pierced a dark cloud, she realized she'd been overthinking the whole thing, went back into the hardware store, and bought two iron fireplace pokers. Solid iron fireplace pokers. When she opened the driver's door on the pickup with the fireplace pokers in her hand, the dog disappeared in a rush of cold wind.

Hallie laughed. She put one of the pokers in the saddle box in the truck bed and set the other on the seat beside her.

Before she could turn the key in the ignition, her phone rang.

"Yeah?" she said.

"Alice Michaels?" A woman's voice, brisk and business-like.

"Hallie," Hallie said.

"Are you acquainted with a Forest Buehl?"

"Who are you?"

"This is Jenna Jamison with the Templeton police. Forest Buehl appears to be missing."

"Missing?" She'd just seen him yesterday afternoon when she picked up the bearing kit.

"Yes, ma'am. Ordinarily we wouldn't be concerned, as it's been less than twenty-four hours, but the ag supply was unlocked all night; the lights were left on. He never closed up and no one's seen him." She said all this in a quick rush, as if this was the biggest thing that had happened since she was hired in Templeton, which it probably was. She cleared her throat, and her voice dropped back to a brisk professional monotone. "We understand that you were one of the last people to see him."

"I was?"

"That's what we understand."

"I don't know what I can tell you," Hallie said. It seemed so removed from everything else in her life, from black dogs and reapers, from iron and blood.

"Can you account for your movements yesterday afternoon?" Jenna Jamison asked.

Hallie almost laughed. Because she'd been with Boyd out at the accident. "Yeah," she said. "I'm pretty sure I can."

"We may ask you to come in and make a statement."

"Sure," Hallie said. "If you think that will help. I hope you find him," she added.

"Me too," Jenna Jamison said.

12

It was midafternoon when she got back to the ranch. Neither Lily, the black dog, nor Hollowell had reappeared. Hallie wished she knew whether the black had gotten rid of Hollowell permanently, hoped like hell it had. She went inside and changed and spent a couple of hours outside checking water troughs and taking hay to the horses. She'd found some old iron nails in the back room and stuffed them in her pocket before she went out, not sure they would help, but at least it was something. As far as she knew, Hollowell could pretty much appear anywhere, and she had no intention of huddling inside until he did.

It was nearly four when she got back to the house, her face red from the dropping temperature and the steady wind. The air felt dry, but she wondered if they might get snow tonight. Seemed about time. She parked the ATV behind the horse barn, covered the seat with a plastic garbage bag in case there was snow, and was walking up to the house when she heard a big truck coming slowly up the drive, heard it pause, drop down into a lower gear, and continue.

Hallie stood at the edge of the yard and waited. Lily's ghost reappeared and drifted cold off Hallie's left shoulder. Too late—the truck was already pulling into the yard—Hallie realized she should have grabbed the iron poker. It couldn't be Hollowell, though. Because why would he need a truck?

In the flat light of a late fall afternoon, Laddie Kennedy climbed down from the cab. A red and white border collie bounded after him. It ran over to Hallie, barked once at her, then ran back and circled Laddie's legs three times before settling with an eager expression under the bare pin oaks at the corner of the yard. The truck was an old medium-sized cattle truck with wooden sides. Hallie could hear thumps, the soft clatter of hooves, breath huffed out. She could smell the cattle too—manure and grain and damp straw.

"You didn't waste any time," Hallie said.

Laddie shrugged and gave her a thin smile. "I ran them over to the Packer place this summer." He walked to the back of the truck and began loosening the pins holding the door in place.

"The Packers don't actually own that ranch anymore," Hallie felt compelled to point out.

"Yeah." Laddie dropped one pin and crossed to the other side to drop the other one. "That's what that deputy told me. Not that I didn't know. Everyone knew. Just didn't figure anyone cared. Promised I'd get them out this week. Thought I was going to have to sell them off. Take what I could get." He started walking back the door, which would serve as a ramp for the cattle once it had been dropped. "It's only ten head. Not much. They've all been bred, though." He looked pleased. "Should calve in the spring. Everything goes good, I can sell the calves in the fall. Buy a few more. Work back up."

Laddie stepped up into the truck. Hallie heard the storm door's muffled slap, and before Laddie had the cattle turned and headed down the ramp, her father was there. No one said anything. The little red and white border collie harried the cattle up the lane, past the horse barn and pasture to the big grazing area just beyond. Hallie jogged ahead to unhook the single-strand electric gate. Laddie, her father, and the border collie moved them through. Fencing didn't enclose the entire grazing area, but it kept the cattle out of the lane, the yard, and the area around the house.

"We'll keep them down here for the winter," Hallie's father said when they were finished. He lifted his cap off his head and settled it back on.

"I'll haul hay tomorrow," Laddie said. "I appreciate you letting them run here."

"Don't worry about it," Hallie's father told him.

They stayed for a while as dusk settled over them and watched the cattle spread out and begin to graze. Ten head of cattle looked like nothing against the flat grassy land stretching to the horizon. Halfway back up the lane, Hallie's father turned off to the horse barn. A few minutes later, she saw light seeping through the cracks in the wall.

"I have a couple more things," she said to Laddie as they approached his truck. "Questions. Can you ask?"

Laddie swiped a hand across his forehead. When they reached the truck, he leaned sideways against the front bumper and crossed his arms. "You know it's not simple, right? Sometimes there's no one to talk to. Sometimes they don't tell me anything."

Hallie took a couple of steps away, turned back, jammed her hands in her jacket pocket, and said, "Have you always been able to do it? Talk to the dead, tell the future?"

It was a minute before Laddie answered. "I don't even really know if I can tell the future," he said. "It doesn't really feel like I can. It's just . . . sometimes I'm right, you know? As for the other—" He turned so his back was against the hood of the truck and looked across the concrete slab that would be the new equipment shed. "All's I ever wanted to do," he said, "was run cattle. Maybe grow a little sorghum on the side. But I figured I'd see the world first, set aside a little money. Ended up in the Gulf War—you know, the first one."

Hallie sucked in a breath, but before she could say anything, Laddie continued. "I didn't die or anything. I didn't even really see much action. I drove the big trucks. Hot and dirty and I never got enough sleep, but I only ever got shot at once. Naw, it was when I was on leave. In Belgium, which you wouldn't think anything strange would happen there. You ever hear of anything strange happening in Belgium?" He didn't wait for her to answer. "No, me neither. But I was out with my buddies. We were at some carnival thing. They told me I should get my fortune told. I didn't believe in it, you understand. No one believes in that stuff."

He adjusted the faded blue baseball cap on his head. The sun sat on the horizon, big and faintly red. "I'd asked Kari to marry me in email a couple of days before and I wanted someone to tell me yes—that she'd say yes, even if they didn't know, even if it wasn't true. So I go in this little booth and the rest of the guys are outside, laughing. We'd had a lot of beer and the whole night seemed kind of super real and fuzzed around the edges at the same time. The fortune-teller . . . she was young or, she looked young—blond hair and dark eyes, thin like she never ate anything. She asked me a bunch of questions. I figured it was so she could 'tell' my fortune, you know.

" 'You've got a little,' she said. And I had no idea what she meant, but I think it was about the cards, because I could always do the thing with the cards—lay them out and make up something that might or might not be true. She took a drawstring bag out of a drawer, said, 'I'm sorry,' and handed it to me." He reached into his shirt pocket and took out something that looked like a large marble. Hallie couldn't see it very clearly in the fading light, but it looked like the colors inside moved on their own, like thin clouds in a darker sky. "It was like grabbing lightning," he said, "or a bad wire. It knocked me flat. When I woke up, she was gone and I could hear 'em."

"The dead."

"I didn't know that then, but, yeah. I tried to get rid of it. I'd toss it in the trash and it would be back in my pocket the next morning. I tried to give it away to this homeless guy, which I felt bad about after, but it didn't matter, because it just came back." He pushed himself away from the truck and slipped the marble or whatever it was back into his pocket. "So, yeah," he said, "it is what it is. You got questions for me? I'll do the best I can."

"Why you?" Hallie asked.

"I got no idea." He laughed. "But if I ever figure it out, I'm getting rid of this thing. I'd like to say it cost me my ranch or my marriage, but it didn't. I'd have lost those anyway. I just don't want it. I want the world back like I thought it was."

Hallie could understand that. She'd wanted that for a while too. But it wasn't something she could give to him or that she figured he could ever really have. Instead, she told him what she wanted—more information about reapers and particularly what their weaknesses were, whether the dead knew anything about what the black dog had said—that things were changing.

"Sometimes they want a price," Laddie said when she was finished.

"Like what?" Hallie asked.

"Doesn't matter. It's a mistake to give them anything. Never ever give them anything." His voice had a developed a distinct edge.

"Thanks," Hallie said.

"Yeah." Laddie whistled up the border collie, who'd been poking at the old yellow dog, trying to get him to play. He opened the door of the truck. The border collie jumped in. Laddie turned back to Hallie. "Mostly, you know, people come by, they want to know if someone's going to fall in love with them or if they can talk to someone who just died. Sometimes they just want to know if the price of corn is going down. I don't know what you're doing." He raised a hand. "And I don't want to know. But it sure is a change."

She thought she heard him laugh as he climbed into the cab.

13

A breeze rose out of the west and rustled dry leaves along the edge of the yard. Hallie decided to walk the quarter mile down the drive and see if Jake had come back to pick up his car. The beginnings of a low cloud cover sat along the western horizon, just beneath the setting sun, heavy and dark, but narrow, like a thin band of winter storm.

It took Hallie less than ten minutes to hit the end of the drive, Jake's car another hundred yards east. Still there. Hallie pulled her cell phone out of her pocket. She didn't have Jake's number, but she called Big Dog's Auto on the chance that Tom would still be there. He answered on the second ring.

"Well, goddamnit," he said when she told him why she was calling. "You know, I tried to call him this afternoon. We got a couple of unexpected rush jobs, and you know Jake, he usually doesn't have a lot going on. Haven't heard from him."

"You know Forest Buehl," Hallie said, "over in Templeton? I hear he's missing too."

"Well, I'm not saying Jake's *missing,*" Tom told her. "I just can't get ahold of him."

"Yeah," Hallie said. It was almost full dark now, stars popping out overhead.

"Maybe it's the flu or something," Tom said. "Tammy Tarracino was in this afternoon, said both her waitresses never showed this morning. Didn't call or nothing. Maybe there's something going around."

"Maybe there is," Hallie said.

Tom told her if he hadn't heard from Jake by the morning, he'd come out and tow the car himself.

Hallie walked back up the drive in the dark, thinking about missing people in Taylor County, about whether it was a real problem, and if it was, about what it meant.

Hallie's father came in, and they ate a mostly silent supper of hamburgers and baked potatoes and canned green beans from someone else's garden. After, her father went back to his office and Hallie was finishing up the dishes when her phone rang.

Boyd.

"Has he been back?" He didn't even say hello.

"Who? Hollowell?"

He was silent and Hallie wished, not for the first time, that he was standing in front of her instead of on the phone, because Boyd said a lot in the silences, in the way he stood, the set of his jaw, what he did with his hands. On the phone all she had were the words he said and the tone of his voice.

"He's clearly dangerous," Boyd continued. "We don't know what he wants or even why he exists. We don't know how he finds you or, I guess, anyone. We don't know, Hallie. And I don't want— I can't watch your back from here."

Hallie could have said, I can take care of myself, which she mostly could, but Boyd knew that. She could have said, Why don't you take care of business down there and let me take care of things here, but he knew that too. She could even have said, You can't make up for something you did or didn't do seven years ago by trying to protect everyone you're acquainted with from everything. And she was pretty sure he didn't know that. Or, at least he knew in the thinking part of his brain. He just couldn't accept it in his gut. And saying it wouldn't change that.

She said, "He wants to use me to get to you."

"How do you know?"

"Well, because he told me so." It seemed pretty simple to Hallie.

Another long silent moment. When he did speak, it wasn't what she expected. "I'm sorry," he said.

"For what?"

"For not doing this right the first time."

"When you were nineteen?"

"People fight wars when they're nineteen," he said.

"I know," she replied. "I was one of them. Just because you can fire a gun, just because you do, it doesn't mean you know anything. It doesn't make you smarter."

"Lily died," he said.

"Yeah, and you didn't. Sometimes that's all you can do."

He didn't answer and she knew he didn't agree with her. She didn't entirely agree with herself. Sometimes being smart mattered. Sometimes what mattered, though, wasn't *what* you did but that you did something.

Finally, she said, "When will you be back?"

"Tomorrow," he said. "Late."

"Have you found anything?"

He paused, like he did, then said, "I found his death certificate. It was misfiled and shoved in a drawer. Then someone found it, but they never refiled it. It was sitting halfway down a three-foot stack of misfiled certificates. He—"

He coughed. Hallie heard a voice in the background and Boyd answering, though she couldn't make out the words. When he came back on, he said, "The thing is, no one seems to know how he died or where his body is now."

"Wouldn't the death certificate say?"

"It says 'undetermined.' Which is . . . unusual; they would have known he'd been in an accident. As well as not helpful. I'm going to try to track down the doctor who signed the death certificate. I'm hoping I can talk to him or her tomorrow."

"Do you think it's important?"

"I don't know. I don't know what's important, that's the problem."

Well, it was *a* problem, anyway. "Are you still in Cedar Rapids? Or at your parents'? Is that where you said you were?" Hallie had only a vague idea where things were in Iowa, though she'd helped Brett trailer a horse down to the Iowa State vet school once when they were both in high school. She was pretty sure Ames, which was where the university was, and where Lily and Hollowell had both died, and Cedar Rapids, which was where Boyd had gone to pick up Beth, were not that close.

"I changed my mind," he said. "Got everything we needed in Cedar Rapids right after I talked to you this morning. We drove over to Ames. Or Nevada." Which he pronounced with a long *a*—Ne-vay-da—not like the state. "That's where the courthouse is and I've just spent three hours going through death certificates."

"Do you really think that the way he died has something to do with why he's come back?"

"I think I want as much information as possible."

He sounded tired and frustrated. Hallie understood that because she was tired and frustrated too. She had a bruised left hip that hurt when she walked, a scrape along her right arm that rubbed against her shirtsleeve, and she felt like she'd been on a forced march for half a day.

The phone hummed, followed by a harsh crackle that hurt Hallie's ear. Outside, the dog barked frantically, as if it had cornered something. "Are you there?" she asked.

"Yeah," Boyd said, though his voice was faint; she could barely hear it. "Hallie," he began, but she lost what he was going to say—if he was going to say anything—in the static. Before she could ask him to repeat it, she heard, "Just . . . be careful."

"I'm always careful," she said.

"Yeah." Something that almost sounded like a laugh. "I know."

After Boyd disconnected, Hallie shrugged into a barn coat and went outside. She didn't see anything, not even the dog—the real dog, not the harbinger, though she didn't see that either. She crossed the yard, figured she'd retrieve one of the two fireplace pokers she'd bought at the hardware store that afternoon. She hoped to hell when Hollowell reappeared they'd prove their use.

She was halfway between the house and her pickup when she saw the shadow again, not so inky black as it had been in the daytime, dimmed under the yard light, and smaller, like it had shrunk, but definitely the shadow. Hallie moved to her left to walk around it. The shadow moved too. She stepped back to the right. The shadow paced her.

Jesus. She didn't have time for this.

She took a step back and the shadow advanced.

"What do you want?" she asked.

As if it had been waiting for her question, the shadow surged forward, quick as a snake, and wrapped itself around her ankle.

Flash. Flash. Flash.

An old man, thin and well dressed with an ebony cane, one hand extended toward her. An entire wall of flame in the middle of desert sand. Bright sun overhead, stark brown sand, fire so hot, it burned white. A farm, not a ranch but a farm, black and white cows in a field by the road, long drive, white house with paint so fresh she could almost smell it, manure and old grain and fresh hay. Three black dogs next to three white crosses.

Then, like landing, she was back in the yard, back at the ranch, bent almost double and gasping for breath. She straightened, wiped a hand across her forehead, and was surprised that she was sweating.

A sharp north wind blew across the yard. Hallie crossed to her truck, grabbed the fireplace poker from the seat, and headed back to the house, actually turning around a couple of times to make sure nothing—not shadows or black dogs or dead men sneaked up on her.

She hadn't asked Laddie about the shadow, because she'd assumed it was something else, something not related to Lily or Hollowell or the black dogs or Pabby. But why was it happening now? Even if what was going on out at Pabby's didn't have anything to do with Hollowell, they were both about death, about black dogs and reapers. So, yeah, that shadow. Hallie added it to the list.

First thing the next morning, after she'd checked on Laddie's cattle and made sure the horses had feed and water, Hallie headed over to see Pabby.

The dog jumped into the truck as she was on her way out to the road. She was almost completely used to the way it jumped right through the door onto the seat. Since she'd seen it appear and disappear in less than the blink of an eye, she was pretty sure it didn't have to go through the door to get into the truck. She suspected it did it for fun.

This morning instead of curling up and going to sleep, the dog sat straight on the seat, looking out at the countryside like it was suddenly interested.

A late-model Nissan with Minnesota plates passed them going north.

"Dead next Wednesday," the dog said, its tongue lolling.

"What?" Hallie's foot hit the brake. "That guy? In the car just now?" She took her foot off the brake and stepped on the gas again, but kept looking in the mirror as the gap widened between her and the car. She wanted to turn around, catch the car, tell the man inside to see his doctor or stay off the roads or hide, just hide. But he wouldn't listen to her. Who would listen to something like that?

"Do you know when everyone's going to die?"

"Yes," the dog said. No hesitation.

"Is Pabby right? Is it her time or not?"

The dog inclined its head. "Times change," it finally said.

Times change.

Well, that was helpful. Though it made a certain amount of sense. Because look at how many things were going on right here, right now. Black dogs, Travis Hollowell, and that shadow. Because Hollowell must have been waiting for something all these years, for something to change before he came after Boyd and whatever it was he really wanted.

But what was it specifically that had changed, what had caused that change, and how could it be changed back? Hallie was getting tired of knowing all the questions and hardly any of the answers.

She asked the dog, "You're a harbinger, right? You're told where to go? Who's going to die?"

"Right," the dog said.

"So how come you're here?"

"Told you. You're interesting."

Hallie rephrased. "How are you able to be here? Aren't you . . . constrained by your function or something?"

"What I told you," the dog said.

"Because times changed? So before, you just went from one person about to die to another? But now you can, I don't know, take a vacation or something?"

The dog looked at her but didn't say anything, which she took for a yes. Reapers and black dogs and who the hell knew what else, doing whatever they wanted to do. That was a problem.

A big problem.

There were almost ten black dogs at Pabby's ranch when Hallie arrived there, lying in the tall grass and in the shade of the gray barn. She had just turned off the truck, her hand on the key ready to pull it out of the ignition when all the black dogs stood up, turned north, and sat, narrow backs straight as arrows. Hallie pushed herself off the seat into a half stand, like that would let her see whatever they were looking at.

"Go now."

The dog turned in a circle three times and pawed at the seat.

"What? Why?"

"Leave." There was urgency in its half-whispered voice. Hallie put her hand on the door handle. If something was happening, she intended to find out what it was. The dog grabbed her arm in its jaws.

"Hey!"

"Stay," it said.

"What?" Hallie asked.

"Reaper."

The word, like the rush of a thousand raven wings, sent the now familiar stab of pain into her skull. The dogs outside pricked their ears. Hallie still couldn't see anything, though the north wind was blowing hard enough to rock the truck.

Then, like she had coalesced out of gray sky and winter cold, a woman appeared. She was dressed entirely in white—white blouse, white flowing skirt, long white shawl with knotted fringe, and white boots. Even her hair was white, a luxurious thick white that seemed to glow in the fading afternoon light.

Hallie couldn't hear anything, the windows were rolled up and she was too far away, but one of the dogs pawed the ground, the same thing they'd done when Hallie talked to them herself.

The woman made an angry gesture and the dog gave a high-pitched yelp and flew nearly three feet before it rolled over and lay still. The other dogs sank down, chins on the ground.

Hallie opened the door and was half out of the truck when the black dog said again, "Wait."

She didn't.

"Why have you not solved this problem?" Hallie heard the woman say as she approached.

"Not our fault." The dog that spoke attempted to sit, but the woman made another gesture and the dog yelped and rolled to its side as if it had been kicked.

"Hey!" Hallie said. She was not defending harbingers of death. She wasn't. Not even harbingers that looked exactly like dogs. She was looking for information.

The woman turned her head and looked at Hallie. Her eyes were cold and pale, not exactly the same as Travis Hollowell's eyes, which had been the yellowed color of bones, but not exactly human either. "You don't see me," she said. Like saying it would make it so. She had an odd voice, a faint vibration running through it, like an echo. She waved a hand and something shimmered in the air between them, but Hallie could still see her, perfectly clearly.

"Yeah, look," Hallie said. "What the hell is going on here? Who are you?"

The woman took a step toward Hallie and Hallie resisted the urge to take a step back. She looked both human and not, like Travis Hollowell, but there was something more, her skin tone or maybe the way she stood, like wind blew just for her and in a different direction than it was actually blowing.

"I am here," said the woman, "because Delores Pabahar's time has come."

"No. It hasn't," Hallie said. But what she was thinking was, Oh, shit, a reaper, which was what the dog had told her, but . . . She should have had the iron poker and paid attention to the hex ring and where was the edge and—

The woman's eyes narrowed. "Don't interfere," she said. With no more warning than that, she reached out and grabbed Hallie with both hands, one on each temple.

Laughter. Bright sunshine, dust, and cold. Early morning, the light so thin, the landscape looks surreal. Hallie turns to say something. Eddie Serrano sitting right there, right beside her. She remembers, remembers what it is she'd turned to say. It is the last thing she ever says to him: Don't forget. About a bet and a chess match. Second to last, actually, she realizes, because she sees the Humvee in front of her go, the blast driving up through the center of the vehicle, stops it cold on the trail and she is going too fast to stop. She tries to steer around it. Too late. Too fucking late. The sound and then the blast in that order. Backwards. "Watch—!" she shouts. Then the world, like a kaleidoscope.

Over over over.

At the end there is black, all black, and words, words she can't hear or understand, but knows they're words all the same.

And black.

14

Hallie blinked.

Instead of the bright brittle light of a cold Afghanistan morning, she saw gray South Dakota skies. She was on her knees, hard ground biting into her skin. She rubbed her eyes and blinked fiercely, because she could still smell it, burnt rubber and blood and singed—

"You died."

Hallie tried to climb to her feet, then sank to her knees again, one hand on the ground in front of her. She felt as if she'd run all day without stopping. And so cold, like half a dozen ghosts had rushed through her one after the other. She'd been touched by a reaper. And she hadn't died. Again. She hadn't died again.

"What?" There was a stabbing pain in her chest, like her heart had stopped and started again. It was familiar, that pain, or at least it was familiar now.

"You've been brought back," the woman—the reaper—said. "Who arranged that?"

Hallie coughed, like clearing her throat would clear her head. With her hand on the ground, she pushed herself up hard, on her feet in one rough motion and stumbling backwards so she wouldn't pitch straight forward into the reaper's chest.

"I don't . . . actually know," she said. Though what she was thinking was shit, shit, shit because until the reaper had touched her, she hadn't remembered what happened when she'd died, hadn't remembered screaming or the sound of the explosion or the sky painted red with blood. And now she did. Like someone had pulled something loose in her head and everything felt different, but the same.

She coughed. Coughed again. "Maybe it wasn't my time," she said.

"That's not how it works," the reaper said. "Your time is your time."

"It's not Pabby's time," Hallie said. "But you're here anyway."

"It's her time," the reaper said, her voice toneless, like something she'd said a thousand times before.

"Pabby says it's not," Hallie said. She felt thick, like she was in two places at once, knew she should be thinking about what this all meant, about how she could make this reaper go away forever, or at least until Pabby's proper time. But all she could really concentrate on was staying upright.

"*Pabby* says? Well, that's convincing. You have no idea what you're in the middle of, do you?" The reaper laughed.

Hallie rubbed at her eyes. They felt gritty; the world looked grainy, as if there were some sort of film over them. "Why don't you tell me," she said.

"You just can't— Shit."

The reaper was gone. Nothing left except dead grass and a rosebush with one last dead flower clinging to a vine. Out past the barn something flickered, like the prairie grass heeled over and back up. "Shit." Hallie echoed the reaper, though she wasn't entirely sure what had just happened.

"What's going on out there?" Pabby shouted from the porch. Her voice sounded thin, like they were high on the side of a mountain and she wasn't getting enough air.

Hallie raised a hand. "It's okay," she said, though of course it wasn't, was probably getting worse all the time, even if she wasn't exactly sure how.

After lingering a few more minutes outside to make sure the reaper wasn't coming back, she went inside and sat at the kitchen table and told Pabby what she knew, which wasn't much. She drank a cup and a half of bad coffee and almost felt warm again. Pabby hardly said anything, and when Hallie said she had to go, she just got up without a word of encouragement or protest and walked with her to the front door. She looked—thinner? Older? Different from the last time Hallie'd seen her. The black dogs were taking their toll.

She was still shaky when she got back in the truck. The black dog was back, waiting for her; Hallie'd expected it would be long gone.

"What was that?" Hallie asked it.

"Reaper," the dog said, the word like a whisper on the wind.

"Yeah, I know that," she said. "Why did you tell me not to go?"

"Because you are past." Wind rattled the truck windows.

"Past?"

"Past time to die."

Hallie paused with a hand on the ignition. She mostly didn't think about death, didn't think about the fact that she'd died. And that had been easy, because she hadn't remembered dying.

And now she did.

I want to talk to you.

She looked around. The words had been so clear that she thought someone had spoken them right here, right in the truck with her. Then she realized they were the words she'd almost but not quite heard when the reaper touched her. Black words written on a black sky. Words from when she'd died.

She sat in the truck with the motor running for several minutes, absently rubbing her chest.

She called Laddie again as soon as she reached the highway.

He didn't even bother with a greeting. "This might be getting into territory you're not prepared for," he said by way of greeting.

"Everything is in territory I'm not prepared for," Hallie said. "*You're* in territory I'm not prepared for."

"Yeah," Laddie said. "Everyone's been talkative lately. More than usual. It's weird. But no one wants to talk about reapers."

"Do you have, like, regulars you talk to?" Hallie asked. "Or just random visitors?"

"Actually, both," Laddie said. "I did learn one thing. Reapers have power, right?"

"Oh, yeah," Hallie said, remembering the accidents at the intersection and at Uku-Weber.

"And that power comes from death."

"That's not really all that helpful." Because wasn't that obvious?

"That's what they're willing to tell me."

He paused, like he was thinking about what he wanted to say next. "But there's something else. Something that comes from death or is created in death or . . . something. Two of them started to tell me. They said something about the moment of death. But then they just wandered off."

"Wandered off?"

"Well, stopped talking to me."

"In the moment of death?"

"I asked them what would stop a reaper. And that's what they said—in the moment of death. Then they wandered off. Or stopped talking."

"Well, what the hell does it mean?"

"Damned if I know."

"Well, shit."

Laddie didn't say anything. Hallie pulled onto the main road and said, "Have you heard anything about people disappearing?"

"Forest Buehl?" Laddie asked. "Yeah, I heard about that. I don't think Forest has missed a day of work since he was fifteen."

"It's not just Forest. Jake Javinovich might be missing too. And," she thought back, "a couple of waitresses over in Prairie City."

"It could be a coincidence."

"Yeah," Hallie said. The way things were going, it probably wasn't. "Can you ask?"

Laddie sighed. "If anyone will talk to me," he said.

Hallie pulled into the long drive up to the ranch and stopped. She rubbed her hand across her forehead. "Look, I know what you're telling me is helpful," she said. It had to be helpful, right? "And I appreciate it, I do. But there has to be a better way. I can't just wait until the right dead person decides to talk to you."

"There's . . ." Laddie paused. Hallie could hear him clear his throat. "I wouldn't trust this person. I mean it, Hallie, don't trust her. But you might . . . you could talk to Prue Stalking Horse."

Half an hour later, Hallie pulled into the parking lot at Cleary's Downhome Diner and Lounge. She'd known Prue Stalking Horse pretty much all her life. Prue had always worked at Cleary's, always tended bar, always been there. Hallie's father said she knew everyone's business, which Hallie figured was pretty normal—she was a bartender, people told her things. But since September, Hallie had suspected Prue knew more, knew about things like blood magic and what Martin Weber had been doing. Hallie tried to talk to her once or twice, but Prue had been cryptic, half-amused, and unhelpful.

But if she had answers that could help Boyd and maybe even Pabby, then Hallie intended to get them. She turned off the engine, got out of the truck, and crossed the parking lot. Cleary's was both a restaurant and a bar. The restaurant side only served lunch until two, but Hallie knew a person could get a burger and fries or a bacon, lettuce, and tomato sandwich anytime on the bar side. She hadn't had anything to eat since an early breakfast and she was starving, figured she could accomplish two things at once: lunch and answers.

Prue set a steaming cup of coffee down on the bar before Hallie even had a chance to sit.

"Thanks," Hallie said. Without looking at a menu, she ordered a cheeseburger and fries. As she sat on the barstool waiting for her food, the black dog walked through the closed front door. It leaped onto the empty stool next to Hallie and sat.

Prue, who had been wiping down the bar, paused, looked at the spot where the dog was sitting, then looked at Hallie.

Yeah, that was interesting.

"See something?" Hallie asked.

Prue looked at her. Though her hair and skin were pale, her eyes were a dark blue, almost but not quite violet. Her lips curved up slightly. "See what?" she said.

"You tell me."

A customer came over to the cash register at the other end of the bar and Prue left to wait on him, when she returned she brought Hallie's cheeseburger with her. Hallie put ketchup on her burger and salt on her fries and waited. The dog sniffed the edge of the bar.

"I see black," Prue finally said. "Not black like a hole. Not quite. But empty, misty around the edges, as if the black bleeds off."

The black dog grinned at Hallie.

"Not a dog?"

"No." Prue frowned.

"Have you ever seen a black dog?" Hallie asked.

Prue's eyes widened, just a fraction, not even noticeable if Hallie hadn't been watching carefully.

"That's . . . interesting," Prue said. She moved several steps up the bar, so that Hallie was directly between her and the dog.

"But you know what one is," Hallie said.

Prue looked around the bar. At three o'clock in the afternoon the entire crowd at Cleary's consisted of Hallie, two men at a table by the kitchen door, and a party of women across the room playing cards and laughing. Prue pulled a black purse out from underneath the bar. She opened it and removed a mirrored case the size of a compact. She opened it so that Hallie could see herself reflected in the lid. After a moment, Prue closed the compact, put it back in her purse, and put the purse back under the bar.

Only then did she say, "You have the mark of death on you."

"Because you're past," the black dog said quietly.

Sometimes Hallie wanted to leave West Prairie City and the ranch and even her father behind with a sudden desire that felt like a knife in her chest. Really, seriously wanted to leave. Wanted to go someplace where people didn't know her, didn't think they knew her, didn't think they knew better than her. She was twenty-three years old. She had never been to college. Absolutely, there were things she didn't know. But she had the mark of death on her. She could see black dogs. She could talk to them.

She couldn't go back to where she'd been. There was no way back from here.

"That's right," Hallie said. "I do."

"I don't mess with . . ." Prue paused. "I don't mess with that sort of thing."

"Sure you do," Hallie said. "You know about black dogs. You can see—what—marks of death? Laddie Kennedy said you might be able to answer some questions for me."

Prue had seemed almost agitated, but when Hallie mentioned

Laddie's name, she smiled. "Laddie Kennedy? Over in Templeton? I hope you haven't been getting your information from him."

"He's been real helpful," Hallie said. She pushed her cheeseburger and fries away. "He told me I should talk to you."

Prue blinked slowly, examining Hallie's face as if there would be a test later. Her gaze moved to the black dog. "I stay out of these situations," she said. "I don't get involved."

She started to move back down the bar, but Hallie reached out and grabbed her wrist. Prue looked at Hallie's hand on her wrist, looked up at Hallie's face. "Remove your hand," she said. Her voice was brittle and cold.

Hallie eased her grip.

Prue's face was tight, but still almost perfectly controlled. "Why are you asking me?"

"Because I think you know."

"You're very young, aren't you?" Prue said.

Hallie leaned toward her across the bar. "You mean I'm naïve? I was in Afghanistan. I shot people. People threw bombs at me."

"You think you can change the world."

"I stopped Martin," Hallie told her. "Look, I'm not asking you to get involved," she said. "I just have a question. Or two."

There was something different about Prue in that moment. Her skin had taken on a yellowish cast, her eyes sank deeper, and her cheekbones hollowed out. "You can ask a question," Prue said. "I may not answer it."

"Let's say, hypothetically, that a reaper came after you. How would you stop it?"

A woman dressed in a denim shirt with apples embroidered across the front, a denim skirt, and blazing white sneakers came to the bar and ordered a boilermaker, a shot of bourbon, and a vodka collins. Prue mixed the drinks and poured the shots, put them all on a small tray, and handed them to the woman, who took them back to a round table near a window where she and two other women were playing what looked like gin rummy, but was probably poker.

After the woman had returned to her table, Prue came back to Hallie. "I'm going to actually give you a straight answer," Prue said. "Not that it will do you any good. There are three things that can keep the supernatural at bay. Iron. Salt. And blood. Maybe blood," she said after a moment's reflection, "because it also provides power. Well"—she raised an eyebrow—"you saw Martin."

"Yeah," Hallie said. "You were a big help there too."

Prue almost smiled. She looked calm and collected once more. "I told you, I'm neutral in all things . . . esoteric," she said. "It's something you should think about."

"What? Being neutral?" Hallie laughed. "I'm never neutral."

"This is big stuff you're messing with," Prue said. "You plunge in like a bull in a china shop and you have no idea."

"I get the job done," Hallie said. "What are you doing? How does being 'neutral' help anyone?"

"I gave you information," Prue said. "In the end."

"And you can give me some more information now," Hallie countered. "I mean, I appreciate the information about the iron and salt. I do. But, Laddie told me something that I don't understand and he thought you might know more."

"It wouldn't be hard to know more than Laddie Kennedy," Prue agreed, which was the first time Hallie'd ever heard her say anything not, well, neutral about anyone.

"He said . . . well, he said something about a reaper and the moment of death, but he didn't know what it meant. What happens then—in the moment of death? Are they vulnerable? More powerful? What?"

Prue looked at her with a level gaze. "I have no idea," she said.

"I don't believe you," Hallie said.

Prue glanced toward the door. She started wiping down the counter again. "Some things should be left alone."

"I'm not leaving this alone," Hallie said.

"Well, I'm sorry. I can't help you any more than I already have."

"Because you're neutral," Hallie said.

Prue looked at her then. "Yes," she said evenly. "You can scoff if you want. It's how I survive."

"Maybe there's no room for anyone to be neutral anymore. Maybe things are changing."

"No," Prue said. "I don't think so. Things don't change." And she smiled that half smile, that seemed to say, Really, I know far more about this than you do. "You need to be careful. These are cosmic forces you're messing with," she said. "Things can go wrong—horribly wrong." She nodded toward the black dog. "You've already attracted attention."

"Yeah," Hallie said, because it was too late for warnings. "Thanks."

"She cheats," the black dog said as they walked out of the bar.

Hallie looked at it. "Who, Prue?"

"She pushes death away. A month, a week, a day. Little cheats. That's all she can do. But we notice."

"Son of a bitch," Hallie said. After all Prue's talk about messing with cosmic forces and being careful. She thought about going back inside, but figured she'd found out as much as she was going to right now.

"Why *are* you here?" Hallie asked.

"Told you," the black dog said. "You're interesting."

"Yeah, I don't believe that," Hallie said.

She had to step back quickly as a woman on a cell phone walked rapidly back and forth in the front lane of the parking lot. One hand waved like conducting an invisible orchestra and she paid no attention to where she was walking or that Hallie had just been talking to empty air.

"No, I told you," the woman said, loud enough for anyone in the parking lot to hear every word, "she hasn't been to work. They haven't seen her. No, she didn't try to call, there are no messages, no missed phone calls. We were supposed to meet here, right here. It's been since, I don't know, almost one thirty. She's two hours late. I haven't heard *anything*."

Hallie looked back at the woman after she crossed the parking lot. She was young, maybe younger than Hallie, with dark hair in a high ponytail, a bright purple fleece vest, and denim shirt. As Hallie watched, she pulled her cell phone away from her ear, looked at it with dissatisfaction, then shoved it in her pocket and trotted up the steps into Cleary's.

Hallie opened the door of her pickup truck. The dog sniffed once, then disappeared. Hallie got in the truck, shifted the iron poker on the seat so it wouldn't hit the gearshift, and headed out of the parking lot.

15

Iron, Hallie thought. Maybe steel, though she still hadn't completely figured out how. Salt. Those were her defenses. And none of them would stop a reaper permanently. Just keep them away. Which, granted, was an important step. But not enough. Not nearly enough.

And then there were the people who were disappearing. Were they dead? Were Hollowell and the other reaper killing them? Like some giant revenge plot? But if it was reapers, where were the bodies?

Hallie's phone rang and she answered it while she was idling at the parking lot exit. She'd hoped it might be Boyd, but it was Pabby. She coughed into the phone for almost a full minute after Hallie answered. "Are you okay?" Hallie asked.

"Fine," Pabby said, like mind your own business, which Hallie tried to do, she did, but it always turned out harder than anyone would think. "Sorry to ask," she continued. "But if you're going to town, can you pick up a prescription for me?"

"I'm in West PC," Hallie said. There wasn't a pharmacy in West Prairie City. There was one in Templeton. And a lot of people drove over to the Walmart in Rapid City.

"It's a pickup at the clinic," Pabby said. "The one on the south side of Templeton."

"Sure," Hallie said.

Pabby coughed again. "Thanks," she said, her voice raspy. There was a brief pause and Hallie thought she might have disconnected, but then she said, "I appreciate what you're doing, with the dogs and all. If you can't solve it, well, I won't be able to tell you. After. But if you can't solve it—"

"I'll solve it," Hallie said. Because not only had she said she would, she was pissed about it now, about black dogs that stayed and reapers who wanted to take people before their time and Hollowell, even though he wasn't Pabby's problem. It all came from the same place, from death, and Hallie didn't like that reapers could just stop doing what they were supposed to be doing and freelance with other people's lives.

"If you can't," Pabby persisted. "I've done all right. And I appreciate the effort." She disconnected without waiting for Hallie to reply.

It was just past four when Hallie pulled out of the parking lot and headed toward Templeton. She thought the clinic was open until five, but considered that it might close at four thirty. It was a flat straight county road between the two towns and she thought she'd make it either way, if she didn't get stuck behind an old cattle truck or a school bus or something.

There was a low rise coming up out of West PC, so gradual, it seemed like it was just another stretch of flat highway until you reached the top and realized you hadn't actually seen what was basically right in front of you. Hallie was trying to figure out if there were some way to find Hollowell or to lure him out, to find iron chains and bind him and then—

One blink and the next—

Hallie stood on the brakes, twisted the wheel so hard to the left that she was pretty sure the two passenger-side tires actually left the ground. The rear of her pickup thumped into the mangled back end of an army utility truck that was sitting crosswise to the road. Then she was across the intersection and straight into the shallow roadside ditch which the truck went through and three yards into the field on the other side, hit a mass of old barbed wire, and stopped to the narrow sound of steel against steel, barbed wire tines scraping across paint.

The engine of the truck whined, then died as it stalled. Hallie threw it into neutral, set the brake, grabbed the fireplace poker, and was out of the truck so fast that it all seemed like one motion. She heard another vehicle on the other side of the intersection, the squeal of brakes, then the loud slam as it hit the wreckage—the military utility truck and a Humvee.

Hallie jumped over a bumper that had come off one of the two wrecked vehicles. She noted a young hawk dead on the edge of the ditch, all the grass dead, of course, and a slender evergreen of some kind on the edge of the adjacent field, dropping needles like rain. As Hallie rounded the big desert camo utility truck, she saw Brett Fowker getting out of a gray dual-rear-wheel pickup. Brett didn't see Hallie immediately, just stood with the door open, looking at the mangled wreckage in front of her, the Humvee crumpled in all along one side and slanted up against the utility truck like it had tried to climb straight over the hood, both of them dusty as if they'd been caught in the middle of a sandstorm.

Brett's cowboy hat had been knocked off and her perfect straight blond hair—perfect cowgirl hair, Hallie and Dell had called it—was shoved up into the collar of her shirt, two strands of it running straight across her face and she didn't even seem to notice.

"Brett," Hallie said.

Brett looked at her, her pupils huge and dark. "They weren't here," she said. "They weren't here!"

Brett Fowker didn't believe in the supernatural or in strange unexplainable things. She'd been with Hallie and Boyd back in September when they confronted Martin for the final time in the old cemetery in Jasper. She'd seen weather that couldn't be explained, had seen—or heard about, anyway—Lorie after she was burned to ash. But afterwards, even after Hallie had explained it all to her, she'd said—I don't think that's how I'll remember it. Honest about it, but determined all the same not to let it change the world she knew.

And yet, here they were. "They weren't here," she said again.

"Yeah," Hallie said, "they weren't."

Brett took a deep breath. Before she could say more, a woman Hallie didn't know climbed out of the cab, sliding across the bench seat to the driver's door because the truck was at a tight angle to the Humvee and the passenger door no longer opened. She wore stiff blue jeans, a yellow silk blouse, and hiking boots that didn't look like she'd ever done any hiking in them.

Seeing that they were both all right, Hallie took a closer look at the accident in front of her. It had to be Hollowell. And she could feel an itch along her spine, because he was coming, had to be coming. This accident felt creepily familiar, but wasn't something she recognized immediately. Maybe it was the military vehicles, the desert paint; maybe it was more.

"Is everyone all right?" Hallie asked.

Brett glanced at her passenger, who nodded, brushing a hand down her arm as if she had to check. The right front bumper of Brett's pickup was hooked under the rear of the Humvee, the headlight on that side had shattered and the grille looked like some of the plastic had broken, but it looked drivable.

"If I—," Hallie began. There was a flicker, like hot air rising, and Hollowell was there, directly behind Brett. He wore black wool pants, black loafers, a black polo shirt buttoned to the top button, and a gray wool blazer.

He grinned at Hallie.

She took a step. Hollowell raised his hand, cupped slightly like he intended to grab Brett by the back of her neck. Hallie stopped. Hollowell drew back his hand. "Leave her alone," Hallie said, her voice tight like twisted wire.

Brett frowned.

Hollowell said, "I want you to come with me."

"No," said Hallie. "I'm not your bargaining chip."

"What are you talking about?" Brett said.

"And you can't kill me." Hallie ignored Brett for the moment. "It doesn't work."

"I can kill her," Hollowell said. "Just one touch."

"Hallie . . . ," Brett said.

The woman with Brett said to her, "Is she okay?"

Hallie said, "Can't they see you?"

"It's not their time," Hollowell said smoothly. "So, no. But I can still kill them."

She was too far away, wouldn't be able to jump him before he touched Brett and probably the woman with her and they died. She stalled. "What is this?" she asked, waving to the wreckage to her left.

Hollowell took a step back, but he was still shielded by Brett. Hallie wished she could will the two of them back into their truck, wished she and Brett had been the kind of friends who'd made up secret languages when they were in third grade, special sign language or secret code that meant—get back in the truck.

"You don't recognize this?" Hollowell asked. "I thought you would. In Afghanistan, the first few months, you had a boyfriend."

"No, I didn't," Hallie said, though she sort of had. He'd been a marine, a few months younger than she was, both of them pretty experienced by that time and everyone else had seemed so young. They'd hung out together, played a lot of poker, slept together twice, and then he died. Hallie remembered what his captain told her, that they'd gone out to recover a broken-down Humvee. A sandstorm came up, they drove right into the Humvee they'd been looking for, and when they got out to inspect the damage, they'd been shot by men who had sneaked into place when they heard the two trucks collide.

So this was that. Sam Paradi's death. Hallie blinked. Damn Hollowell anyway.

Brett stepped forward.

"Tell her not to move!" Hollowell said sharply.

"Brett," Hallie said, her voice sounding surprisingly calm even in her own ears. "Do you trust me?"

Brett stopped, took a deep breath. "Hallie," she said.

The other woman put her hand on Brett's arm. "I can—," she said.

Brett said, "Wait."

"One minute," Hallie said. "Just don't move for one minute."

"Are there—?" she stopped, couldn't bring herself to say "ghosts," Hallie figured.

"Sort of," Hallie said. "I'll explain. I can explain."

"Just . . . take care of it," Brett said through tight lips.

"Yeah," Hallie said.

"I will kill them," Hollowell said. "I have no compunction. Why should I? This is what I do."

"I don't understand," Hallie said. "Why now?"

"What you think is not important to me," Hollowell said.

"Too bad for you," Hallie said. "You shouldn't have stuck a traffic accident in front of me on the highway."

Suddenly, the black dog materialized in midair just in front of her, hit the ground, leaped again, and hit Hollowell hard in the chest. There was a flurry of fur and man, Hallie couldn't actually tell what was happening. She ran forward. Brett saw her coming, grabbed the woman in the yellow silk blouse, and flung them both sideways. The dog fell back, hit the ground hard. Hallie planted her feet and threw the fireplace poker like a spear right at Hollowell's chest. There was a noise, a weird snapping sound, Hollowell disappeared, and the fireplace poker dropped to the ground in a cloud of dust.

The dog popped back to its feet, shook itself all over, like shaking off water. "Thanks," Hallie said.

"Jesus Christ," Brett said, scrambling to her feet, "what was that?" Brett didn't swear very often, mostly when she was around Hallie.

The yellow silk blouse woman said, as Brett offered her a hand up, "Is your friend—? Is this the friend you told me about?" She looked at Hallie, a crease across her forehead. "And what about these—? Why is no one here?" She seemed remarkably calm, but Hallie could hear a quiver in her voice, as if she hoped projecting coolness would be the same as actually feeling it.

"Fine. It's fine," Brett said. She closed the distance between herself and Hallie, grabbed Hallie's arm, and said in a fierce whisper, "This was over. In September. I thought that this was over."

"Yeah," Hallie said. "I thought so too. Who is that?" indicating the yellow silk blouse woman with her chin.

"I don't think that's really important right now," Brett said. "What is this? What just happened here?"

Hallie took a step back. She walked over to Brett's pickup and retrieved her fireplace poker and then walked back to Brett. She hefted the poker in her hand, felt the weight of it shift and settle. "Do you really want to know?" she asked.

Brett sighed. "No, actually," she said. "No, I don't." She stepped back, then stepped in close again. "Will it—whatever it was—will it be back?"

"I don't know," Hallie said honestly. "You should maybe . . . Here." She handed Brett the fireplace poker.

Brett looked at the iron poker. She looked at Hallie. "I didn't see anything," she said.

"Salt should help," Hallie said. "Line your doors and windows. I think. I think salt will help."

Brett looked at Hallie. She looked over her shoulder at the yellow silk blouse woman.

Hallie heard the sound of an approaching car. No sirens—so someone had either called it in, saying everyone was walking around, or were about to call it in when they saw the stack of cars. Hallie touched Brett on the arm and stepped away to speak briefly to the dog. "Is he coming back?" she asked.

The dog had dropped to the ground in the shade cast by the bed of Brett's pickup truck, as if it had just run a race. It gave her a long look before it said, "If he doesn't have an assignment, then it will take him a few hours, maybe longer. Has to climb back out."

"Really?" Because that would at least be something.

"You're trouble," the dog said.

"I thought that was why you liked me," she told it.

The dog laughed. Hallie turned back to face Deputy Teedt coming around the corner of the utility truck, looking it and the Humvee up and down as if he couldn't actually believe they were sitting here. He looked at Hallie. His expression changed to something approaching resignation. "I should have known," he said.

Hallie grinned at him. "Things happen," she said.

"Yep," Teedt said. "I suppose you can explain this?"

"No, not really," Hallie said.

Teedt sighed.

16

It was late when Hallie got back to the ranch. Her father was already in bed, one light left burning over the kitchen sink. It wasn't until she'd taken off her boots, scrounged a sandwich from the refrigerator, and sunk down at the table with a tired sigh that she realized Boyd had never called her. And he was supposed to be back. Late today, he'd said. He should have called.

She pulled out her cell phone.

No answer.

No messages.

She dialed again.

Nothing.

She left a message. "Where are you? Are you home?" Because he would have called if he were back in Taylor County. Right?

It wasn't that Boyd couldn't take care of himself, because she knew that he could. But Travis Hollowell was out there. And he was looking for Boyd. The dog had said Hollowell might not be back for a while, but there'd been plenty of time for him to find Boyd before he created the wreck at the intersection.

She called again.

Still no answer.

She wasn't worried about him. Something had delayed him, and he hadn't called because . . . well, he hadn't called. She wasn't worried. It was just that she wanted to talk, about reapers and vehicles that looked and smelled like Afghanistan and friends who had died, about black dogs and Pabby. To talk.

He never answered.

She put on her jacket and went back outside, but stopped with her hand on the door of her pickup truck. Where was she going? What was she going to do when she got there? She put her head against the cold glass of the driver's-side window. If he wasn't home, was she going to drive to Iowa? Which road? How would she find him?

You better be okay, goddamnit, she thought.

The sky was clear, the stars bright points of light above her head. The temperature was already below freezing and dropping quickly. Tonight would probably—finally—be the first hard frost. Hallie turned around and leaned her back against the truck, her hands shoved in her pockets. When she thought of leaving, which she'd thought a lot before all this latest—Pabby and Boyd and Lily—she remembered this, the cold and the quiet. Not silent, because you could always hear things on the prairie—the rustle of dry grass, the wind around the corner of an old building, distant trucks on the highway—but quiet. Hallie'd been to Berlin and London and New York City and she liked the pace, that things happened there, that you could always find something, but she liked this too, that sometimes things just stopped.

She hadn't thought about Kate Matousek's job offer since she'd mentioned it to her father—hadn't thought about it much at all for the last two days, to be honest—not that she didn't still want it, didn't still think it was a good fit for her, or that she didn't still plan on leaving. But there were immediate things—Pabby and Hollowell and Boyd, always Boyd. Who better be all right, she thought again.

Because she needed him to be.

She pushed herself away from the truck and started back across the yard. She heard the wild flutter of a flock of birds taking flight from the bushes west of the house. The shadow when it came this time was long and narrow. She didn't even see it until it was right there, next to her. Before she could react, it wrapped itself around her ankle again.

Flash. Flash. Flash.

A roan horse alone on the open prairie. An orange tractor burning against a cold winter sky. Blue silos. A school bus with a slash of bright green paint across aluminum windows. Hallie didn't know any of these scenes. Not her life and not her death. But they kept coming. An ice cream stand with boarded-over windows, NEVER AGAIN painted in fluorescent yellow across the front. An autumn tree with brilliant red leaves. Sunset. Sunset. Sunset. Winter storm. She tried to close her eyes. But it didn't matter. She didn't even know if she could close her eyes, if she had a body. Would it be like this forever? Had dying finally caught her? Here? Like this? For no reason at all?

An old man with a cane.

Hallie didn't know how long he'd been standing there before she realized that he was there somehow outside the flashing scenes, though those scenes continued flash, flash, flashing behind him. He was tall and very thin with elegant long fingers that curled around the cane's knob like, despite his age, he had lost very little of his strength. He had a hawkish nose and one pale blue eye half-sunk in its socket. Over the other eye, he wore a black patch. He looked at her. And waited.

"Who are you?" she asked him, surprised that she had a voice at all, because if she couldn't close her eyes and she couldn't walk away, how could she talk?

"I am Death." He frowned, as if he wasn't entirely sure why he'd said it.

"I'm not going," Hallie said.

And she wouldn't. She didn't know how she would stop him, but if he was really Death, if there really was a Death, well, he'd left her behind once. As far as Hallie was concerned, he didn't get a second chance. This time, she would have a say. And she was really pretty stubborn.

"The natural order of things," he said.

"What?" Hallie said.

"I maintain—" Brief pause. "—the natural order of things." Like a skipping record.

"I don't understand," Hallie said, which seemed to her to encompass pretty much everything—what was going on right this minute, Travis Hollowell, dying and coming back.

"Martin Weber went against the natural order."

Huh. Because she'd expected him to say that she did, because she'd died, because that's what everyone else kept telling her. "That was kind of the point, wasn't it?" she said. "His point, I mean, to disrupt the natural order and control the weather."

Death—if that's who he was—inclined his head. "Thin. The walls. Always, always thin. But now they're too—" He spoke in stops and starts. "Thin. Too thin. I don't— I can't— Tracking is very hard."

"Why are you telling me?"

Death smiled, but his one eye looked confused or frightened or maybe both. "Because I can," he said.

Hallie coughed and found it impossible to stop. Coughed under the blue white arc of the yard light with her hands like frozen blocks of ice, palms raw from the hard cold ground and bitter cold wind across the back of her neck. But Death was gone and the flashing vertiginous scenes were gone and goddamn what the hell?

Was that a dream?

Because it hadn't felt like a dream.

Still coughing, she heard the voice again: *I want to talk to you.*

About how things work. I want to talk. She heard it twice, the exact same thing. Then nothing.

Her chest ached like she'd been clobbered with a two-by-four. She pushed herself up and sat for a minute on the near-frozen ground. Black dogs and reapers and now Death. Yeah, her life wasn't weird at all.

After a few more minutes, she got to her feet, almost not shaky.

She looked around—for the shadow, for the black dog, for Lily's ghost. None of them were there. Just Hallie. And the yard light. And the cold north wind.

Okay, then, the hell with it, she thought. Because this sort of thing didn't resolve itself just by standing around and worrying about it.

She went inside, poured herself a glass of water, and drank it. Then, she drank another. The whole supernatural world was knocking on her door. Boyd wasn't answering his phone. Every auto accident ever was probably going to be reenacted in front of her in the course of the next few days. And people were disappearing.

She spent the next twenty minutes pouring salt from a big box out of the pantry along all the windowsills and doorframes. She didn't want to wake her father, so she went back outside and laid salt all along the outside wall below his bedroom.

She went upstairs with the box of salt. And the fireplace poker.

She didn't sleep.

17

At seven o'clock the next morning, still no call from Boyd, and as she was getting into her pickup to head into town, Ole, the Taylor County sheriff and Boyd's boss, called her.

"Where the hell is he?"

"Hi, Ole," Hallie said. "How are you?"

"Yeah, okay, fine. I don't have time for that shit, what do they call it, small talk? He should be at work right now. He told me he'd be back yesterday. He's my most reliable deputy. Always exactly where he says he'll be. So where the hell is he?"

"Boyd?"

"Yes, Boyd! Keep up."

"Why are you calling *me*?" she asked.

"Figured you'd know," Ole said. "You seem to know everything else."

It took her forty-five minutes to drive to West Prairie City, longer than usual because she ended up behind an old Pontiac going forty and had to detour around a bridge that the county was rebuilding. By the time she arrived, she felt like screaming or hitting something or driving a hundred miles an hour down the main street. Because where was he? Where the hell was he?

She drove past the sheriff's station, which had what looked like all the Taylor County patrol cars parked in front along with two state troopers' vehicles. She didn't stop, turned onto Main Street then left at the next intersection, followed that street right to the edge of town. She called Patty Littlejohn, the sheriff's dispatcher. An unfamiliar voice answered.

"Where's Patty?" Hallie asked.

"She's not here today," the voice, a man's, answered. "Can I help you?"

"Like a day off or just didn't show up?" Hallie asked.

"Who is this?" the voice asked suspiciously. Hallie disconnected.

Jesus. What was happening? What the hell was happening?

She pulled into the driveway of the small bungalow Boyd rented.

It was a cold morning, no wind. The clouds were thin, like a dark film across the sky so that the sun seemed distant and faded. Jake Javinovich. Forest Buehl. Patty Littlejohn? All missing. There were waitresses who didn't show up for work, people who missed their lunch dates. And Boyd? Was Boyd missing like they were missing? There were reapers on the ground and black dogs. The barriers growing thin, that's what Death had said.

Jesus.

Lily's ghost appeared in the passenger seat next to her, close enough that Hallie's right elbow was instantly numb from the cold she radiated. No black dog. Hallie wondered if it could possibly be gone for good, but she'd wondered that about the ghosts once or twice too, and look how that had turned out. She looked around carefully as she got out of the truck, because Hollowell seemed to find her way too easily. And despite what the dog had told her yesterday afternoon, she was pretty sure neither of them knew the exact timeline for Hollowell's reappearance. She wasn't generally cautious, but she could be careful.

First point, Boyd's Jeep Cherokee wasn't here. Which meant he wasn't here. Still wasn't here. Which she'd expected, of course, because if he were here, he'd be answering his phone or calling her or . . . something.

The front and back doors of the house were both locked and the windows too. Of course. Because it was Boyd's house.

The yard was both deep and wide. Behind and to the north was a garage that was really more like a barn, two garage doors and a loft overhead, the whole thing almost as big as the house. The small side door of the garage was locked. She tried one of the overhead doors. There were outside lights, so there was electricity to the building. She couldn't tell, though, if the garage doors had openers or were just locked, because either one was likely. In any case, they wouldn't open.

She made a quick search of the outside perimeter, the back porch, and the landscaped areas around the house and garage in case he'd hidden a key to the house somewhere. No such luck. Of course. She really didn't want to go into his house, because what was she going to find? A note, saying, If I'm not back by Wednesday, I'll be at the following address? But she had to do something and this was something she could do.

Lily's ghost bumped against her spine. Hallie circled the house one more time and was just coming back around to the drive when a sheriff's car pulled in behind her truck.

"Find anything?" Ole said as he climbed out of the car.

"He locks everything," Hallie said. "Who does that?"

Ole shook his head, hitched his gun belt a half turn to the right, and crossed the drive. "Maybe that's how they do things in Iowa," he said.

"You seriously haven't heard from him?" Hallie said.

"I told you." Ole sounded irritated. He passed Hallie and headed for the back door. Twisted the doorknob in his hand like maybe Hallie hadn't done it correctly.

Hallie eyed him for a minute. "Maybe I have a key in my truck I forgot about," she said.

"Maybe?"

"You could do something else while I look."

Ole rolled his eyes. "I have to go call something in," he said.

It was a plain button lock. She and Dell had figured out button locks one rainy afternoon playing with the one on the front door they never used back home. On this one, Hallie had to pry off a metal strip before she could slide a debit card between the latch and the doorframe, but it was still pretty simple. Ole watched her from the car. She got a hammer from the saddle box in the back of her pickup and tacked the strip back onto the doorframe before entering the house. The back door led into a tiny entry with stairs leading down to the basement and three steps up to a big bright kitchen with white cabinets, a countertop that looked brand-new, battered hardwood floors polished to a dull shine, a bright rag rug in front of the sink, and a small painted table with two chairs and a vase in the center with white and purple silk flowers.

"Jesus," Ole said, coming in behind her.

"Well, he's neat," Hallie said.

"He's particular is what he is," Ole said, opening one of the cupboards to be confronted by glasses sorted according to height. "Most particular man I know. If he says he'll be back on a certain day, says he'll make his shift, I count on that." He paused, opened a lower cupboard, and closed it again. "Because I can."

"Do you count on Patty Littlejohn?"

Ole looked at her, a piercing gaze. "Do you know something?" he asked.

"No," Hallie said, which was almost the truth. "I really don't know anything."

"I been getting missing persons calls all morning. Well," Ole amended, "five. Five missing people. No one saw them go. No one knows anything about them. That's a hell of a problem. And I don't like it."

Lily's ghost drifted between the two of them. Hallie followed her into the dining room—table, six chairs, a china cupboard with two shelves of white ironstone dishes, two bottles of single malt whiskey and a bottle of Russian vodka, all with the seals still intact. There was a row of low bookshelves underneath the double window, mostly nonfiction about the Civil War and astronomy, with a half shelf of old mysteries on the bottom and two large-format books laid flat that appeared to contain pictures of old tractors and combines.

In the living room, Hallie picked up three days' worth of mail, which had been dropped through a slot in the front door.

"You're not going to read that," Ole said.

Hallie flipped through the envelopes—nothing, nothing, nothing—two letters from a B. N. Hannah. Lily's ghost touched one of the envelopes, her fingers going clear through, like the envelopes or, more accurately, her hand wasn't there at all. Hallie tucked the two envelopes in her back pocket. "No," she said to Ole. "That would be wrong."

"Damn right." Ole went back out into the kitchen and punched the button on Boyd's answering machine. He turned up the volume and Hallie could hear it as she continued to explore the living room.

There were three messages on the machine—none of them from Hallie, since she'd been calling his cell phone. One was from the sheriff's dispatch, asking him to call in. One was from the farm supply in Templeton saying they'd got in the carburetor kit he'd ordered. The last was from someone named Beth, who Hallie had to assume was Lily's sister because wasn't that what Boyd had called her—Beth? "I don't know if this is the right number. I tried your cell. . . . It's almost five. I thought you were going to be here, well . . . earlier. I'm not *panicking* or anything. But I thought—" There was a loud clatter, a high-pitched sound that might have been a scream abruptly cut off, then silence.

Hallie looked at Ole.

"It's Beth Hannah from Cedar Rapids," Hallie said because it was what she knew and it was all she could do. "Can you find the address or get someone over there or something? Can you *do* something?"

"Oh hell yes," he said. His cell phone was already out of his pocket and he was punching in numbers.

There was probably nothing to it. She'd talked to Boyd since then and Beth had been with him, hadn't she? But it felt like doing something.

While Ole was on the phone, Hallie went back into the dining room and through it into the bedrooms. It felt wrong. If he wanted her here, he'd have invited her, but something had happened. She knew it. Hell, Ole even knew it. Boyd's privacy was worth nothing if she couldn't figure out where he'd gone or what had happened.

The small south bedroom had a desk and three bookshelves. The top of the desk was clear, nothing but a desk lamp, a pencil holder with three pens, and a leather blotter. She went through all the drawers—there were a bunch of labeled file folders, all taxes and bills, a ruler, a tape measure, a small jar full of paper clips, and some unused stationery. A small laser printer sat on one corner of the desk next to a second telephone handset.

She left the office and went into the bedroom. The shades were pulled and the light from outside filtered the room in gray and gold, like time stopped here. Lily's ghost drifted into the doorway behind Hallie, but stopped on the threshold, as if she didn't want to enter. Like the rest of the house, everything was neat, precise. And yet, it wasn't sterile. It felt like Boyd, like he lived here. It took only two short strides to cross from the door to the bed. On the nightstand was a clock, and next to the clock was a small black journal and a pen.

Hallie picked up the journal. She knew what it was. Because Boyd had told her once that he wrote down all his dreams, made lists and charted the commonalities. It was the thing that made him both who he was and who he didn't want to be.

The thing.

Like Hallie's ghosts.

She picked up the notebook, shoved it into an inside jacket pocket, and left the room.

"Well, that was damned unhelpful," Ole said when they left the house. He twisted the knob on the door after Hallie locked it, like it was automatic, like he always checked.

"Yup," Hallie said.

"Cedar Rapids says they'll check, but that call was a couple days old. Who knows if they'll find anything. You know where he went, right?" Ole eyed her like she'd been holding back important information.

"Iowa," Hallie said.

"That covers a lot of ground."

Cedar Rapids, where the call had come from, but as Ole had said, it was a couple of days old. She considered. "Maquoketa, maybe. No, he was in Ames last time I talked to him. So, there. I think." Like she knew anything about any of those places. But she could read a map. She could get there if she had to. And if Boyd wasn't coming back here or answering his phone, then she would go find him. His dreams could be wrong. Or he could be interpreting them wrong. She could probably leave South Dakota. She probably wouldn't have a problem. Probably.

She pulled out her phone and dialed his number again, as if something had changed since the last time she'd done it. Ole took a few steps away from her and pulled out his phone too.

Nothing.

"Goddamn," said Ole after he hung up from his third phone call in as many minutes.

"Ole," Hallie said, quiet for her, though she felt like shouting. "How many people are missing?"

Ole drew in a breath. She wasn't sure he was going to tell her, but then he said, "Looks like two or three a day the last three days."

"Jesus."

"Yeah." Ole drew the word out, like it had three syllables. "But this is different, right? You know where he went."

Before Hallie could respond, she saw something that made her catch her breath. The still-green lawn in front of her, across the drive and past Boyd's house, was dying. Like a line of death marching straight toward them.

Hallie stepped in front of Ole, like she could stop whatever was coming before it reached him.

"Excuse me?" Ole said.

The black dog flashed into existence beside her, its hackles raised and a low growl on its lips. Lily's ghost disappeared in a silent puff of winter frost.

Travis Hollowell appeared, like he'd just stepped from an invisible room.

He looked at Hallie, looked at the dog sitting at her heels. He smiled, but Hallie thought it was a bit strained, not as cool and relaxed as it had been the first time she saw him.

"You picked the wrong side," he said to the dog.

The dog's snarl deepened. "My side," it said.

"Things have changed," Hollowell said. Then, he added, this time directed more at Hallie than at the dog, "Your side is losing."

"I hear that all the time," Hallie said.

"Who the hell are you?" Ole asked. Hallie looked at him, looked at Hollowell. Yesterday at the accident, no one had seen him but her.

Now, Ole could. That meant something. She had no idea what. But it probably wasn't good. And it better not be Ole's time. Not here and not now. Not if Hallie had anything to say about it.

"He killed Boyd's wife," Hallie said, by way of explanation.

"What wife?" asked Ole. He put his hand on the flap of his holster.

At the same time, Hollowell said, like Ole wasn't even there, "I keep looking for him and I keep finding you."

"Good," Hallie said.

The black dog growled.

"Look," Hallie said. "You better not do anything to Boyd. Because if you have, I will make you wish you'd never come back."

"You know nothing," Hollowell said. He was dressed exactly as he'd been the first time Hallie saw him, same clothes, same shoes, like he had two sets of clothing and he alternated between them. "You should not have talked to him," he said.

"What? Who?"

"What?" said Ole at the same time. "Listen, mister—"

"What did he tell you?" Hollowell asked; there was an expression on his face Hallie couldn't immediately identify—anger mixed with fear and something more, some element that seemed not quite human. Which made a certain amount of sense, since he wasn't human.

"Are you talking about Boyd?"

"Death."

Death. Hallie'd half convinced herself that last night was a dream, though given the things that happened, that kept happening to her, she should have known that it wasn't. But what had Death told her? Not very goddamned much. Nothing about Hollowell, for sure. And even if he had, she wouldn't share it with him.

Ole grabbed Hallie's arm. "Who the hell is this guy?" he asked in a low voice.

Hallie ignored him, didn't dare divide her attention.

Hollowell drew himself up so that he looked razor-thin and almost skeletal. "He's had things his way for far too long," he said.

"Death?"

"I will get what I want, and neither you, Boyd Davies, or that old fool will stop me," Hollowell said.

"This is like that damn stuff back in September, isn't it?" Ole said, still in that low voice. Hallie nodded, though she didn't know if Ole would know it was directed at him. She wanted to tell him to get out, wanted to tell him to run while he could, but it probably wouldn't help. It was probably too late already.

"What exactly is it that you want?" she said to Hollowell, because the whole conversation—Death and what Hollowell wanted, which she'd thought was some combination of Boyd and Lily's sister, was not becoming clearer.

"Immortality."

And, finally, that was pretty clear. Except, "Don't you have that already?"

Hollowell raised a hand, palm open toward her. "Enough. You will not talk to him again."

"That'd be great," Hallie said. "Except I didn't decide to talk to him in the first place." She had one of the fireplace pokers in her truck. She just had to get to it.

Ole had been moving slowly around Hallie as she and Hollowell talked. She put out an arm to stop him, but he was already a foot beyond her reach.

Hollowell smiled. He looked at Ole, who had his right hand on his gun. "Is he important to you?" he asked Hallie.

Ole returned Hollowell's gaze with an even, steady look that said, You may have appeared out of nowhere, but that doesn't change how this will turn out. "Who the hell are you?" he said. Hallie was pretty sure Ole didn't usually ask for anything twice.

Hollowell seemed amused. He raised his hands.

Hallie pulled iron nails from her pocket and flung them at him.

Before the nails hit him, Hallie felt the push, saw the young maple tree by Boyd's front porch shatter like old firewood. She grabbed Ole and shoved him backwards toward the big garage at the end of the yard. A window in Boyd's house burst outward and showered them with glass. "Run!" she said, and pushed Ole. He stumbled and it was too late anyway. The ground heaved up underneath and threw them. Hallie felt herself flying, saw Ole flying in front of her and tried to grab him. She could smell dirt and fire and things that weren't here, not here—burning oil and gunpowder and—someone screamed and the only thing she was sure of was that she wasn't the one screaming. Then the sky went black and cold.

So cold.

18

"Hey."

Quiet. Familiar.

"Don't move."

Hallie moved.

"Ouch."

"I said—don't move."

That voice—Boyd. Hallie opened her eyes and, with some effort, sat up.

"Where have you been?" she asked. Not, hi, or I'm glad you're okay, though afterwards she wished she'd said one or the other. But, really, where the hell had he been?

"Take it easy," Boyd said. "Is anything broken?"

She moved cautiously. Everything hurt, from the top of her head to her feet, but it all worked. "Nothing's broken," she told him.

She looked around.

Half the roof on Boyd's big garage was gone. The entire front yard was dirt and broken tree limbs. It looked like a battleground, like it had been hit by a mortar. Hallie scrambled backwards without thinking, because she could smell it. Afghanistan.

A quick breath and it was gone. Ironic that Boyd's hand on her arm and the arctic cold of Lily's ghost against her spine were what rescued her from that other place. Not so ironic about Boyd—but the ghost, that ghosts were home, that was ironic, like she really had died and was just too stupid to know it.

Hallie tried to rise to her feet—a flash of pain through her rib cage, though she was still pretty sure nothing was actually broken.

"Ole?" she asked. Because he wasn't just some guy. He was a guy she knew and he was only here because of things he didn't know anything about and probably wouldn't believe if he did. If he was dead—

"Ambulance is on its way," Boyd said. He had a streak of dirt down the side of his face. "Ole's . . . I think he'll be okay, but he's definitely got a broken arm, maybe a concussion. He's unconscious. He has a fairly deep three-inch gash on his right temple. There's a lot of blood," he cautioned, like Hallie hadn't seen blood before. He left Hallie then, moved like he was as stiff as she was, like he'd only been waiting for some evidence that she knew where she was and wasn't going to completely flake out on him—and when had she ever flaked out on him? He returned to where Ole lay a few feet away.

Ole was clearly unconscious and Boyd was right, there was a lot of blood, though it looked like nearly all of it was from a long gash across his right temple. A woman Hallie'd never seen before was applying direct pressure to the wound. When Boyd stood beside her, she made a move like she would relinquish her position, but he waved at her to continue.

Hallie watched them for a few minutes before she tried to get up again. She felt like there was dirt in her left eye and she couldn't stop blinking. Everything seemed oddly quiet—no birds, no traffic, no wind. Hallie felt both defenseless and yet, like things weren't that urgent. Maybe she had a head injury herself. Because that was wrong. It was wrong. Things were urgent.

She needed to think. Hollowell had been here and he hadn't taken her, even though she'd been unconscious on the ground. Wasn't that what he'd been trying to do for days?

She struggled to her feet, took a step, and stumbled, even though the ground was pretty even. She caught herself but not before she felt a sharp ache again along her rib cage. She took another step and then another, each one easier than the one before, though everything still hurt and her eyes were still not quite focused.

The black dog trotted out from behind Boyd and Ole and the woman Hallie didn't know, trotted across the broken dead lawn like it didn't have a care in the world.

"Where is he?" she asked.

"Got a call," the dog said. "Still can't ignore a call."

"What? Like to kill someone?"

"Because it's their time," the dog said.

Jesus.

"Pretty damned convenient," she said. Not that she wasn't grateful.

"Might not have been real," the dog said.

"Really?" Because the dog had done it? *Could* the dog do it? Or Death had done it? Which was really disturbing if she thought about it much.

The dog looked at her and panted.

She saw that Boyd was watching her, a tight frown creasing his forehead. He probably thought she was talking to herself.

"Where have you been?" Hallie asked him because this probably wasn't the time to explain that the dog he couldn't see was here. "You didn't call."

Before he had a chance to answer, the ambulance pulled into the yard.

Deputy Teedt arrived right behind the ambulance, like they'd been taking a coffee break together or something. He swore when he stepped out of his car and saw the destruction of Boyd's front yard, the shattered dining room window, and the unroofed garage, but he stood back while the EMTs loaded Ole into the ambulance. Ole regained consciousness as they moved him. "What the hell?" he kept saying. "What the hell was that?" Over and over, like it was the line pulling him back from wherever he'd gone.

Hallie tried to stay out of the way, but her shirt was torn from the blast, she was covered in mud and dirt, and she had blood on her hands. In the end, when Teedt asked her, she couldn't think of anything to say but the truth. Some of the truth.

"You were just . . . here?" Teedt asked skeptically. "And then there was an explosion."

"Pretty much," Hallie said.

"As if we don't have enough trouble," Teedt said. And Hallie couldn't even bring herself to be pissed. He flipped his notebook closed and stuck it back in his shirt pocket.

"Are you all right?" Boyd had come up behind her and she hadn't heard him, startled badly when he put his hand on her shoulder. She wondered if there was something wrong with her hearing, which would be really weird, since it hadn't actually been an explosion, not in the "loud noise" sense. It had been death—not the personification of, but dying, leaf and tree and grass, dying to fuel a reaper.

"I'm fine," she said, dragging her fuzzy brain back to the present and Boyd's question. And hadn't she already told him that? She looked around, felt like she'd completely forgotten to do that, to look around. Where was Lily's ghost? Where was the black dog? Hadn't it been here a minute ago? Was it important, that they weren't here? Or normal.

Maybe she *had* been hit on the head.

In some way that seemed mysterious to Hallie afterwards, the ambulance pulled away. Teedt got back in his car, talking to people, possibly random strangers, on his radio. Eventually, he also pulled away. Hallie found herself standing on Boyd's front porch.

"What happened?" he asked her, standing in front of her looking calm and patient. But wasn't he the one who'd been missing? Wasn't all this about him? He pushed her toward a chair, but she didn't move. She couldn't sit down yet, because she wasn't doing it, wasn't letting go, until something—at least one thing—made sense.

"We should go inside," she said, because they were in the open here. Anything could happen. She wasn't sure they'd be safer in the house, but then again, they might.

Boyd unlocked his front door. It seemed randomly funny to Hallie, that his door was locked, after everything, after she'd already been through his house looking for clues, after shattered windows. The woman, who Hallie finally realized must be Lily's sister, had retreated to a corner of the porch, hunched between the railing and the living room window. Splintered wood hung off what was left of the railing. She had auburn hair that curled wildly to her shoulders, a ruby red tank top, short leather jacket with a fake lambskin collar that just skimmed the top of her low-rise jeans, high-heeled boots, and a bright orange purse big enough to fit Boyd's entire house in. Hallie'd initially figured her for mid-twenties, but as she looked closer, she realized she was young, maybe no more than eighteen or nineteen.

She looked cold, but Hallie couldn't tell if she really was cold or just frightened. Boyd looked at Hallie as if to make sure she wasn't going to fall over right in front of him, then went over to the young woman, and with an arm on her elbow and one lightly touching her shoulder, he steered her toward the front door.

As she passed, Hallie could hear her say, "It's too late, isn't it? It's already too late."

Then Boyd was standing in front of Hallie again and she couldn't figure out how he'd done that, like a minute or two had slipped away from her entirely. "Let's go inside," he said. He hesitated. "Hallie, you're—" He reached toward her face and she flinched. "—you're bleeding," he finished, awkward because his hand was still hanging in the air halfway between them.

"What?" Hallie said.

"Maybe you should have gone with Ole," Boyd said as he waited for her to precede him into the house.

"Maybe," Hallie said, by which she meant no.

She already knew where the bathroom was, so as soon as they were inside, she headed straight for it, went inside, and closed the door.

It was a tiny bathroom, just space enough for the sink, toilet, and tub. She flipped on the light and looked at herself in the mirror. She had a shallow cut above her right eye, which hurt when she touched it, though she hadn't felt it at all until right that moment. Her face was streaked with dirt, and when she ran her fingers through her hair over the sink, coarse dirt rained down like hail. Bruises were already blossoming on her arms and along her right jawline. She could feel a stab of pain where her hip bone had connected with the ground, layered over the bruising she got out at Uku-Weber the day before.

She ran water in the sink, found a stack of towels and washcloths in a narrow cupboard behind the door, and washed the worst of the dirt and blood off her face and hands.

Boyd knocked on the door. "Are you all right?" he asked.

"It's fine," Hallie said. Not, I'm fine, because she wasn't and she needed a moment to stand there and breathe and stick a couple of butterfly bandages on the cut on her forehead. Because of course Boyd had butterfly bandages. He had six boxes of bandages, more kinds than Hallie had known existed.

Because he was Boyd. Because he had to.

He opened the bathroom door and handed her a clean plaid flannel shirt.

"Thanks," she said, but he was already gone.

When Hallie finally opened the bathroom door, she felt ready to face whatever was out there. Lily's ghost had returned and floated past her in a chill breath of arctic air. Boyd stood in the small hallway that separated the two bedrooms.

"Do you have coffee?" she said, because she just needed him to back off some. Seriously.

Boyd blinked. "Sure," he said after a moment. He went into the kitchen and Hallie walked out into the dining room, rolling up the sleeves on the shirt Boyd had given her. The girl was there, near the windows, pulling her hair back against the nape of her neck, then releasing it.

"Who are you again?" Hallie asked, not that anyone had told her in the first place, or had a chance to. Not that she didn't know, or was at least pretty sure, but it would be nice if someone said it.

The girl startled, like she'd thought for some odd reason she was alone. Lily's ghost drifted toward her, reached out a ghostly hand, and touched her curls. The girl moved sideways abruptly, as if she'd felt a sudden draft. She looked out the window, like looking over her shoulder.

"I'm Beth," she finally said. "Beth Hannah. Boyd—well, maybe he should tell you because it's all a little crazy." She paused and Hallie could see her take a deep breath, like a gulp.

"I'm Hallie," Hallie said, even though Beth hadn't asked. You shouldn't just trust that I'm not going to hurt you, Hallie thought. But Boyd had let her in the house and maybe Beth trusted Boyd.

"You should sit." Boyd's voice, right next to her, made her jump. He put a hand on her arm and when she turned, he handed her a white ironstone mug filled with hot coffee. She accepted it without a word and crossed into the living room to sit in a chair between the fireplace and the front windows, where she could see the yard and the street just beyond it.

"He's coming back," she said.

"How soon?" Boyd asked.

"I have no idea," Hallie said. "He's never around very long." Huh. She'd just realized that. "But he comes back."

Boyd's nod was tight, like anything more would be extra motion. "Okay," he said. "Okay." Like he was going to figure this out if it killed him. He was wearing a dark red barn coat with a pair of jeans that looked brand-new, a dark blue button-down shirt with thread-thin white lines making squares like grid work, and freshly polished boots. He looked like he had a bruise along the left side of his face, but Hallie couldn't tell if it was that or the light above their heads casting shadows.

"But he'll be back." Hallie thought this was the important point.

"He'll be back," Boyd said grimly.

"Catch me up," she said. "Why is she here?" Then, because even Hallie realized that was rude, she said it to Beth. "Why are you here?"

Beth took a step forward, her arms out wide, intense. "Because he *wants* me," she said, like that would explain everything.

"For what?" Hallie asked.

"We don't know," Boyd said. "Probably for the same reason he wanted Lily."

"But he's dead now."

"Yeah," Boyd said heavily, like he spent half his days wishing the world would make sense.

Beth took a deep breath, looked at Boyd, then started pacing in the narrow space between the front door and a set of low bookshelves underneath the windows.

"Okay, see, I've been seeing him on and off for the last week.

Mostly just in different places, like if I was at the mall, I'd see him in the parking lot. Or if I went to the grocery store, he'd be in the produce aisle. You know?" Like everyone had a stalker, like that was the way things were.

"Three days ago, he came to my apartment—I live in Cedar Rapids, you know. Iowa," she added unnecessarily. "I think he thought I wouldn't recognize him, because I was a kid when he used to come around, when he wanted Lily to—" She stopped and looked around the room as if looking for something familiar. Boyd gave her a slight nod when she looked at him. "—when he wanted Lily."

"But you recognized him?" Hallie said. Boyd had crossed the room again after handing Hallie her coffee, and he leaned against the front door as if to keep things out. In the better light he looked pale. And that was definitely a bruise. She looked away from him and back at Beth. Right now, she wanted to know only two things—when was Hollowell coming back, and how did they stop him?

She hoped whatever Beth was telling them right now would help her figure out the answers.

"Oh, yeah," Beth said. She'd lost some of her fear as she spoke, looked more angry and less terror-stricken. "I recognized him. But I knew it couldn't be him. Because he died. I knew he'd died. I thought maybe it was his evil twin or something."

"His good twin," said Hallie.

"What?"

"Well, Travis was the evil twin, right? He killed Lily. I mean, if they'd been twins. Which . . . they weren't," she finished awkwardly, reached up to rub her head, then stopped because moving her arm like that pulled at her injured ribs. Boyd frowned at her, made like he would move across the room toward her, but she waved him off. She was fine. She was. She drank the rest of her coffee.

"Okay," Beth said, the word drawn out like it was half a question.

"Well, anyway, he asked if he could come in and I didn't even know what to say. You know, it's not all that often that your dead sister's dead stalker comes back to haunt you."

"Like probably never," Hallie said.

"Like, exactly," Beth said.

After a brief moment, she continued. "He didn't try anything. He said he just wanted to talk. He said he remembers me and he always liked me and he misses Lily. Which I would say is the creepiest part, except he's dead, you know. That trumps all the other creepy by, like, a hundred."

"What did he say when you asked him about it?" Hallie asked. "About being dead."

"He laughed."

"Did he tell you what he wanted?"

Beth stopped pacing. She stood in the middle of the living room and didn't look at either Hallie or Boyd. "He said I could see her again. If I went with him. He said he could take me to see Lily."

19

Jesus."

"Yeah, like I would go."

Hallie wondered if he could, though, if he could take someone to the other side, if she—or anyone—could cross to the other side, if she could see Dell again. Or Eddie Serrano. Or her mother.

She blinked.

"And then the wrecks," she said. It wasn't really a question.

"Yeah, like the next day." Beth's eyes were wide, as if she couldn't quite believe any of it, couldn't believe she was here, in this house, in South Dakota, telling this story. "And I was scared shitless, let me tell you. I expected him to show up any minute. I went home and grabbed my stuff and I went and hid in a church."

"In a church?"

"Well, I thought, you know, that maybe he couldn't go in there, because he was dead and it would be sacred ground."

"Did it work?"

"I don't know. That was when Boyd came. We went back to my apartment and we didn't see him at all. But maybe he just wasn't around."

"But you've seen him since."

"I don't think he just knows where someone is," Boyd said. "I think he has to find them."

He knows where I am, Hallie thought, though she didn't say it. Her head was hurting worse and she wanted to go back in the bathroom and look for aspirin. Instead, she said, "He can't cross iron."

"What?" Boyd looked at her like maybe she hadn't been listening to anything they said. Or like maybe he'd lost track of the conversation himself somewhere.

"And I think," because Hallie had to get this whole thought out of her head and into enough order that it actually made sense before she could go back and explain what she meant. "I think he's here because the walls are getting thinner."

"What does that mean?" Boyd seemed irritated beyond the specific conversation they were having.

"I—" There was movement out the window, a dark shape. Hallie looked, expecting the black dog maybe. But it was Hollowell. "Hell," she said. "He's back."

"Shit." Which was always a surprise, coming from Boyd. He crossed quickly to the window while Beth retreated to the corner of the living room away from the windows.

"Why is he doing this? What does he want?" Beth said. She looked like she wanted to hide in or under something, and Hallie could hardly blame her.

Boyd turned and left them—to lock the back door? Hallie wasn't sure. She stood. Hollowell was just standing there, looking at the house. What was he waiting for?

Boyd returned with his service pistol still in its holster and the flap unsnapped. "I'm going out there," he said.

Before Hallie could say anything or move—and when had she

gotten so slow?—he had the door open and was out on the porch and going down the steps.

"Goddamnit!"

Hallie made to follow him, but Beth grabbed her arm. "What should we do?"

Boyd was walking across his devastated front yard, and Hollowell was standing there, just standing there.

Can't cross iron.

The fireplace poker. Which was in her truck. Which she'd have to go past Hollowell to get to.

But, iron, yes. That had been amply demonstrated already. She headed into the kitchen, ignoring Beth, who was safe for the moment, if only because Hollowell was still outside. And he was going to stay outside if Hallie had anything to do with it.

Boyd had pots and pans in the drawer under his stove, but no cast-iron skillet. She went halfway down the basement stairs, but as soon as she saw there was no workshop or anything except an old furnace and a row of shelves stacked with plastic tubs, she reversed and ran back upstairs and straight out the back door.

At the garage she didn't hesitate, just lifted her foot and smashed in the side door, feeling the impact all the way up her spine. There was a red tractor with narrow wheels in the middle of the garage, parts laid out in rows on the concrete floor. Tools hung on the walls, and Hallie grabbed a prybar though she wasn't sure how much iron it had in it, but what had the dog told her? It had said something when she'd asked about the hex ring, about why it worked, because buried iron didn't last and the hex ring definitely had.

Dead man's blood and sacrament. That was what made steel as good as iron.

But you couldn't get a dead man's blood just anywhere, not even in a cemetery, not after embalming fluid and all that. Goddamnit, she didn't have time for this.

Wait.

She'd been dead once. Right? Maybe it counted. The dog and Hollowell and even the reaper out at Pabby's had all treated her like she was different. It was what she had, right now. And right now was when she had to have something. She left the garage, ripped off the butterfly bandages, scraped the cut on her forehead hard to start it bleeding again, and rubbed the blood on the tip of the crowbar. She didn't really know any sacraments, just, "Now I lay me down to sleep. . . ." It would have to do.

She arrived in the front yard in time to hear Hollowell say, "I simply want to talk to her."

"You've already talked to her," Boyd said. "She doesn't want to talk to you." He didn't have anything to back him up, to stop Hollowell from doing pretty much anything he wanted. He must have known there was hardly any chance the bullets in his gun would work, but he stood there like they would, like he had the entire Taylor County sheriff's department backing him and maybe the state police besides, like Hollowell could never move him.

Like he would defend this spot to the death. Which Hallie knew he would.

"I'd like her to tell me that," Hollowell said. He sounded so smooth and urbane, as if this were any conversation, as if he were confident that he would prevail in the end, as if he hadn't tried to kidnap Hallie, hadn't tried to kill Brett, hadn't just visited destruction on Boyd's yard.

"No." Boyd brought his own brand of steel. Hallie could hear it in his voice.

But all the backbone in the world wasn't going to do him any good;

one touch from Hollowell and he'd be dead. And he didn't know it. Though Hallie knew he'd stand there anyway, even if he did.

Hollowell tilted his head and looked at Boyd as if he were some particularly odd bug. "I should have killed you when I had the chance."

A muscle twitched just under Boyd's cheekbone. He shook his gun out of the holster.

Jesus.

Hallie stepped straight in before either of them could do anything else and hit Hollowell square in the chest with the crowbar. "Does that hurt?" she asked. He flickered—actually flickered, but then he came back. Steel, not iron. Maybe this wouldn't work. Then Hallie hit him again. He stayed gone.

"What the hell was that?" Boyd asked her.

Hallie stumbled. Boyd caught her by the elbow. It felt like something had gone out of her when she'd hit Hollowell. Not like the headaches she sometimes got, more like hollowed out, like something gone inside her.

"We need to get out of here," she said.

Boyd nodded, focused and direct, but he said, "He can find us anywhere."

Hallie had some thoughts about that, because he seemed to be able to find her—her, not Boyd or Beth—all the time. But her thoughts were so muddy, swirling in her head with black dogs and Death and everything that had been slammed across Boyd's yard. "I know a place," she said. "Where Hollowell can't get to Beth. But we need to go now."

Boyd was moving almost before she finished talking, striding ahead of her into the house and back out again with a shotgun in addition to the pistol he was already carrying, three boxes of shells, and Beth following him, bewildered but also looking kind of pissed, which Hallie understood and which would probably get her through this thing, whatever this thing was, better than being afraid. She also thought the pistol and shotgun were kind of useless, but she didn't say it.

Boyd had brought a first-aid kit—because of course he had an extra—which he tossed to Hallie as he passed. She turned and followed the two of them—Boyd and Beth—to the vehicles and realized only when they were standing in front of them that the second vehicle in the driveway was not Boyd's red Jeep Cherokee, but a late-model metallic gold SUV with Iowa plates she'd never seen before.

"What's this?" she asked as Boyd slid the shotgun into the back.

Boyd straightened and looked square at her. "We had a little problem," he said.

Hallie might feel as if her thoughts were thick and slow, but she figured that out quick enough. "He found you down there?" Because that shot her theory all to hell, her theory that he could find her but not them, what they did next depended on that one specific fact.

Because she was past.

"No," Boyd said, then, "No, no. It was just . . . it was stupid. Some truck, a gravel truck, its brakes failed and it hit us in an intersection. My phone got smashed. Your number was stored in my address book. I'm sorry."

"Really? That seems—" Well, actually, it seemed like exactly the kind of thing that happened right when you needed it not to happen. But he could have called the ranch, because that was in the directory. "Are you all right?" she asked suspiciously. "Because—"

"Are we in a hurry?" Boyd asked. "I thought we were in a hurry."

"Right," Hallie said. "Okay." Because Boyd was right—they could talk about the details later. She backed up a step, away from the SUV, and Boyd stepped toward her. Beth was already in the passenger seat, adjusting her seat belt and looking straight ahead out the windshield, like, Let's get on the road already. Hallie held up her hand to hold Boyd off and tried to think things through. "I don't know if I can explain this well," she finally said. And then she didn't explain it at all. "I think he'll find me before he finds you," she said.

Boyd was standing really close to her now, his gaze locked on her face. "I don't think we should split up," he said, as if he were already ahead of her.

Hallie put a hand on his face, so natural and automatic, she didn't realize she'd done it until he raised his hand to hers. "We have to make sure Beth is safe," she said. "That's what's important right now."

"You're important too." He pulled her hand down and held it.

"But I've got this," she said, holding up the prybar. "You saw what it did. And," she added, "I can handle myself. You know that."

"I do know that," he said. "But I don't like it."

Hallie liked it, liked parts of it anyway. She liked the part where she might get into a straight-up fight. And she liked the part where Boyd and Beth might be safe. She didn't like the part where they didn't know where Hollowell was or when he might appear. She particularly didn't like the part where she didn't know whether this would work.

But Hollowell kept finding her. Not Boyd. Not Beth. Her. It made sense that she could draw him off, head away from Pabby's ranch while Boyd and Beth headed toward it. He couldn't kill her—she was pretty sure—hurt her, maybe. Kidnap her, which was the real danger of this plan. Or that it wouldn't work at all, that Hollowell would find Boyd and Beth on the road and Hallie wouldn't be there.

"I don't like it either," she said. "But it's what we've got." She took the prybar and Boyd's extra first-aid kit, carried them back to her pickup truck, and slid them behind the seat.

She turned back to Boyd, glad at the moment for the extra distance between them. She wanted desperately to stop, to get her bearings, to sit with him somewhere quiet, for him to tell her everything that had happened in Iowa. But those were not the options on the table. And if the army and Afghanistan had taught her anything, it had taught her to go and keep going, because sometimes that was all that got you through. She sucked in her breath.

"You know Pabby Pabahar, right?"

"Delores?"

"Okay. Yes."

She gave Boyd directions to Pabby's ranch and explained as much as she could explain about Pabby and the hex ring. "Beth will be safe there," she said. "You and I will have some time to plan our next move, specifically how to take care of Hollowell. Because there has to be a way."

She didn't tell him that Death was talking to her, because frankly she didn't think there was much to tell. She also didn't tell him about the people who had disappeared, even though there was a lot to tell there, even though they absolutely needed to figure that out. And how weird had her life gotten that she expected their disappearance was related to everything else that was going on and not, say, a random serial killer.

Boyd wrote down a phone number in the small notebook he carried in his pocket and handed it to Hallie. "Beth's cell phone," he said, and Hallie realized she should have thought of that, thought of how they were going to stay in touch when they split up.

"Listen," she said. She stepped over and took the iron fireplace poker out of her truck. She still had the prybar, which worked if not quite so effectively. "Take this," she said to Boyd. "It's like the hex ring—iron. Not that he can't cross it, but if you see him, if you hit him with it, it will stop him."

Boyd unloaded his shotgun, put it in the SUV on the floor. He fastened the pistol in its holster to his belt and took the poker from Hallie. "Hit him with this?" he said, though he had seen her with the prybar.

"Don't let him touch you," she said, and couldn't keep the tension from her voice. "He's a reaper. He'll—" She couldn't say it. "Don't let him touch you."

"I don't—," Boyd began.

"I know." Hallie cut him off. Because he didn't like it and he didn't want to do it this way and there wasn't any other way to go. It had to be like this. "I think I can make iron shot," she said. "Cast iron crumbles; it should be doable. We just need to find some—like a skillet, or old pipe. We can smash it up, load it into shells."

"We need to know what he wants," Boyd said.

"He wants me," Beth said. She'd rolled down the passenger window of the SUV.

"But why?" Hallie asked. "And why doesn't he just take you?"

"Why didn't he just take Lily?" Boyd said. "It's as if he doesn't just want to have her or to marry her—he wants her to want to marry him."

"He said he was sure I'd do it—go with him—if I just took the time to understand," Beth said.

"Would you?" Hallie asked.

Beth wrinkled her nose. "No," she said definitely.

"All right," Hallie said. Though it wasn't, was getting more and more messed up all the time.

Boyd kissed her before he left, by her pickup, close and awkward, like high school freshmen about to board separate buses. Hallie wanted to laugh, though there was nothing to laugh about, wanted this moment to be lighthearted: See you in the funny papers, as her grandfather used to say when she was five. But it wasn't lighthearted and she didn't laugh. She didn't even say good-bye.

20

Hallie watched Boyd and Beth pull out of Boyd's driveway with mixed feelings. If she was right, then they would be safe driving out to Pabby's ranch. If she was wrong . . . well, she'd better be right.

There was a crack in the windshield that she hadn't noticed until she was sitting behind the wheel. It began low in the center directly underneath the rearview mirror and went straight up and to the right. Faint spidering ran from the original point of impact, dirt driven hard into the glass. She started the engine and put the truck in gear. One more thing she'd worry about later. She drove out of West Prairie City and took a left toward Templeton. If she didn't see Hollowell, she'd stop at the grocery store over there and stock up. If Pabby was going to be putting them—or at least Beth—up for several nights, she'd need more food. She should probably get that prescription she hadn't managed to pick up last night. There wouldn't be another opportunity for a while.

Hallie thought she saw Hollowell just at the edge of West Prairie City, but it turned out to be Will Tolliver, whom she'd been in high school with, standing in his parents' driveway. He was dressed like a banker in a white shirt and tie, which was what had fooled Hallie—also that she hadn't seen him in four or five years. She waved at him as she drove by and he waved back, though she was pretty sure he had no idea who she was. Then, as she watched—and it happened fast, because otherwise she'd have been past him and missed it—he took a step forward and disappeared. Hallie slammed on her brakes and sat there with her truck idling in the middle of the road, too stunned to do anything else.

Had there been a flash of black, like the world had gone negative? She thought maybe—maybe there had. Then he'd been gone.

Jesus.

Jesus.

She pulled the truck to the curb, left it running, and got out. She walked to the spot where Will had been. She thought the grass was a little flat, but it was all low and brown and hard to tell. The sky was dark enough though it was still midafternoon that things had a faded flat quality. Hallie reached out tentatively and touched the ground. Pain like a pinprick through her fingertips.

Everything is thin now, she thought. And it works both ways. Reapers and black dogs come through to our world; we fall into theirs. If they didn't stop Hollowell. If they couldn't fix this. She didn't even want to think about what that would mean.

At the intersection between SR 54 and the county road, she thought she saw the shadow, Death's shadow. She stopped the truck and got out. She jumped the fence into an ungrazed pasture, her ribs twingeing at her. She could see it—or what she thought was it—bending the grass over like a breeze that wasn't there, heading straight into the field away from her.

Damn it.

She walked back to her truck, put it back in gear, and went on.

She didn't see anything suspicious the rest of the drive to Templeton or running errands. Besides the grocery and the clinic, she stopped at the ag supply where there was someone new at the checkout and picked up a box of steel shot. Self-loaded cast-iron shot would be good, but she could make the steel shot work too—or so she hoped. Halfway out the store she went back and got some steel-jacketed bullets. Maybe they could make Boyd's pistol useful too.

She stopped at Laddie's, but he wasn't there. She called him. He answered on the second ring.

She didn't waste time on a greeting or small talk. "I need more," she said. "I need to know what the 'moment of death' thing means." Because it better mean something. It better not be a waste of time. Hallie couldn't afford to waste time.

"They're not talking to me," Laddie said.

"What?"

"The dead. I've been trying to get someone to talk to me for the last day and . . . nothing."

"That can't be good."

"Yeah, I don't think it is," Laddie said. He sounded worried, like maybe the dead were getting out of town before disaster hit.

"Laddie, it's—" Hallie had told Laddie some of what was going on, but she wasn't sure whether he understood that they were talking life-or-death. But then, they were talking about reapers. Wouldn't it always pretty much be life-or-death? "I really need to know."

"Did you talk to Prue?"

"She wasn't exceptionally interested in helping."

"Where are you?"

"I'm at your place, but I'm heading out to the Pabahar ranch from here." She told him about the hex ring and why it was important.

"Look," Laddie said after she was finished, "I'll talk to her."

"Prue?"

"Yeah." He drew the word out long, like in his head he was still talking himself into it. Hallie told herself to talk to him about his history with Prue after all this was over. If there was an after.

"Thanks, Laddie." She paused, then added, "Laddie, this is—I think this is more than just one rogue reaper. And I think it's getting worse, like a lot worse. If you want to walk away, it's okay. You can still run your cattle."

"You know," Laddie said. "People come to see me. Some of them, they come in kind of sideways, like they hope no one will see them, like they're kind of embarrassed by the whole thing. They want to know if someone will love them or if their wife will leave them or they want to talk to their kid who died in Iraq or something. They hate asking and they don't want to want it. After, it's like they won't look me in the eye. I go to the feed store or down to the Viking or the cattle auction all the way over to Pierre, because people come from all over. And they won't look at me, don't hardly want to admit they know me. People say it's because I'm bad luck, because I lost the land or my wife left me, but it's because I tell them things they don't want to know or want to know so bad, it makes them cry.

"This, what you're doing, feels important. Like it matters. And I'd give a lot to do something important. It's been a while since I've done that." He was silent for a long moment and Hallie wasn't sure if he'd disconnected or not. Then he said, "One of the dead, she's been around a long time. She says she once heard of a man who fought off his own death. That he could see the reaper and when it touched him, he stabbed it in the chest with a . . . well, I don't know what it was, but the reaper disappeared."

"The moment of death?"

"Yeah. Maybe?"

Maybe. Because that was what she had these days.

A mile outside Templeton, heading south, she finally saw Hollowell. He was standing in the middle of the road, facing her as she approached, like he owned the road and everything surrounding it.

It took more will than she'd expected to step hard on the gas and drive straight at him.

He disappeared.

Something hit the side of her truck with a loud bang.

She punched down on the gas, wondering as she did it if you could outrun a reaper. Maybe she should have asked Laddie that, back when the dead were still talking to him. Another heavy thump against the bed of the pickup. A quick glance in the rearview mirror showed her Hollowell standing in the truck bed. He swayed slightly—she was going close to eighty—but otherwise looked untouched by the speed or the wind that buffeted him.

Hallie slammed on the brakes and swerved to the side of the road. She was out the door with the prybar already in hand, the momentum from the sudden stop still pushing her forward. Before she could reach her arm back to swing, Hollowell was out of the truck bed and had slammed her against the open door, his right hand clenched in the folds of her jacket and jerking it up tight against her throat, choking her.

"Where. Are. They?"

Hallie's breath rasped against Hollowell's choke hold. "Who?" she whispered, like she didn't know perfectly well.

Hollowell's grip tightened. "Don't play games with me," he said.

The way they were standing, Hallie couldn't take a full swing with the prybar, but she could give him a short tight thump in the ribs, which she did. He flinched and took a step back. "Kill me," Hallie said. He couldn't. She knew that. And he did too—or, at least, she'd told him. But maybe he would try anyway. Maybe it would be close enough. Maybe.

Moment of death.

That was what the dead had told Laddie. Told him more than once, so maybe . . . maybe.

Hollowell smiled at her, the thin-lipped grin of a ghoul. He put his hand on her face.

Wham!

Just like that, she was there. Explosion. Dirt. Pain. Afghanistan.

Ignore it, she told herself. Hollowell was in front of her. Directly in front of her. Right here. The desert, the explosion, the sound of someone screaming. Old and done. It was done.

But it was so real. She could feel it. And yet, she could feel something else too, like someone trying to tear her head from her neck. She realized what she should have realized before, it wasn't just a reaper's touch that could kill her. He could break her neck, right here, right now, like a regular human killer.

She raised the prybar, which she couldn't feel, but which she knew was in her hand. Had to be in her hand. She jabbed it hard into Hollowell's side, couldn't reach his chest; he was holding her too tightly. But jabbed it so hard, it had to penetrate, right underneath his ribs. She felt something, something like a rip in the air around them, saw the gray South Dakota sky, then, in the middle of that other place. She drew back and hit him again, as hard as she could, as if it could penetrate stone. Or human flesh.

Snap!

She was back. On her knees on the cold pavement.

Hollowell was gone.

I'm sure you wonder why I'm talking to you.

Who are you?

You've died. And you have a choice to make.

I haven't—I'm not dead.

I can send you back. And I'm going to. But the time may come when I'll ask you to make a choice.

What are you talking about?

Or . . . you may never hear from me again.

* * *

After a moment, Hallie became aware of the hard ground, of the cold wind across her face, the quick spatter of rain on the dry roadbed. She hauled herself to her feet, leaning heavily against the door of the pickup, the cold metal biting through her jacket. She kept getting these fragments of conversation, a conversation she'd had when she was dead, back in Afghanistan. With a reaper? With Death? With someone who wanted something from her, but she had no idea what.

Yeah, well, he could just get in line.

Her forehead burned where Hollowell had touched her, like he'd brought some hellfire right out of hell with him. Her neck was sore where he'd tried to—what? Choke her? Break her neck? Whatever he'd been doing, it hadn't worked. But what had *she* done? Had she actually killed him as he was killing her? The moment of death? Or was he just gone, like before? Because she'd had the prybar? Maybe it was all bullshit, what the dead had told Laddie. Why would they know, anyway? They were dead. Killing a reaper at the moment of death obviously hadn't worked for them. If they'd tried it. If they'd even known before they died, because although it startled Hallie sometimes, how much people did know if they paid attention to the supernatural, most people didn't pay attention. It might well be the sort of thing you didn't learn until it was too late.

When her breathing was marginally less ragged, she pulled out her cell phone. Then . . .

Right. He didn't have a phone.

She dug through her pockets with shaky hands. She found the notepaper where Boyd had written Beth's number, smoothed it out, and dialed.

"Hello?"

Beth sounded scared even across cell towers.

"Can you put Boyd on?"

A pause, then, "Yes?" the one word more abrupt than Hallie was used to hearing from him. She wondered how much sleep he'd had the last three days. Then she wondered if he'd been dreaming about the future or what might turn out to be the future, if he had any idea what was coming, what was already here.

"Any trouble?" she asked. "Where are you?"

"The Pabahar ranch. We've been here almost an hour. You?"

"Yeah." Hallie's throat felt razor-edged and raw, but she was pretty sure her voice sounded perfectly normal. "He was just here."

"Damnit, Hallie! We should have stayed together. I'm—"

"I'm fine," she said, which was almost not a lie. "But I wanted you to know. It took him," she checked her watch, "over two hours to come back and to find me. I'm heading to the ranch now." She paused. "Look," she said. "This is more than just Hollowell and what he wants from Beth. Call in. Ask Teedt. He can tell you what's been going on."

"Hallie," Boyd began—like, Don't leave me hanging, like, Tell me right now what you're talking about.

"I'll be there," she said; then she disconnected, like it was a promise, like a promise would be enough to hold him.

After she put the phone away, she stayed where she was, leaning against the truck. Her head ached, and there was a blackness crowding her vision that made her reluctant to start driving right away.

She was about to push herself upright and get back in the truck when she saw something moving out in the field. It said something about how lousy the whole day had been that she briefly considered just driving away. But she didn't. She grabbed her shotgun from behind the seat and walked out into the field to meet Death.

When she reached the shadow this time, she walked straight into it instead of letting it come to her. It felt like falling. She scrambled to catch herself, but there was nothing to hang on to. After what seemed a very long time, she stopped, though it didn't feel as if she'd hit bottom. It didn't feel like anything. Except stopping.

After a moment of nothing—no sound, no light, just her own breathing and the ache of the bruises on her ribs—the kaleidoscopic images began, though they came slower than the other times, like an old-style slide show. A brick schoolhouse with the windows painted over. A man on horseback riding away. Yellow tulips in rows in a field stretching to the horizon.

And Death.

He looked younger, though not young—gray hair instead of white, a face with laugh lines at the corners of his eyes and a crease along his forehead: his eye, the one she could see, was dark, not blue. Still thin, still with a gold-knobbed cane, still dressed in black. Still Death. He still had a black patch over one eye and a deep slash across the other cheek, which looked painful though he didn't seem to notice it.

"Have you seen her?" he asked.

"Who?" Hallie still didn't feel as if she were standing on solid ground, and it disoriented her and made her feel vulnerable, which made her mad.

"What?"

"Her. 'Have you seen her?' That's what you said."

"I did?" Death looked at her. "I must have meant— I meant you."

Jesus.

"Hollowell is totally out of control," she said. "Aren't you in charge down there?" Not that the idea exactly inspired confidence.

"Over," Death said.

"What?"

He stared at her. "Not down," he said, then frowned as if he'd forgotten what he was going to say. "Not down," he finally said again. "Over. A separate space."

"Huh," Hallie said. By which she meant, I don't care. Because she didn't. Because she was talking to Death. Talking. To Death. Where Death lived when he was at home seemed like a minor and petty detail.

For a moment there was silence, as if neither of them could recover from that brief unnecessary side trip. Then Hallie said, "Hollowell. And the white reaper, the one who's after Delores Pabahar. Shouldn't you be able to control them?"

"Yes," Death said. Although he definitely looked younger, he seemed, conversely, to lean more heavily on his cane than he had the last time. And that ugly slash. Hallie wanted to ask him about it, but it seemed like another unnecessary side trip.

"Reapers cannot—have not—cannot—" He stopped, thought. "Have been under my control. That is their debt."

"So what exactly is going on now?"

Another silence, and this time Hallie wasn't sure he was going to answer at all. His lips moved, like he was talking to himself. He inclined his head. "The walls," he said. "Very thin."

"Because of Martin."

"I don't—know."

But hadn't he told her it was Martin? Maybe it wasn't just the walls that were getting thin. Because it sure looked like he was too.

"People are disappearing," Hallie said. "Because the walls are thinning. You need to send them back."

"I don't—" Death frowned. "There are strangers," he said. "They're . . . I know they don't belong. But I'm not—"

"If I stop Hollowell," Hallie said, interrupting him, "will it end the problem? Will the walls go back up? Will things be solid again?"

"Hollowell," Death said. Hallie wanted to shake him, to say, Come on, you know. You're the one with power. I'm just along for the ride.

"If I stop him, does it stop the rest, the thinning walls, everything?"

"Stop him," Death said. Hallie wasn't sure whether it was an answer to her question or if he was repeating what she'd just said.

"You talked to me once," she said. "Back—back when I—over in Afghanistan."

"I don't remember that," he said. He leaned on his cane, and his expression seemed serene to Hallie, like none of this mattered as much as it ought to. And it ought to matter a lot because . . . well, because it was pretty important that there be a line between the living and the dead. Like, pretty damned important.

"You need to do something," Hallie said.

He looked at her for what felt like an uncomfortably long time. "I am doing something," he said.

"What?"

"I have you."

"What? You don't have me. No one has me. You can't—"

And she was back, like a curtain falling, on her knees in the field twenty yards from her pickup.

Her heart pounded like she'd run a marathon, her head pounding in sympathetic vibration. She thought she was going to be sick, but she closed her eyes and breathed through her nose and it passed. Until she tried to stand up and almost fell.

Another minute and she could stand. Two more and she could walk across the field to her truck. It was a good five minutes before her heartbeat slowed, another ten before the pounding in her head subsided, and longer than that before she drew her first unshaky breath.

She turned the key in the ignition and put the truck in gear. She was not Death's dogsbody. Or Death's anything else. And what did he want, anyway? Did he even know what he wanted? For her to stop Hollowell? Well, she was going to do that. As soon as she figured out how.

But she wasn't doing it for him.

She felt close to normal by the time she reached Pabby's. Or as close to normal as someone who had been blown up, attacked by a reaper, and had talked to Death could feel. She'd taken an extra fifteen minutes on the way to stop back at the house, grab her father's shell loader and necessary makings, and leave him a note that said,

Helping Pabby. May be late. Or tomorrow.

As she went up the long drive to Pabby's house, she passed at least twenty black dogs. Boyd wouldn't have seen them when he and Beth had arrived. She wondered if Pabby had said anything about them. Or if it mattered.

She saw that Boyd had driven his rented SUV right up into the yard and she followed suit, parking parallel to him so that both their vehicles were well inside the ring. The dogs moved aside as she passed, then moved back, like closing the gate behind her.

Pabby came out on the porch with her rifle raised as Hallie got out of her truck, even though she must have recognized the pickup.

"It's me," Hallie said as she stepped out of the vehicle.

"What the hell happened to you?" Pabby said. Hallie took that to mean that she looked like hell, which was probably just about right, even though she'd tried to clean up some in the truck. She felt like hell, felt like her bones ached, felt worse in some ways than when she'd woken up in the field hospital outside Kabul. Although, maybe she just didn't remember how bad that had been.

Or maybe dying had been easier.

Boyd came out of the house right behind Pabby, not running, but moving quickly. His limp was showing, as it did sometimes when he was tired. When he reached her, she took a step back, like he was too close, though he wasn't. She regretted it, because Boyd noticed things, noticed practically everything. It was just—it had been a hell of a day, and most of it there'd been someone or other right up in her face.

"I was worried," Boyd said. He didn't say it like an accusation, but even in the lowering light of late afternoon, Hallie could see how tight he was wound, showing more than he usually showed, probably more than he wanted to.

"Why? What time is it?" she asked, because it couldn't have taken that long, talking to Death.

"Past four," Boyd said. "We've been waiting three hours."

That didn't seem right. "I brought groceries," she said, not as an explanation but, well, because she had.

Boyd tilted his head and looked at her, and she knew that he saw more than most people, though exactly what he saw or thought he saw in this instance she had no idea. He looked back at the house, as if thinking about the reason they were all here, behind an iron ring on someone else's ranch. "We should have stayed together," he said.

"No," Hallie said, shaking her head. "No, because you got here and Beth is safe and that's what counts."

"What took you so long?"

Hallie wanted to say, Nothing. She was tired and her body ached and she couldn't figure out how to talk about it—which might have been the oddest part. Usually she didn't worry about how to do things; she just did them. But Death was talking to her. And that felt—well, she didn't know how it felt, that was the problem. She said, "It's weird—really weird—but it's not Hollowell. I would need to—I don't know—I need to think about it first."

She watched him adjust what he was thinking and what he wanted to do, watched him fold back his need to know and leave her room to operate. It was—she couldn't even articulate how much that meant—that he wanted and probably needed to know what was going on, but that he listened to what she was saying, what she needed and, right now, in this minute, when she needed it, let her have it.

He nodded. "All right," he said. "All right."

21

They went on in the house and Hallie headed to the bathroom to clean up.

Boyd found her there five minutes later.

"Are you all right?" he asked, standing in the doorway of the small bathroom so that Hallie felt trapped, then pissed off because she felt that way.

"I'm fine," she said. "Hollowell can hurt me, maybe. But I don't think that he can kill me."

"What do you mean he can't kill you?" Hallie wasn't sure the skin across Boyd's cheekbones could stretch any tighter.

"Because I died," she said.

He rocked back on his heels, like she'd hit him.

You forgot, didn't you, she wanted to say. You forgot that I died. Because he didn't see ghosts every day or black dogs. Because shadows didn't grab him. He'd told her more than once that he wanted her to stay in South Dakota, wanted to see what kind of future there was between them. But she sometimes wondered if he wouldn't be better off if she did leave. No more ghosts. No more reapers. No more people who used to be dead.

A muscle in Boyd's jaw worked hard against the bone. "He can hurt you," he finally said, indicating her temple, where she'd just put a new bandage. He ran a hand along his jaw. "I shouldn't have let you get involved."

Hallie examined her forehead in the mirror, because if she spoke too soon, she was going to say something they'd both regret for a long time.

Finally, she turned to face him.

"You know," she spoke carefully, because this stuff counted, "you know that I can take care of myself. That I choose what I do and don't get involved in. You know that. And I'm involved in this. You don't get to change that."

Boyd turned and walked away from her, as if he hadn't heard a word she'd said. Quick steps, like he wanted to run but couldn't—wasn't going to anyway, because it was one of the things she liked about him, that he didn't run. He walked from the bathroom door into the large living room, paced it in half a dozen long strides, then turned when he reached the sideboard by the dining room door. His face was shadowed. Hallie couldn't see his eyes.

"We can't hole up here forever," he said, his words clipped and short, as if Hallie had misunderstood the situation, as if she hadn't realized what was at stake.

"We know he can't get past the hex ring. It buys us time." And it was weird, though in line with all the other weirdness of the day that she was the one saying, Wait, think, and he was the one saying, Go.

"We don't know where he is. Or when he's going to be here. We don't even know where he comes from."

"We know where he comes from," Hallie said. "He comes from the other side."

"What does that mean, Hallie?" Boyd asked, like if she couldn't answer that, then she didn't know anything. "He comes from the other side? There is no other side."

What was wrong with him?

"What's wrong with you?"

Boyd took a deep breath and let it out. He unbuttoned his jacket. With careful deliberation, he took it off, folded it, tucked it under his arm, and shoved his hand in the front pocket of his jeans. When he spoke again, his tone was measured, as if he'd reverted back to type, to calm and rational. He didn't fool Hallie. She could see the muscle jumping along his jawline. "I'm tired of guessing," he said. "We're always guessing. We never know what we need to know. Never. We guess and we're wrong and people die."

"Yeah," Hallie said after a minute. "All right. Here's what I know." She ticked things off on her fingers. "I know Travis Hollowell is a reaper. I know what a reaper does. I know that the walls between living and dying have gotten thin. They're getting thinner all the time. I know the hex ring keeps them out and that iron or the combination of steel, blood, and sacrament can hurt them. That's what I know."

"That's not enough. It doesn't solve anything," Boyd said when she was finished.

"It's more than nothing." Hallie was irritated too. She wondered if this was what he wanted, if he wanted a fight. It had been a long day, her ribs and head ached, and she was tired. But she didn't want to fight with him, not when he was angry and not when he was looking for one. "We will figure this out. We figured out Pete and Martin and we'll figure this out too."

"Why us? Why now? Why here?"

"I don't know," Hallie said.

"Yeah," said Boyd. "Exactly."

"What are you so pissed off about?" she said.

He tilted his head when he looked at her, and though she still couldn't read his expression it felt like he was looking down his nose at her. "What?" he said. "Do you think you're the only one who gets to be angry? You think you're the only one bad things happen to?

Lily was my wife. I should have protected her. I should have saved her. It was the only thing she asked and I couldn't do it."

"She saved you. Is that what you can't deal with? That she saved you? Maybe she was never asking you to save her. Maybe she just wanted you to be her friend."

There was a stillness about him that nevertheless seemed like tension, like wound so tight, there could only be an explosion. Hallie didn't care. She liked explosions.

And besides, he'd started it.

"But I wanted to save her," he finally said, quiet like the prairie after a storm.

He left before Hallie could reply.

22

Fine, she thought after he'd left.

After a minute, she went back out to the kitchen where Pabby was bustling around the stove. She'd managed to draw Beth from her huddled form in the kitchen chair and set her to work chopping vegetables. She turned her head when Hallie entered.

"Supper'll be ready in an hour," she said. "You want to tell that boy?"

Despite things and the way they were, Hallie grinned at the idea of Boyd as "that boy," though her own father called him the Boy Deputy—because he looked younger than he was. He probably looked younger than Hallie did these days. Because Death follows me around, she thought as she grabbed a jacket and went outside.

The yard and corral lights came on as Hallie walked back through Pabby's yard toward the barn, casting the area in yellow light and lengthening shadows. The wind, still out of the north, was cold and dry. It carried the scent of old leather and horse manure and damp hay. She heard Boyd before she saw him, a rhythmic banging, like he was hammering on something.

Pabby's barn was fairly small with a shed attached to the northeast side with a high slant roof and three dirty cobwebby windows on the long end. Hallie could see light and movement in the shed, but dirt obscured the detail.

She reached the doorway and paused. The shed held a heavy oak workbench and, on the far wall, wooden base cabinets with open shelving above. Boyd had found some old cast-iron pipe and was smashing it to bits on the workbench with a light sledgehammer. He'd hung his jacket on a hook by the door and rolled up his shirtsleeves.

She slipped back out the door and went to her pickup to get the shell reloader she'd put there earlier and the steel-jacketed bullets. She came back to the shed and gathered the scrap iron Boyd had created, laid everything out on a second bench built into the wall, and started making shells and fixing the bullets so they'd actually be useful the next time Hollowell appeared. They worked together for a good fifteen minutes, neither of them talking, comfortable in a way that Hallie loved more than all the conversations they'd ever had. And they'd had some good conversations.

The hammering stopped.

"Things are complicated," Boyd said.

When she stood, he was right there, right next to her. "That doesn't bother me," she said. She put her hand on his arm. "What are you dreaming about?" she asked.

"Hell," he said.

Her hand tightened. "Literal hell?"

"In my dream, everyone I know is there. They're all dead. And they're in hell. And every mistake I ever made, everyone who's ever died because I couldn't save them, they're all there." He looked at her. "You're there, Hallie."

"Well, I'm not going to die," she said.

"You don't know that," he said. "You don't know." He looked haunted and Hallie remembered that he'd told her once that it wasn't just the dreams, but the feeling when he woke from them, as if the world had ended, as if everyone had died.

"I'm sorry," she said.

He shrugged a shoulder and it was one of those gestures that made him look young, years younger than he really was, Boy Deputy young. "It's just a dream," he said, though they both knew that it wasn't.

"I'm not angry at you," he continued. She could see the lines around his mouth relax, as if telling her made things easier. "Or at anything you've done. I know who you are."

Hallie set the shell she'd just finished loading on the workbench and put a hand on the back of his neck. She brushed the short bristles of his precisely cut hair.

"You are not my type," she said.

He smiled, a slow smile, not like his usual quicksilver there-and-gone smile. "Yes, I am," he said.

He kissed her, and for the first time in a long time, even in that brief time between Martin and the reapers, Hallie felt safe. Not safe like no one was attacking them, or she couldn't handle a fight when it came to her. Like time enough and space enough. Like this moment belonged to them.

She kissed him back. He tasted like sunrise and ocean breezes and warm winds in January.

She was about to kiss him again when she heard the sharp rattle of someone knocking on the loose door frame. She turned to find Beth standing in the doorway of the shed. Boyd's arm was still around Hallie's waist, her hand on his chest. Beth ducked her head, but Hallie thought she saw a tiny smile.

"Mrs. Pabahar sent me to find you," she said. "She says if everyone isn't at the table in six minutes, she's throwing the food out the back door for the birds."

"Six minutes?" Hallie said.

"I know," Beth said. "But that's what she said."

23

It was a little more than ten minutes by the time they walked back to the house and Boyd and Hallie washed up and made their way to the kitchen.

"I thought you were giving it to the birds," Hallie said. The kitchen smelled of roast beef and steamed potatoes and warm applesauce and— "Is that pie?"

"You can clean up after," Pabby said as she slapped a plate of butter and a pitcher of milk onto the table. "Since you weren't here to help."

"Oh, I will," Hallie said. "This looks terrific. Thanks."

"You been helping me all week," Pabby said gruffly. "I appreciate it."

The meal was eaten mostly in silence punctuated by talk about the weather and the late hay crop and the price of cattle at the Rapid City auction. Like kissing Boyd in the work shed, it was a moment out of time. No one mentioned black dogs or reapers or death.

After, Boyd and Beth went with Pabby to strip the beds upstairs and replace the sheets. Hallie was putting the last dish in the rack when she heard a huge racket outside—howling dogs, a piercing scream, and a low rumble that sounded like thunder.

She grabbed her shotgun from where she'd left it by the front door and ran outside.

Curving around the hex ring on the field side were at least forty black dogs. And Hollowell. So it hadn't been her moment of death out there on the road and she hadn't managed to kill him. Good to know.

At the opposite end of the line of dogs was the reaper in white. Behind them was a phalanx of men and women. All of them dressed in a varied assortment of white and black. All of them screaming.

Hallie heard pounding footsteps behind her, and Boyd and Pabby joined her on the porch.

"What's that screaming?" Pabby said.

"What screaming?" Boyd asked.

"You can't hear that?" Hallie had to yell to hear herself over the dogs and the women.

Boyd grabbed her arm just above the elbow. He frowned. "No."

"What?"

"No!"

"Stay here," Hallie said to Pabby. She grabbed Boyd and headed to the edge of the yard.

"Shut them up," Hallie said when she and Boyd finally faced the line of dogs. Both the unnamed reaper and Hollowell had paced her as she approached, so the two reapers were now next to each other. The white reaper looked at Hollowell with a sour expression on her face. Boyd stood next to Hallie—so close, she could almost feel his shoulder against hers, which was good, helpful to know that he was there and that he trusted her.

"I can see Hollowell," he murmured in her ear, "but nothing else. I don't *hear* anything. Is there something else?"

Hallie nodded but she didn't answer him. Even with the hex ring between them, she didn't want to get distracted.

The reaper in white raised her hand. The dogs stopped howling. The screamers stopped screaming.

"Let me in," she said.

"No. It's not Pabby's time."

"Is that what she told you?"

"You know it is, we had this conversation already."

The reaper looked at her with a disconcertingly steady gaze, like she knew a secret she thought Hallie ought to know. And she probably did. Reapers were all about secrets. Hallie's secret was she didn't care.

"Things are getting worse," the reaper said. "All I'm trying to do is redress the balance."

"You think this is Pabby's fault?" Hallie said. She shifted the shotgun. The iron-loaded shot was back in the toolshed, so the shotgun was more or less useless. But she felt better having it in her hands. "I want those people back. The ones who've disappeared."

"And then you'll bring her out?" the white reaper said.

"This isn't a negotiation," Hallie said.

Hollowell stepped in front of the white reaper. "I'm tired of playing games," he said.

"This is not your space." The white reaper glared at him. "You shouldn't be here."

Hollowell looked down his nose at her. "Rules don't matter anymore," he said. "You're wasting your time."

"Everything matters," the white reaper said. "It's all ripples. What you're doing now, changes everything."

"Still here," Hallie said, because couldn't they argue with each other somewhere else?

The white reaper said, "Ask him why he's here."

"I know why he's here," Hallie said. He wanted Beth Hannah.

"Shut up," Hollowell said to the white reaper; his face was a mask, but Hallie could see that he was angry.

"You think what you want hasn't been tried?" the reaper said. "You think others haven't wanted that?"

"You never had the courage," Hollowell said. "None of you."

"Wanted what?" Hallie said.

"To be a real live boy," the reaper said, and laughed.

"What's going on out there?" Boyd asked. "What else is out there?"

"Like he wants to be human again?" Hallie asked, ignoring Boyd momentarily. "And immortal?" Because he'd told her that himself, that he wanted to live forever. "How does Beth fit into that?"

"That's the key, isn't it?" the reaper said. "Ask yourself what two sisters have that no one else has. No one." She cocked her head again like she was listening, though even Hallie couldn't hear whatever it was she was listening for or to. "Gotta go," she said. "Tell Delores I'll be back."

She disappeared as reapers did, with just a breath of wind.

Hollowell started to say something, stopped abruptly; then he disappeared too. Something darker than the evening, something that looked almost like a tornado though it was the wrong time of year and the wrong weather rose up a hundred yards out in the field and just as quickly died.

The screamers had already faded. Only the black dogs remained. One by one they stood and trotted into the grass until three were left—one standing, one lying like a sphinx, and one sitting.

Hallie didn't realize until she shifted the shotgun again that she'd been holding it tightly enough to make her fingers ache.

"What was that?" Boyd said after a moment.

Hallie turned away from the open field to look at him. "I think it was interoffice politics."

"What?"

She drew a breath and began walking back to the house. As Boyd fell in beside her, she said, "Okay, there's Hollowell, right? But there's also another reaper who's trying to take Pabby, and it's not Pabby's time."

"How do you know?"

Hallie grimaced. It was complicated. Like everything. "Pabby told me. And it goes with everything else, with why Hollowell is here. Things are changing."

Boyd stopped walking and Hallie faced him. "What things?" he asked. She felt like they'd had this conversation but she was pretty sure they hadn't—he'd been gone.

"Did you talk to Teedt? Did he tell you? People are disappearing. People all over Taylor County just . . . gone." She ticked items off on her fingers. "Hollowell, Pabby, Beth, black dogs. What are we supposed to do about it? About any of it?"

"We sit down," Boyd said. "We go over each and every piece of information we have. We write things down. We see where things connect and where we have gaps. And we fill them in." He said it so calmly, so reasonably. And Hallie wanted to believe him. She did.

She drew a breath, let it out. "All right," she said. "Who knows? It might actually work."

"Yeah," Boyd said. "Sometimes it does."

Briefly, Hallie told him everything Hollowell and the white reaper had just said or at least enough to make sense out of the half he'd been able to hear.

Pabby and Beth came off the porch to meet them. Pabby was half-bent, like she'd just tried to lift something too heavy for her and she looked frail, which Hallie hadn't noticed before—older and frail. Hallie hoped she was okay. Beth had her arms wrapped around her chest in a now-familiar posture.

"Who was the woman with Travis?" Beth asked. "Is she helping him?"

Hallie looked at her. "You could see her?"

"Well . . . yeah." Beth looked at Pabby and Boyd and back to Hallie. "I mean, she was right there."

Hallie looked at Boyd. He frowned, but he didn't say anything.

"She looked—," Pabby began, then stopped. She shook her head, like shaking something off, then said in a much stronger voice, "Come back in the house. I'll make coffee."

Five minutes later, they were sitting around the kitchen table once more.

"Do you know why Hollowell wanted to marry your sister?" Boyd asked Beth when they were all finally seated. "Did your stepfather ever say?"

"Old Daddy. That's what we called my stepfather. O.D. Actually. Odie." Beth smiled. "He wasn't a bad guy. Not really. But he always cared about my mama more than he cared about Lily or me. And . . . I don't know. Not that I didn't love my mother. Or she didn't try to be good to us. But—" She paused, wrapped her hands around the white coffee mug as if she were suddenly cold. "—I never said this. It's not something we talked about. But Mama was married to Odie before I was born."

"So, you and Lily were half sisters?" Boyd asked.

Beth looked up, an expression on her face that Hallie couldn't quite place. "No. Oh, no. That'd be simple, see. And nothing was ever simple in our family. No." She looked down, then back up, first at Hallie, then at Boyd. "No, Lily was five when I was born. Mama'd been married to Odie almost three years. But Lily and I, we had the same father."

Boyd tapped an index finger against his coffee mug. "Odie. You called him Old Daddy. But he was Hollowell's age, wasn't he? He must have been—what? Forty? Seven years ago? He wouldn't have been that old when he and your mother got married. In his twenties?"

Beth shrugged. "I guess. He was just one of those guys that was always old. You know? He always acted like it didn't bother him. Lily and me. That we called him Odie. But maybe it kind of ate at him. Maybe that's why he thought Lily ought to marry Travis. Because we owed it to him." Looked at the table again. "I was only twelve for all that. I really don't know."

"But," Boyd hesitated, "who was your father? When your stepfather—Odie—when he was trying to force Lily to marry Hollowell. I thought your father was dead?"

"Well, yeah, he was," Beth said, "I mean, we never knew him. We used to talk about it, Lily and me. What he was like. Mama said he was her dream. We thought that was romantic. Like he was a dreamboat, I guess. She said Lily looked like him a little. And I wished I looked like him. But I don't think I do."

"What about Hollowell?" Hallie asked. "Was he around? Could he have been your father?"

Beth looked at her like, are you *nuts*? "He was around," she said. "But no, I'm sure not. It just—no. We did see him a lot, though, and maybe that was why he wanted to marry Lily. I mean, at least at the beginning maybe he thought she liked him. Even my mother used to like him. Before Odie borrowed money from him and things got weird. Back when I was, maybe, eight or nine, my mother and Odie and Travis used to talk about things, things they'd stop talking about when we came in the room. Travis brought old books and what I think were journals and he and my mom—I asked them once if they were on a treasure hunt and Travis laughed. He said, 'We're trying to figure it all out.' But I never knew what he meant."

"Did you ever die?" Hallie asked. Because Beth could see reapers.

Everyone looked at her. "What?" Beth asked.

Hallie tapped a finger on the table. "Like, had to be resuscitated. Like saw a light at the end of a long tunnel. Like that."

"No," Beth said. "No! I've never even been to the hospital. Well," she considered, "when I was born."

Boyd put his hand over Hallie's. "Do you have a picture of your father?"

Beth frowned. "Why? What difference does it make?"

"I don't know," Boyd said honestly. "But Hollowell doesn't want just anyone. He wanted Lily. And he wants you. He came back from the dead for you. There has to be a reason."

There was a long stretch of tired silence. Too much had happened, and it had been too long a day to think through it all clearly. Pabby slapped her hands on her legs and stood. She said she didn't know about anyone else, but she was going to bed. She gave Boyd a pillow, sheets, and a blanket for the couch in the living room, and she and Beth went upstairs.

It wasn't much past nine, and Hallie went out on the front porch. The temperature hadn't dropped all that much after sunset. It felt as if it was still above freezing, a light breeze out of the west. The black dogs were out there, outside the hex ring. She could see their eyes glitter when they lifted their heads.

She heard the front door open and ease softly closed as Boyd joined her, but she didn't turn around. He stood behind her for a moment; then he put his arms around her waist. She could feel his warm breath against her neck. She wanted to stand like that forever, while the sun rose and set and they stood there, breathing. She put a hand over his.

"I've been dreaming," she began. But that wasn't right. "I have—" She thought about turning to face him. But she would have to step back to look him in the eye and though she wanted to look him in the eye, she didn't want to step back, so she looked across the yard at the black dogs and the prairie and the tall light over the corral. "I see a shadow sometimes," she said, "and when it comes near me, it's Death."

His hands tightened around her waist. "Like the future?" he said. "Like someone dying?"

He didn't say, Like you're going to die, but she knew that's what he was asking. "No," she said. "Like Death, like a person, like he wants to talk to me."

She felt embarrassed, like she'd just confessed to reading porn off the Internet and she wasn't sure why. Out in the toolshed, he'd said he was her type. But he wasn't. Hallie knew he wasn't. Except right now, in this moment, he was what she wanted.

"Death talks to you?" Boyd said, not like he didn't believe her, more like he didn't know how to respond. And she didn't blame him. Because this was new territory. Even for them.

"Yeah," she said. "He does."

"What does he say?"

"That the reapers are out of control."

"That's helpful."

"Yeah."

"If this shadow comes again, can you tell me?" he asked.

"It won't come while we're in the hex ring," Hallie said, not that she knew she was right about that, but she was pretty sure.

"We're not staying in this ring," Boyd said.

"Yeah," Hallie said. "Okay." By which she meant she wasn't.

24

The temperature dropped. Hallie could hear the horses moving in the paddock by the barn. She didn't want to go inside, didn't want to break this moment, like a step out of time. Like reapers weren't chasing them, like Death wasn't lurking, like Hallie could stay here with Boyd forever and go anywhere in the world she wanted, both of them at the same time.

When her phone rang, it was like an electric shock, as if the sound of it shattered the air around them. Hallie stepped away like she'd been stung. Boyd stepped back too, fetched up hard against the house, like he'd forgotten where they were.

"Hello?"

"Boyd there?"

It was Teedt.

"How did you get my number?"

"Boyd gave it to me." Like he was explaining to a slow child. "Is he there?"

Hallie handed the phone to Boyd.

He listened for a minute without saying anything. "I know it's a problem," he said, "but I won't be in tomorrow."

Hallie tapped him on the hand and when he looked at her, she indicated the barn. Boyd frowned and she held up a hand—five minutes—not asking his permission, telling him she was going. She left him to his conversation and trotted across the yard to the work shed. The shed was just at the edge of the yard light and even leaving the shed door open, everything was black with a few streaks of grainy, overexposed gray. She felt her way along the wall to the cabinets and then over to the workbench she'd been sitting at. She gathered up the shotgun shells she'd loaded and the steel-jacketed bullets she'd smeared with blood and recited the only real prayer she remembered. She stuffed the shells in an outer jacket pocket and the bullets in another pocket and headed back across the yard.

Next time reapers and screaming women came, she—and Boyd—would be prepared.

She found Boyd in the living room making up the couch. The only light was from a sconce on the wall by the dining room doorway. He was tucking the corners of the sheet under the couch cushions—square corners and everything. Hallie wanted to laugh and then she didn't because it was so . . . Boyd and normal. And in that moment she wanted normal so bad, she could taste it. There were no ghosts here, no reapers. Tonight, just for once, nothing could touch them.

"How's Ole?" she asked.

Boyd didn't turn, kept smoothing the sheet so there would be no wrinkles. "He's going to be fine. Teedt says he's planning to be back at work tomorrow. And he probably will be. Teedt said when he came around, he talked about death marches and invisible dogs and they thought they might need a psych eval. After he was awake, he told them they must have heard him wrong, that he was talking about gas explosions and saving the dog. I don't think anyone has the nerve to ask him, 'What dog?'

"Something else," he said as he shook out the blanket. "Teedt says that Jake Javinovich is back."

"Back? Like alive? Like okay?"

Though Boyd's back was to her, Hallie could see his shoulders rise and fall. "Apparently. Turned up in Frank and Sarah Jeter's backyard. He was surprised to find he was missing days. He says he doesn't remember anything."

"But he's alive." Which was the best thing Hallie had heard all day.

"He's alive," Boyd agreed.

"Son of a bitch." By which, she meant good.

Boyd put the blanket over the sheet on the couch, tucked in the corners, and smoothed it as carefully as he'd smoothed the sheet.

"I have something," Hallie said after a minute. Boyd straightened and looked at her.

When she first met him, she'd been unable to get over how pretty he was, not handsome, pretty like the boys who starred in Hollywood teen movies—smooth skin and fine features—and saved only by that short, precise haircut and quiet stubbornness. He wasn't her type. Seriously wasn't. But when he turned and looked at her and a slant of light highlighted the planes and angles of his face, she didn't care.

She crossed the room, took his hand, and put the steel-jacketed bullets into his palm. "I got you silver bullets," she said.

"What?"

"Yeah, not really," she said. "But I—" For some reason, right then, she didn't want to say, "coated them in my own blood," so she said, "—I primed them. They should actually work on Hollowell."

Boyd held a bullet up to the dim light. "Really?"

"Well, I haven't tested them, but in theory, yeah." She turned away; Boyd grabbed her by the wrist. She turned back, an eyebrow raised, and smiled.

"Hallie, you know—"

"Shut up," she said, and kissed him.

He kissed her back with an intensity that might have frightened her, except she'd known, she had always known that there was a part of him that could kiss like that, like fire and lightning and open prairie. She shoved her hands up under his shirt. Then there was unbuttoning and shirts coming off and fevered like the first time or in a long time and— "Wait," she said.

He paused with a hand on her hip. "I've done desperate," she said. "I've done 'we could die tomorrow.' I don't want to do that. We don't have to be desperate. We're not going to die tomorrow."

He smiled and it was neither the quicksilver smile nor that grin when he'd told her he was her type. It was slow and deep and she didn't even care if it was just for her, because it was just for this moment. And that was enough.

Later, Hallie woke, startled and not sure what had startled her. Boyd was beside her, but he was sitting straight up, staring at—well, Hallie didn't know what he was staring at, because she couldn't see anything herself.

"Boyd," she said quietly.

"I'm sorry," he said, but he didn't look at her. "I didn't mean to wake you."

Hallie sat up. She put a hand on his knee. "Is it a dream?" she asked.

"I—" Boyd laid his hand over hers. It almost felt to Hallie as if it was shaking. "He wants something, Hallie. Don't give him anything."

"Hollowell?" Hallie asked. "He's not getting anything from me."

"Death." Boyd turned away from whatever nothing he'd been staring at and looked at Hallie. "Look," he said. "Maybe—I'm not saying this because I want to protect you or save you." Though Hallie knew before he'd even finished the sentence that he was and he did. "But maybe you should stay here. Inside the circle. Until everything's finished. I mean, until we figure out how to handle Hollowell. I just—I can't explain it, but we could make that work. Couldn't we?"

"We can make it work," Hallie said, by which she meant, no. But she didn't *say* no. Because he'd asked her in the middle of the night, because it clearly was important to him, and because he already knew the real answer before he'd even asked the question.

She pulled him back down beside her, but it was a long time before either of them fell asleep again.

Hallie woke again much later, warm for once and comfortable even though she was lying on the floor and it took her a minute to figure out where she was. Then she remembered. Pabby. And Boyd.

She opened her eyes. She was alone, though she could still feel the warmth from his body, like he'd just gotten up a moment before. She sat up, raised her knees to her chest, and listened. She didn't hear sounds from the bathroom or the kitchen, didn't smell coffee. She pulled on her jeans and padded barefoot to the kitchen. No one there.

It was just after six by the kitchen clock, the sky outside predawn gray. Her feet were cold on the old linoleum floor. Boyd's jacket was gone from the row of hooks by the back door. Hallie abandoned her initial idea of making coffee, grabbed her own jacket, and went back in the living room for her boots. A moment later she stepped out onto the front porch. Breath puffed out in front of her like crystal smoke, the morning temperature brisk enough to frost the tips of the grass and sharpen the air as she breathed.

She saw Boyd up by the corral feeding grain to the horses. He looked up at the sound of the front door closing. Hallie lifted a hand and he raised his hand back. She headed over to her pickup truck for the cell phone she'd left in there last night and the steel prybar. She didn't need it here unless she went outside the ring, but it was good to have, more useful outside the truck than in.

Look out!

Dog's voice inside her head and Hallie was dropping and rolling and something arched past her, so close, she could feel the breath of its passing on the back of her neck. She scrambled to her feet, the prybar in her hand. What looked like a steel dart, though it couldn't be steel, protruded from the ground just in front of her. As she watched, it disintegrated in a nasty-smelling puff of smoke leaving nothing but a charred circle where it had been.

Magic. Couldn't survive in the ring, but it had gotten in somehow. There had to be a gap.

"Boyd!" she shouted. She heard snarling, the sound of bodies thumping together and teeth snapping as she came around the side of the truck and saw three of the black dogs attacking a fourth. Too many against one, harrying it back until the one was against the edge of the hex ring and had nowhere to go. Hallie didn't think; she hurled the prybar. It landed in the middle of the fight, and all four dogs disappeared.

She hoped it would be okay, the black dog, wherever she'd just sent it, but didn't have time for any more thought than that.

"What's wrong?" Boyd looked from Hallie to the thrown prybar outside the fluttering hex ring markers.

"Not that," Hallie said. "There's a gap in the ring. Someone shot a dart at me. Or it looked like a dart," she added. "It disappeared."

Boyd didn't swear or ask if she was sure. He said, "Did you see where it came from?"

Hallie shook her head. "It can't be big—the gap—or they'd be through."

"Look out!"

Boyd grabbed her and pushed her to the ground as another dart flew past. This one burst into flames and disappeared before it even hit the ground.

"I saw that," Boyd said, incredulous, because, Hallie figured, he didn't see black dogs or reapers or—

"Because it was inside the ring?" she speculated, but Boyd wasn't listening, already headed across the lawn, where Hallie didn't see anything except a couple of ring markers, but where Boyd must have seen the trajectory of the dart as it arced across the yard.

Hallie dived for Boyd's rental SUV, wrenched open the front door, then the back door, found the fireplace poker on the floor of the backseat, grabbed it, and followed Boyd.

Pabby came out on the porch with her rifle.

"Stay there!" Hallie shouted.

Then she saw it, something on the ground, sliding through a gap no more than an inch, not black like the shadow, gray like mist. It began to burn as soon as it passed the hex ring, already disintegrating, but moving so fast, it didn't matter.

"Look out!" Hallie shouted at Boyd.

It hit him low on the leg, then flamed into ash. Something even Hallie couldn't see howled, and Boyd dropped to the ground.

Past the barn, at the edge of the pasture, a wall of black began to rise, like the black Hallie'd seen at Uku-Weber, darker than the predawn sky, higher than the roof of the barn. Hollowell appeared out of nowhere, like he'd been outside the hex ring the entire time, waiting. He turned away from Hallie and Boyd, toward the black, raised his hands, and said, in a voice that resonated through the chill morning air, "My power now." His voice was quite calm. He made a broad gesture with his hand, like he was throwing something, and the black dissipated in a rush of cold wind.

Hallie reached Boyd and hauled him up. Boyd was still steadying himself on his feet, reaching for his gun, when a half dozen of the darts shot through the gap in the hex ring.

"Hallie!" Boyd dived for her at the same time she grabbed his shoulder and pulled him sideways. Both of them hit the ground and rolled. Hallie was back on her feet, scrambling for the fireplace poker, when she realized that Boyd, getting to his feet more slowly, was outside the ring.

"Give me your hand!" she shouted. But it was too late.

Hollowell had already grabbed him.

Boyd collapsed in his hands like a puppet whose strings had been cut, and for a stark unreal moment, Hallie thought that Hollowell had killed him. Then she saw Boyd shift like he was trying to wake up and stopped her wild plunge forward, though not before she thrust the fireplace poker into the ground, closing the gap with a snap that was actually audible.

Hollowell looked at her. He grinned. "Well," he said. "Shall I kill him?"

Hallie's hands clenched into fists so tight, they numbed her fingers.

"No," Hollowell went on, smug and confident, not waiting for her to answer. "This is the deal. The deal that I wanted two days ago, if you had just cooperated," he said. "You bring me Beth Hannah and I give him back. You have three days."

"What? No," Hallie said. She didn't make deals.

"Oh, yes," Hollowell said. "Three days. Otherwise, you'll never see him again."

"What?" Boyd was awake again, though he looked groggy and confused. "Hallie," he said, "Don't—" But he had no time to finish his sentence before he and Hollowell disappeared straight into the ground.

25

Hallie threw herself across the buried railings and clawed at the ground like she could find them both and haul them back, like it didn't matter that Hollowell could come back for her, like nothing else mattered except getting Boyd back. She knew it was stupid and futile both, but she dug anyway, wrenching up clumps of dried grass and soil.

Boyd was gone and Hollowell had him.

She heard laughter and looked up. The white reaper.

"Wow," she said. "That was something. I bet you weren't expecting that."

Hallie scrambled to her feet. She shoved the reaper hard in the chest. "Where did he go?" she demanded.

The reaper stumbled several steps backwards. Her eyes were wide and her lips curved back into something that resembled a snarl.

"Don't touch me," she said, her voice brittle and hard.

"Tell me where they went," Hallie said.

A cold and bitter wind rose out of the east. The light at the edge of Pabby's yard flickered out, then came on with a buzzing snap, casting Hallie and the reaper in blue white light like winter.

The reaper took a breath and Hallie could see her shoulders relax. "You should be more careful," she said in a calmer tone. "I know you think we can't kill you. But the rules are different every day. Anything can happen."

"Like stalking Pabby?"

"You know it's her time," the reaper said coolly.

"No." Not like she hadn't had this conversation already. Not like she had time for this. "It isn't."

"You don't know as much as you think you know," the reaper said. She stepped closer. "And I have no interest in your problems." Her lips creased into a cold smile.

"Tell me where they went." Hallie grabbed the front of the reaper's shirt. It was made of some sort of gauzy material that felt as if it would slip right through her hands.

The reaper's brows snapped together. She brought her hands up and clapped her palms to Hallie's temples. Hallie felt a short sharp shock, like she'd been pierced with needles. Everything went white. Her knees buckled.

Then . . . nothing.

"You are really annoying, do you know that?" the reaper said, stepping back and gathering the shredded front of her shirt around her.

"I'm going to get a lot more annoying if you don't tell me where they went," Hallie said.

"There are stronger beasts than I in the under worlds," the reaper said. "You have no idea."

"Where. Did. They. Go," Hallie said. Minutes were passing. Important minutes that could mean the difference between finding Boyd and not finding him. Between getting there in time or failure. And right now, for the next three days, failure was not an option.

The reaper raised an eyebrow. "Let's make a deal," she said.

"What?"

"You know what I want," the reaper said. "You could get it for me."

"No."

"All you'd have to do is confuse her about where the line is. Such a small thing."

"Did you not hear me? No. I'll figure it out myself."

"You'll be too late."

"I'll show you."

Hallie turned to see the black dog, returned from wherever she had sent it with her prybar earlier. An entire phalanx of black dogs sat behind it, their eyes reflecting the stark cold glow of frost-fresh dawn. One of them was growling, or maybe more, like the rumble of distant thunder.

"You cur," the reaper said with a sneer. "If he catches you, he'll send you all the way down. All the way. And he will catch you."

"What's he going to do when he catches you?" the dog asked. Behind it, the other dogs howled, like a Greek chorus. Hallie wasn't sure whether they were howling at her, the reaper, or the black dog who was talking to her.

The reaper laughed, but it was a brittle sound, like breaking glass. "Don't say I didn't warn you," she told Hallie. To the dog, she said, "Don't cross my path again." Then she disappeared into the earth like Hollowell and Boyd.

Hallie turned, prepared to face a pack of angry black dogs, but they'd already dispersed, back to lurking at the edges of the hex ring, like Hallie wasn't important enough to interest them.

"Seriously," she said. "You can take me?"

"I can show you the way in," the dog said. It seemed more agitated than usual, its tail whipping back and forth like a metronome, one front paw scratching aimlessly at the ground.

"Why?"

The dog tilted its head. "Because."

"What does that mean? That's not helpful. I want to know if I can trust you."

The dog stretched into a long play bow, then sat, lifted a paw and inspected it, then set it back down. It had a scratch along its muzzle, white against the black fur. "Trust is overrated," it said. "If I say I'll do it, it's done."

Hallie looked at it for a minute. Minutes, seconds, the microscopic bits of time consumed by her heart beating and her lungs expanding and contracting pounded against her like a vast ocean tide. This moment and this moment and this, and Boyd was farther away and in more trouble and she had to go. Right now.

No.

Not yet.

No matter how much she wanted to go, to keep going, to stop for nothing until Boyd was back, there were other people in the world. Things were bigger.

"Can you meet me in—" She did a quick calculation in her head. "—three hours?" she asked the dog.

"Three hours?" The dog tilted its head, considering. "I thought it was important."

"I have three days, right?" When the dog didn't answer immediately, "Right?"

"Time is different underneath," the dog said. "You should hurry."

Well, shit.

There were still things she needed to do, though. "Two hours," she said.

The dog nodded agreement. And disappeared.

"You're leaving me here?" Beth's voice rose. "I want to talk to Boyd. Where is he?"

"He had to go," Hallie said, and each word hurt, like grinding her insides out.

"He wouldn't leave without saying anything," Beth said, her face pinched in the single light of an old floor lamp. "He said he'd help me!"

"He's going to help you," Hallie said impatiently. "*I'm* going to help you. But right now I'm going to help you by leaving."

Pabby was at the kitchen table, her rifle beside her, looking through a stack of photo albums. "Where are you going?" she asked Hallie.

And seemed surprisingly unsurprised when Hallie said, "Well, hell, I think."

Pabby nodded like it was just what she'd expected. "That other reaper," she said. "Is she out there?"

Hallie frowned. "She was, not now. Why?"

Pabby shrugged. "Thought I might talk to her," she said. "Maybe talking would help."

"Yeah," Hallie said. "I don't think so." She looked at Pabby closely. Pabby flipped through a few more photos. "Be careful," Hallie said, though it didn't seem as if any of them knew what "careful" meant anymore.

She spent forty-five minutes loading the rest of the iron from the pipe Boyd had smashed the night before into shells. She debated whether to add blood and sacrament. This was actual iron, so theoretically it should work anyway. In the end, she decided better safe than sorry, carefully swiped blood on each shotgun shell and repeated the parts of the Lord's Prayer she could remember over the whole stack. Then she headed out. To the ranch first, because in her family they weren't good at saying good-bye. The assumption was always, We'll see you again. That hadn't been working so well—her mother gone and Dell.

So this time she was saying good-bye. Or at least, See you later.

Of course, her father was nowhere to be seen and his truck was gone when she got to the ranch.

Damn him. As if he could have known that she was going to be leaving, that she might not be coming back. And then she wondered if he had already left—disappeared. But she was going to fix this, right? She and Boyd, they were fixing this.

She had no idea what she'd be able to take with her, but she went upstairs and changed, adding several layers because it might be cold or it might be hot—who knew?—and it was easier to wear than carry.

She dug an old backpack out of the very back of her closet and filled it with the shells, three bottles of water, a couple of pairs of socks, a box of crackers, though she was a bit uncertain how long they'd been in the cupboard, and a hat and gloves.

She relaid salt along the back door and several of the windowsills, her father having apparently swept the kitchen.

She tried to call her father on his cell, but since he rarely charged it and almost never answered it, she wasn't surprised when he didn't pick up. Except for the part where he might be among the disappeared. Except for that part.

She went into the office, took paper out of the printer, and wasted ten valuable minutes writing him a note. She didn't generally spend a lot of time thinking about what she was doing next or about things as simple as writing a note. *Hi, I'm not here, I'll be back,* was her usual. She tried to figure out how to say, I'm going to hell to get the Boy Deputy back, without sounding crazy. But realized pretty quickly that wasn't actually possible.

In the end, all she wrote was,

Gone to get Boyd. Out of state. Be back in a couple of days.

Hallie

P.S. Leave the salt alone.

She grabbed a flashlight and stuffed it in the backpack. Then she turned out the lights, closed the door behind her, and went out to her truck.

She checked the time—an hour left. An hour was a long time. And Boyd was in hell or purgatory or wherever dead people went. And he was alone. When he said, "Don't—" just before Hollowell had taken him, he probably meant, Don't come. But he must have known she would.

He must have.

The sun was peeking over the horizon, muted by a gray sky that seemed to turn darker the nearer it came to dawn, when Hallie turned into the long drive to Brett Fowker's house. There was a hard turn to the right at the halfway point, which Hallie'd never been able to figure out. The approach was pretty much flat, no creeks or low spots.

"Maybe your dad wanted to stop a sneak attack," Hallie had said to Brett when they were eleven.

"Maybe he did," Brett had replied.

Once she'd made the turn, Hallie could see the Fowker front yard and slant shadows against the house, cast by the big yard light near the edge of the drive. Beyond the light was a series of smaller lights around a corral and bracketing the doors on the end of the horse barn. As Hallie pulled into the yard, she could see that even though it was not quite seven, the lights were on in the house. She parked next to Brett's old gray Honda. Another car sat on the other side, something new and cream colored.

Brett was waiting for her when she reached the side door. "Are you going to tell me what's going on?" she said before Hallie could even say hello. She was wearing jeans and a flannel shirt and she had a dish towel slung over her shoulder. Hallie could smell coffee and bacon.

"What are you talking about?" she said as she walked blinking inside. The big modern kitchen had a center butcher block island, rough tile floors, and light oak cabinets. A small table near the archway into the great room was set for two people. Brett moved across the kitchen and turned the heat down on the stove.

"Is your dad here?" Hallie asked, because she thought she'd heard that he'd gone to Arizona to pick out horses.

"No," Brett said. She turned from the stove, leaning against the sink with her arms crossed. "I have a friend over." She didn't look impatient, or like she wished Hallie wasn't there, but then Brett almost never did, calm and sensible—or at least, if not sensible, then always appearing as if she were. "And you know what I'm talking about," she went on, refusing to be distracted, "—the accident out of nowhere, talking to thin air, fireplace pokers." Which Hallie could see leaning against the refrigerator. She looked behind her. A thin trail of salt ran across the threshold of the kitchen door.

"Look, it's not a big deal," Hallie said. "I have to leave for a little while. Out of state." Way out of state. "I need someone to check up on Pabby while I'm gone. She can't leave the ranch right now, and she'll need food and maybe help with the horses. Also, my dad, if you could check on him when you're by that way. I should be back in two or three days."

"But you might not be."

"What?"

"That's what you're not saying. That something might happen, that you might not be coming back."

"That's what I *didn't* say."

"It's what you should have said." Brett pushed herself away from the sink. The center island separated her from Hallie. "Because you never come here without calling first. Because you didn't ever ask me to look in on your dad when you were gone four years in the army. Because Pabby's never needed help in her life." She refolded her arms over her chest. "So, what's really going on? It's got something to do with yesterday, right? Of course it does. Sally says those trucks couldn't have just dropped out of nowhere, that it must have been an optical illusion. Or a collective hallucination or something." Brett paused. "But I remember September."

"Sally?"

"Who was with me yesterday."

Hallie looked at the clock. Time was almost up. "Remember when I explained what happened in September? Remember how you didn't believe me?"

Brett's hands loosened and Hallie could have sworn she turned a little pale. "Martin's dead," she said flatly.

"Yeah, it's not him," Hallie said. "And I don't really have time to explain. Except, listen, what I'm asking from you isn't dangerous. Well," she temporized, because people were disappearing and she didn't know how to keep Brett from disappearing too, not yet. "I'm almost sure you won't see anything you don't want to see."

"Damnit, Hallie! It's not about what I do or don't see or want to see. It's about how the world should work. Does work. It's about how the world works. Martin was an anomaly. Yesterday was an *anomaly*. Right? Because otherwise everything is bullshit."

Hallie had no response. That Martin had existed, that he had practiced blood magic, that his magic had endangered all of them. Those were facts. Shit happened. That was Hallie's attitude. And if that shit was something that you'd never believed in and shouldn't exist, well, you adjusted your worldview and went on.

"If you can't do it, just tell me," Hallie said. "I mean—" She mentally backed up a step or two because Brett deserved more than that. "—I trust you, Brett. We've known each other a long time. You're smart and you're loyal and you come through in a pinch. So it would help a great deal if you could do this. But if you can't, that's okay. Really. I'll figure something out."

Brett frowned, like she thought maybe Hallie was just buttering her up, but Hallie figured she should know better. Hallie never buttered anybody up.

"Look, you know I'll do it," she finally said with a quick glance back at the poker against the refrigerator.

"But?" Hallie said. Because this whole conversation was about things neither one of them was saying.

"When you come back," Brett said, "you explain it to me, what this is all about. Even—" She half held up her hand. "—even if I don't want to hear it. I get to decide that. You tell me. I decide what I hear."

That sounded screwier to Hallie than just seeing things and accepting them, but if it worked for Brett, it worked. "Thanks," she said. "I owe you."

"Yeah," Brett said. "You do. So, come back."

"Yeah," Hallie said, because she was going to the underworld, the land of the dead, hell. And suddenly she wished she'd spent more time with her father the last month, with Brett who was her best friend from all the way back to elementary school, with Boyd. "Thank you," she said. "Tell my dad . . . tell him, if he asks, that I'll be back in two days." Because she would. She had to be. That was the whole point.

26

Hallie sat in her pickup truck in Brett's driveway and made several quick phone calls. She called the hospital to check on Ole, called the sheriff's office to tell them Boyd wouldn't be in for the next three days (but he would be in again, he would). She called Laddie Kennedy, and when he answered, it sounded as if she'd woken him up.

"Are the dead talking to you?" she asked.

"Not a word," he said. He sounded worried, like the world had changed again without warning or asking him.

"Did you talk to Prue?"

Hesitation. "Here's the thing," Laddie said. "You can't trust her. I know people around here like her, but what's she ever done? Listen to them when they talk? She doesn't solve their problems."

"She doesn't have to," Hallie pointed out.

"No, I get that. I do," Laddie said earnestly. "And I charge people money to tell their future or talk to their dead grandmother. So it's not like I'm pure. Or can afford to be pure." He laughed. "Well, really, no one can—not around here. But I'm a volunteer on the fire department. And I helped Cass Andersen bring in her late hay last month when two of her wagons broke down the same day. People call me and ask me to help," he said, as if that were important. "I don't just take."

"Okay." Hallie shifted in the seat, pulled the phone away from her ear to check the time. "But did she tell you anything?"

"It's like riddles," he said, "the stuff she tells you. Like she can pretend she's helpful and not taking sides, both at the same time. So, yeah," he continued. "She says the moment of death? She says that's right. But it has to matter."

"Okay, first, that doesn't work. And, second, what does that mean? It has to matter?" Hallie tried not to let impatience creep into her voice, because Laddie was helping and he wasn't getting all that much for it, even if he said it was worth it. But she was out of time.

"She said," Laddie continued, an edge in his voice that hadn't been there before "to tell you that if you're equipped to handle whatever it is that you're trying to handle, that you'll know what it means."

"Well, that's helpful." Which it wasn't. It wasn't helpful at all. She'd tried it already. Even though Hollowell couldn't kill her with a reaper's touch, he had tried to kill her. And she'd tried to kill him, right then, right in the moment. It hadn't worked. And "it had to matter"? What the hell did that mean?

"I could take a look at the cards," Laddie offered.

Which might or might not tell them something, Hallie thought. "Thanks, anyway," Hallie said. "You've been a help."

She could hear Laddie pull in a deep breath. "If Prue knows something more—" He paused. "—I got some stuff I know, I might be able to pressure her."

"I'll work with what I've got. Thanks," she said again.

"No," Laddie said. He sounded more energetic than any of the other times Hallie had talked to him. "It's good. This matters."

"You don't even know what this is." Because she'd never explained it, not entirely.

"No," he said. "And I don't even want to. You know too much, it's always trouble. Always. But from the questions you're asking . . . yeah, I bet it matters."

"Yeah," Hallie said. "It does."

She was halfway down the road back to Pabby's when the black dog jumped into the truck through the closed passenger-side window. Hallie swerved slightly to the left, then recovered.

"Don't do that," she said.

"Turn around," the dog said, settling itself on the seat. It sat upright this time, looking forward out the windshield.

"What?"

"You're going the wrong way."

"I'm going to Pabby's."

"Go to—" The dog paused. "—the storm," it finally said.

"I have no idea what you're talking about."

"The center of the storm."

Hallie pulled to the side of the road. The sun was fully up now, just above the eastern horizon, but muted by thin gray clouds so it looked red and diffuse behind them. "There's no storm," she said.

"The thunder building," the dog said. "Lightning in the floor."

"Uku-Weber?" Because the building had a lightning mosaic in the floor of the large central atrium.

The dog didn't respond, just looked at her with bright eyes.

"Jesus," Hallie said. She made a quick three-point turn and headed down the road in the opposite direction. The sky in this direction, west, was several shades darker, clouds still thin but black, reminding Hallie uneasily of Death's shadow.

"So Uku-Weber, what?" she asked, trying not to hunch her shoulders, like the dark was weighing her down. And it looked like that was what they were doing, driving down, going under. "It's got an entrance to the underworld?"

"Yes."

"It just happens to be there?"

The dog didn't respond.

"Are there other entrances?"

"Sixty-two."

"Sixty-two? Why? Don't you just come and go?"

The dog looked at her. "Everything has entrances and exits. Sometimes you need escape routes."

"Really?"

"Sometimes," the dog said.

"All right," Hallie said after a minute. They bounced over a bump where the road had cracked and settled. "And there's one at Uku-Weber. Did Martin know that? Is that why he came here? Built here?"

"They move," the dog said. "Where things are thinnest."

"But there are sixty-two."

"Today."

Jesus.

Hallie had just turned onto the county road when a mid-sized cattle truck with one headlight out came toward them. Hallie lifted two fingers from the wheel and the driver lifted two fingers back. She could smell the faint odor of cattle as the truck passed. She looked over at the black dog. "This place," she said, "how exactly . . . big is it?"

The dog sat very straight and looked at her. Its eyes might have blinked. "I don't know what you mean," it said.

Hallie frowned. "You don't know what I mean? I mean how big is it? As big as West Prairie City? As South Dakota? As the world?"

The dog huffed out a breath. "No," it said. It didn't say anything for a long moment and Hallie hoped it wasn't finished, because she might have to swear. "It just is," the dog said.

"How do I find Boyd?" Hallie persisted. "I mean is he going to be right where we go in? Is he going to be six thousand miles away?"

"Bring something that belongs to him," the dog said.

"I don't—" But then Hallie remembered the journal she'd taken from Boyd's bedroom. When everything had happened, she forgot she had it, and when she'd finally remembered, she just stuffed it in the glove box and planned to give it back later. "Yeah, okay," she said. "I have something."

"Okay," the dog said.

Less than a mile from Uku-Weber, the dark clouds grew thicker and low, like the sky itself had lowered. Though it was past eight o'clock in the morning by now, Hallie kept her headlights on, like driving into midnight.

At the building, the parking lot proved empty, which wasn't surprising.

"Inside?" she asked the dog. "The entrance is inside this building?"

"Down," the dog said, which she took to mean yes.

The sun was now completely blocked overhead, but Hallie could look down the road toward West Prairie City and see shafts of sunlight slanting onto the road. So, dark here, but not everywhere. Here. Like this was the center of something and Hallie wasn't sure she wanted to know of what.

She hopped into the pickup bed and opened the saddle box. Her father had at least one set of bolt cutters back at the ranch, which would have been handy, but it was too late now to go back and get them. She grabbed a small hammer and the prybar she'd retrieved as she was leaving Pabby's, because they would be handy and fit in her backpack both. She started to close the saddlebox, looked up at the building, then reached back inside and grabbed two flashlights, a big one like a torch and a smaller one that she could strap to the barrel of her shotgun if she needed to.

She jumped back onto the ground, grabbed her backpack from the front, and slung it over her shoulder. She took the shotgun from behind the seat, loaded it with five of the iron shot shells, and started across the parking lot. It still surprised her how empty the place looked, because it had been only a couple of months. But it looked as if no one had been there for years. Cracks in the concrete, yellow parking stall lines already fading. Someone had scored jagged lines along one of the pillars lining the main sidewalk, and there were chunks knocked out of the curbs, like kids had come to skateboard—which actually wouldn't have surprised her. There was no skate park or even much concrete in Taylor County. Whether there were any kids with skateboards . . . one thing Hallie'd been learning lately, if it didn't seem likely, then it probably was.

There was a scent in the air that she hadn't noticed when she visited the building earlier, pungent, like acid with an underlying hint of something rotten.

She came around the first set of pillars and stopped. The stone fountain, the one she'd examined the other day, the one Martin had clearly had plans for, was nearly invisible. Black clouds rolled out of its base, like polluted dry ice or a perverse fog machine. The black drifted over the rim of the fountain, then rose like heavy oily smoke, rising above the building like a black roiling shaft of anti-light until it hit the low clouds and spread, the layer of heavy black widening across the sky. Something was clearly happening here, but Hallie had no time, not right now, to figure out what it was. She gave the fountain a wide berth, not sure what would happen if she touched the stuff, but sure she didn't want to find out.

She circled the building quickly, in case a door had been left unlocked. She assumed the building had a security system, assumed that when she entered, someone somewhere would know it. Once she was inside, she needed to move quickly.

She walked back to the front, looked at the black dog, who had been pacing silently behind her, took a long breath, and blew a hole in the bottom half of the main door with her shotgun. The sound of shattering glass was loud and brittle in the morning air. Afterwards, everything seemed extra quiet—as if sounds she hadn't even noticed suddenly ceased.

She used the prybar from her backpack to clear the jagged glass, ducked low, and stepped inside. She paused. Light filtered through the two-story windows. The space was cold, colder than outside. Breath puffed out of Hallie's mouth like smoke. When Martin was alive, there had been a barrier just inside the door that kept ghosts from entering the building, dropping grit from the ceiling—she guessed now it was salt—like a fine powder curtain. With the power off, that barrier no longer existed and the black dog trotted in beside her.

"Where are we going?" she asked.

"Down," the dog said again.

The elevator wouldn't be working, but there had to be stairs. Hallie headed to the back, flipping on the big yellow flashlight. The shadows deepened as they got farther from the big front windows.

Hallie could hear her own feet, boots sounding loud in the quiet, no hum of air handlers or buzz of lights overhead. The place smelled clean and cold. Halfway down the back hall, she found a door marked STAIRS. She opened it, shone her flashlight into the dark well, and saw bare concrete steps leading down.

"Down here?" she asked.

The dog nodded.

One flight down, they were confronted with a door marked UTILITY and a second door at right angles to the first. The second door glowed all along the edges, like something cut from fluorescing paper, but when she shone the light directly on it, the door disappeared. Hallie looked at the dog.

"Yeah," it said.

"All right," Hallie said. "Okay." Because they were going to hell.

Or purgatory. Somewhere there were dead people walking around and reapers and black dogs, all those things in a place they belonged. Hallie would be the outsider.

And Boyd. Who was already there.

She switched off the flashlight, put it in the backpack, checked the shotgun and that she still had the knife strapped to her belt that she'd been carrying ever since Hollowell's first attack. She could hear the dog panting.

She reached for the door, then stopped.

"Do you have a name?" she asked.

The dog huffed. "Maker."

"As in 'I Am The Maker'?"

"Widow Maker."

"Hmm . . . ," said Hallie.

She put her hand on the door handle; it was ice cold in a way that made the muscles spasm all the way up her arm, ghost cold.

"Wait," Maker said. Its panting was loud, harsh in the tomblike silence of the stairwell.

"This is the door, right?" Hallie said.

"There are rules," Maker said. It sounded reluctant. It had backed away from her, though there wasn't much room in the narrow space, jammed tight into the corner behind the ghost door.

"What rules?" Hallie said, because she was all about knowing the rules. She liked to know the lines she was crossing when she crossed them.

"Outsider rules," Maker said. "Three rules."

"Okay." Hallie took her hand off the door handle as the cold began to spread up her arm and into her neck. She thought the temperature had dropped since they reached the bottom of the stairs, but she couldn't see her breath anymore, so she wasn't sure.

"Three rules," Maker repeated. "For outsiders. Remember why

you came. Think about why you came. Because if it can make you forget, it will."

"It?"

"The under."

"The place?"

"The place," Maker agreed.

"Okay," Hallie said.

"Two," Maker continued. "He has to agree to leave."

"Yeah, well, he's not going to want to stay," Hallie said.

"Three," Maker went on. "You have to go out the way you came in."

"Okay," Hallie said. "All right. I can handle that." Because she wasn't likely to forget what she'd come for and she didn't know any other way out than this. "Anything else?" She put her hand on the door handle and pushed it down.

"Reapers have—" Maker stopped, coughed harshly, then tried again. "Reapers have one weakness."

"Jesus," Hallie said. "Really? What is it?"

Maker shook its head rapidly, like it had something in its ear. "You know."

"I don't—," Hallie began.

Before she could finish, Maker said, "Watch out for monsters." And disappeared.

She hesitated. It was unlike her, but she hadn't realized until Maker disappeared how much she'd been relying on it coming through the door with her.

But . . . Maker had never lied to her. So far as she knew. And it wasn't as if she had a choice. She pushed the handle down, shoved the door open, and stepped through.

* * *

She stopped, blinking. From the near total darkness of the stairwell, she'd stepped straight into a scene lit bright as noonday sun. She looked behind her. The door was gone.

Hell.

Where the door would have been if there were still a door, open prairie stretched to the horizon. The thigh-high grass was heading out, and the sun, or what would be the sun if she were back in the world, which she was pretty sure she wasn't, was high overhead. It looked like late summer. It smelled like grass and cedar needles and goldenrod in flower but underneath was another, more acrid, smell, like unwashed jeans. Or old blood.

To her right was a forest, like a wall, heavy dark evergreens with old elm trees around the edges. One huge tree, the roots pulled out of the ground and taller than Hallie's head, had toppled straight into the forest, bending the other trees and snapping several of them so that they were nothing more than jagged spars spiking into the stark blue sky. In front of her, the landscape was all rough rock and shale, sloping sharply upward. A breeze hot and damp blew down the slope toward her.

Something resembling a road, smooth and graveled, ran thirty yards to her left, carving right through the rock and shale as if it had been specially engineered. It seemed like a trap, probably was a trap, for her or for someone else, didn't matter. Hallie preferred the prairie to the forest or the rock and shale slope. Less protection, but she could see what was coming.

First things first, though: Which of all the possible ways laid out here was Boyd?

"Run!"

The sound came from everywhere and nowhere and before she even thought about it or who had said it, Hallie ran, across the rock-strewn flat in a heartbeat and up the slope toward a group of large boulders. She vaulted over the shortest into a small protected space, boulders in front of her and granite rock wall behind. The sun—or whatever—still bright in the sky. She slid slowly upward and peered over the protective rock.

Below her, sniffing in the shale, were two of the biggest creatures she'd ever seen. They looked more like dogs than anything, and they didn't look anything like dogs. They had prick ears, black eyes, powerful rear legs, and large broad snouts. Short hair like bristles and long incisors. One of them raised a head, sniffed the air, and the two of them, as though they'd communicated with each other, started slowly up the slope together.

Hallie sank down with her back against the rock.

Maker had told her there were monsters.

Jesus.

There was a strong smell in the air like filthy wet dogs and old carpet. Loose gravel trickled quietly down the steep slope beyond the boulders. Clouds blotted out the fake sun and suddenly it felt winter-blizzard cold, like being surrounded by ghosts. Hallie could hear the creatures scraping their way up the slope, slow, like making certain there were no mistakes. She thumbed off the safety on her shotgun, put her hand back, and unsnapped the belt sheath for her knife. She raised herself up, set her shotgun to her shoulder, and fired at the closest one, the sound like an explosion, like the only real thing in the place. The creature howled and tumbled backwards. She hit it a second time and it disappeared with a pop.

The second creature, which had been carefully sniffing the ground as it moved, snapped its head up and came straight at her at a dead run. Hallie didn't have time to bring the shotgun to bear, barely had time to brace herself before the massive creature barreled into her and knocked her flat. She rolled out from underneath before it could swipe her with its long front claws. It lunged. Hallie scrambled up a rock; the claws swished as they passed the tip of her nose.

She grabbed the knife from her belt and launched herself. Despite its size, it was incredibly fast, sidestepped her easily, and hit her with a backhanded swing of its claws. Hallie managed to stay on her feet—barely—and stumbled backwards to regain her balance. Her ears rang and sparks flickered across her vision. She could hear the creature breathing, loud like it echoed off the rocks. Its breath smelled like rotten bananas and abandoned buildings.

It sat back on its haunches and looked at her.

"Out," it said. Its voice rumbled deep in Hallie's chest and made her think of dead cats on roadways, collapsing bridges, and serial killers.

"Listen," Hallie said. "I'm just—"

"Out!" The creature lunged at her, one clawed paw reaching for her. Hallie stumbled on a rock, and the creature might have had her then, except Maker suddenly reappeared, snapping wildly, throwing off its aim. The creature roared and swung blindly, connecting hard with Maker, who was thrown sideways, collapsed in a heap, and was still.

"Goddamnit!" Hallie threw herself forward—better to attack than die against a wall. The creature turned, threw its paw up, and hit her a glancing blow even as she was ducking away. She hit the ground, and the creature was on top of her before she could even draw a breath. Its claws curved around her left arm, effectively pinning her to the ground. It lowered its heavy head, jaws slavering. Hallie's lips drew back in an involuntary snarl.

She jammed her knife into the crease between the creature's front leg and its chest. It roared and shook, like shaking off a flea, tossing Hallie sideways and slicing her arm as she slipped out of its hold.

She scrambled to her feet. Almost stumbled, her arm feeling like a thin electric wire had been injected straight into her veins; the pain sang through her bones. Maker still lay unmoving, ten feet away against the uphill slope. Unconscious or dead, Hallie couldn't tell. The creature crouched in front of her. So big and it didn't even look like it was bleeding where she'd jabbed it.

Steel. Sacrament. Dead man's blood. Did it work in here too? Iron did.

And at this point, she had nothing to lose.

She swiped the knife across her arm where the beast's talons had slashed her, then launched herself while the creature was still gathering itself for a final lunge.

She yelled, "Jesus Christ, die!"

And stabbed it. More wildly than skillfully. The knife met soft resistance. Hallie shoved hard as the beast slammed into her. She hit the ground, braced for the impact of the beast—*pop*—it was gone.

27

Hallie's heart thumped against her chest, her breath rapid and shallow. The creature had been solid muscle and hot breath, stinking of old bones and wet fur, capable of crushing her or ripping her head off. And now it was gone.

She rose stiffly, scoped the surrounding landscape for more creatures. It was cold enough now that she expected to see her breath, but she couldn't. A loud crack, and one of the largest trees in the forest below toppled over followed by the *pop, pop, pop* of smaller trees breaking under its weight. Blood dripped from the cut on Hallie's arm. She wiped the knife on her shirt, stuck it back in its belt sheath, picked up her shotgun, and crossed the small space to where Maker lay.

It was breathing.

She returned to the rocks, picked up her backpack, and returned. The sun reappeared and the temperature rose and it was suddenly hot, like stepping out of a walk-in freezer into a heated room. She settled both Maker and herself inside the few inches of shade tight up against the rock wall. Then she sat cross-legged with her back to the slope, facing the direction the creatures had come, her shotgun in the crook of her elbow. She took one of the water bottles she'd brought, some gauze, and bandages.

The beast had torn a three-inch gash in her arm with its claw, but it was a clean slice and the bleeding had pretty much stopped. It still hurt like shorting electric wires, but Hallie could handle that if she had to—which right now she did. She sluiced the gash clean with water, took out an antibacterial wipe, and dried the area as best she could with some of the bandaging material she'd brought. Then she bandaged it with clean gauze, wrapped it, and taped it secure.

By the time she'd finished, Maker was blinking awake again.

"Are you okay?" she asked.

Maker growled.

"Do you need a drink of water or something?"

Maker climbed to its feet, shook itself like shedding water, then sat down and began to lick its right paw. Like nothing had happened.

Okay, Hallie thought. "What the hell were those things?"

Maker stopped licking. "Unmakers," it said.

"What does that mean?"

"Unmakers. They unmake."

"Unmake what?"

"Dogs, demons, reapers. The unliving. Unmakers make you gone."

"Like, for good?"

"Forever," Maker agreed. "Unmade."

Hallie eased herself back to her feet, her back pressed against the rock. "Boyd?" she asked. "Will they be after Boyd?"

Maker sniffed. "He's living."

"So, they're after me."

"Abomination."

"Yeah, don't call me that," she said. Then, "So, they'll be back?" From their current vantage, she could see a good half mile across the open prairie below, see the entrance to the woods on the up side of the plains. Nothing moved.

Maker stretched first one back leg and then the other. He sat. "They are not unmade," it agreed.

"How long?"

If a dog could shrug, Maker shrugged. "Sometime," it finally said.

All right, then. Time to move.

"So it is you."

Hallie turned quick, raised the shotgun, then stopped. Because—of course. Perfect.

Crouched on a small outcropping maybe six feet or so above her was Lily, Boyd's dead wife.

She looked like her ghost, except not gray and wearing different clothes—short hair bleached blond with dark layers underneath, pale skin, dark eyes, wearing a shirt the color of old parchment, faded blue jeans, and Doc Martens. Her bangs were long enough to hang in her eyes, and she brushed them aside at the same time as she jumped down from her perch. Hallie didn't know what Lily'd looked like when she was seventeen. But she didn't look any older than that now.

"Lily," Hallie said.

"Yeah," Lily said. "I've been sort of waiting for you."

"Do you—?" Hallie lowered the shotgun a fraction, though she also took a step back and turned. "Is this where you—" She started to say "live," realized that was exactly the wrong word, and changed it. "—where you are?"

"There's not really a 'here,'" Lily said. "There's just 'not there.' Not in the world."

"That doesn't actually make sense," Hallie said.

"It doesn't make sense to *you,*" Lily said.

Okay. It wasn't as if Hallie needed it to make sense. She just needed to get through it, find Boyd, and get out. "Are you here to help?" she asked.

"I want to see him," Lily said, which wasn't an answer.

"Boyd?" Hallie asked. "Do you know where he is?" I'm talking to a dead person, she thought.

"I know he's here," Lily said. "But it's—"

"Should go," Maker said.

Hallie scanned the surroundings. "Are they back?"

"Better if we're moving," Maker said.

Yeah.

"Where is he?" she asked Lily.

"If I could find him myself, I wouldn't be standing here, would I?"

Jesus.

Earlier, Maker had said that she could use something of Boyd's to find him. Hallie dug Boyd's journal out of her backpack. The latest entry began with the date and time—3:21 A.M. His handwriting was so neat, it looked machined.

> *Components: Steel. Fire. Evening/Morning.*
>
> *Setting: Unfamiliar. Unfinished high-rise. Unidentified city. High steel. Fire. Hot blue flame.*
>
> *Symbols and/or principals: Bones. Death. Hallie. Lily. Dog (unknown). Monsters (several). Car engine (rusted). Ghosts (army).*
>
> *No one goes down without a fight. Everything burns.*
>
> *Repeat: 4. Time frame: 3 weeks.*

Great. That was clear. She held up the notebook. "This is important, right?" she said to Maker. "This helps us get there?"

Maker didn't say anything. "Do you have a problem?" Hallie finally said.

"She shouldn't be here," it said.

Lily bared her teeth at him. "*You* shouldn't be here," she said.

"I have a purpose," Maker said.

"So do I."

"Enough," Hallie said. "How does this work?"

"You attract him. He attracts you."

"Like a magnet?" She reslung the backpack, settled the shotgun more firmly, and held the journal out toward Maker, like maybe he would take it from her and show her how it worked. It grew cold suddenly, in her hand. She drew it back. The cold lessened. She took two steps away from the rocks behind her. The journal got colder again. She turned around and faced the rocks and it got warm.

"It looks like we go over the top," she said.

"Can I see that?" Lily asked.

Hallie didn't want to let her. It seemed private, personal, which it was, but it was Boyd's private and personal notebook, and she'd already taken it and opened it and read it. "It's Boyd's," she said.

"I know it's his," Lily said. "I want to see it."

Hallie stuck it back in the back pocket of her jeans. "You should ask Boyd," she said.

There was a narrow path up and around the rocks, so Hallie struck out along that rather than dropping back down to the plains. It widened out in a few short yards. Maker trotted ahead of them, like it was just a dog, like this was just a walk. Lily moved up beside Hallie. Woods stretched out below and to their right nearly to the horizon. A stark rock face to their left. Clouds covered the sun again, a thin cover so the air felt dry and cold, miserable but not unbearable.

"Boyd says you saved him," Hallie said to Lily. "That you died for him."

Lily turned and walked backwards, as if she wasn't worried about walking right off the edge. "The world fades after you die, you know," she said. "It's not that you forget, which would be simpler. It becomes less important. Like someone dropped a curtain on your memories."

Laddie had said that too. That the dead didn't remember things.

"So, I don't know," Lily said. "That's what I'm saying. It's not," she added, "that I don't remember dying, because I do. I remember the moment at least, the specific moment. It's not like I'm going to describe it to you or anything, but I do remember it. But other things? I remember Boyd. I remember he was . . . he was nice to me, you know. I think I loved him. But that doesn't matter so much here either."

"Is this—?" Hallie paused, figuring out what she wanted to say. The path was curving to their left and sloping down, rock rising to Hallie's right almost matching the wall on her left, so they were in a narrow canyon. The razor-sharp edges of stone left by old rockfalls or the idea of them protruded from the narrow walls so that they had to turn sideways in places and edge their way through. The light faded so that they seemed to be walking in twilight. Water, or something Hallie didn't want to investigate too closely dripped down the rock face.

Just as Hallie thought she couldn't stand it anymore—too close and tight and the air heavy with the smell of something she didn't even dare try to identify, the canyon widened out and they stepped out onto a steep gravelly slope edging downward onto open ground.

"Is this where the dead go?" she asked Lily. She didn't want to ask about heaven or hell or which this was, but—

"Because of the ghost." Maker spoke up from the other side of Lily though it had been almost completely silent since Lily appeared.

"What?" Hallie asked.

"The ghost," Maker said. "It holds her here." It trotted up between Hallie and Lily, though it kept its head cocked toward Lily, as though it expected her to try something sneaky at any moment.

"Is that why there aren't any people?"

"What?" Both Maker and Lily said it at the same time.

"People," Hallie said. "Shouldn't there be people here? Where is everyone?"

The dog and the girl stopped walking and looked at her. "It's full of people," Lily said. "There are people everywhere."

Hallie stood on the sloping path and looked. "Really?" she said.

"Because I don't see anything." And Hallie was used to seeing things, to seeing more than other people did.

"Everywhere," Lily said firmly. "They're all kind of caught up in their own stuff. Because we can kind of still see the world. And we kind of want to be back there."

"You want to be back there?" Hallie asked.

Lily looked at her squarely. "Wouldn't you?"

Well, yeah.

"Is everyone here?" Hallie asked. Was Dell here? Was her mother?

"They move on." Maker looked pointedly at Lily. "Mostly."

Hallie reached back to shift the backpack higher on her shoulder.

Maker's ears pricked forward. "What is that?" it asked.

"What?" Hallie searched the surrounding landscape. Rock behind them, and in front, shallow sloping grasslands punctuated by stands of trees and cut through by paths both narrow and wider out to the farther horizons.

"That." Maker touched her arm with its nose.

Hallie had to look because even though it still stung, like a burn, she'd forgotten about being injured. She shrugged. "That thing," she said. "It caught me with a claw. It's not a big deal. It hardly even bled."

Maker took three quick breaths. "It's a big deal. Big deal. You have to leave. Leave now."

"What? Why? I'm not leaving until I find Boyd."

"Unmade. You will be unmade," Maker said.

"I feel fine," Hallie said. Which wasn't completely true, but close enough.

Maker cocked its head sideways. He looked like a cartoon dog, almost human and yet clearly not. "Unmakers touch the unliving," it said.

"Which I am not," Hallie said. She wasn't dead, right? So she didn't count.

"When you're in here," Maker said.

"When I'm in here, what? I'm dead?" Because that would be truly creepy.

"When you're in here, you are one of us. Out there, you're not."

"So, I have to leave or I'll die?"

"Unmade."

"Worse than die?"

"Worse than anything."

Hallie looked at her arm, which still looked fine to her. "How soon?" she asked Maker.

"Half an outside day."

All right, then. Twelve hours. Hallie could do that. Find Boyd. Get them out. Not be unmade. Easy. Right? She looked at the sky. Couldn't tell anything from that. The sun wasn't even visible. And anyway, it wasn't actually the sun. She had a watch but it had stopped keeping time when she came through the door. But okay. It would be okay.

A hot strong wind blew across their path, sending small bits of gravel running down the slope and whipping a miniature dust devil that danced down the remaining slope, then died. Lily had gone ahead as Hallie talked to Maker. She was maybe twenty yards down the slope, waiting for them. "What about Lily?" Hallie asked. "Can she be unmade?"

Maker shrugged. "Death rules here. Mostly," it said. "He would not allow it."

"Death wouldn't? Why?"

"She is Death's daughter."

Hallie stopped. She stared at Maker. "What?"

Lily had bent down to tie her shoe, and Hallie was momentarily distracted by the question of where shoes came from in hell. Or clothes. Or—

"What do you mean, she's Death's daughter?"

Maker looked at her like she'd said something stupid. Like, Catch up.

"That's what this is about," it said.

"This? What, this? Hollowell?"

"If you marry Death's daughter, you live forever."

"Really?" Then, "*Really?* So why is she dead?"

"Because she died."

Hallie looked at Maker. "Well, okay." Was she being dense? She didn't think so.

"You live forever," it said. "But you can die."

"You don't die from old age."

"Yes."

"And you don't get ill." Because hadn't Hollowell had cancer? "But people can kill you."

"Or you can kill yourself."

"Wait, Hollowell must have known this, right? That's why he wanted either Lily when she was alive or Beth now. How did he know? Who knows something like that?"

Maker gave her a look that clearly said, How would I know? But then it said, "Death knows."

"Why would Death tell Hollowell?" She looked at Lily up the path. Would he have told Lily's mother? Or would she have discovered it somehow? Because what had Beth said? That Hollowell had come to their house with old journals, that there were conversations that had stopped when she and Lily came into the room. So maybe?

"Will Boyd live forever?" she asked. Was that why he looked so young?

Maker looked at her. She wished she could tell what it was thinking. And why it was telling her this now. "No," it said.

"Jesus."

28

Past the canyon and down the slope, the grass was short and green, and though it wasn't particularly warm, Hallie could feel sweat against her chest underneath the backpack straps.

Half a field length in front of them was one of the stands of trees, gathered at what looked like a small creek. No people, no matter what Lily and Maker claimed. Among a host of disconcerting things, it was unsettling to have gone from the person who saw things no one else did to the person who didn't see anything, even the things everyone else saw.

"We're close," Maker said.

"Close to what?"

It looked at her like it meant to roll its eyes, but instead it turned away and trotted down the gentle slope.

"No, seriously," Hallie said. She hated this place even more than she'd expected to, particularly hated this, which looked like . . . anyplace, like it was safe. Hallie jogged to catch up, but though the land looked smooth and gentle, it was rough underfoot, holes appearing where there didn't seem to be any, jagged ends of old vegetation, and she stumbled hard twice before she caught up with Maker. "Seriously," she repeated. "What's going on here?"

"This is his," Maker said.

"His? Whose? Hollowell's?" And then she knew. "Boyd's." Because this was Iowa, past the gravel slope, here in front of her, all green and gentle hills and just enough trees that you could tell where the creeks and rivers and farmsteads were. "But why? Why make it look like this? Why isn't it just . . . well, *hell*?"

They reached the stand of trees, and Hallie leaned her shotgun up against one of them, took her second bottle of water from the backpack, and drank, careful not to drink too much, though she was hot and incredibly thirsty. It had to last until she reached Boyd, until they could walk back out.

She could have drunk the whole bottle and another one besides, but she recapped it, returned it to the backpack, and settled her shotgun in the crook of her arm. She felt a little ridiculous carrying it in this place, so peaceful, so not hell, but she wasn't stupid. No matter what she saw next—church, priest, children getting out of nursery school—she meant to be prepared.

"I remember this," Lily said as she stood at the edge of the road. Her voice was so soft, Hallie barely heard the words.

Hallie wanted her feelings about Lily to be predictable, to be jealousy, because Lily had once been married to Boyd, or anger, because they were all in this mess either for or because of Lily, or even sadness, because she, Lily, had died. She wanted to wish Lily far away, to never have met her or seen her or known her as anything other than a misty gray ghost. But the Lily in front of her just looked lost and seventeen.

"Was it nice?" she asked.

Lily looked at her. Her eyes had a certain flatness to them, as if they weren't quite hers or they weren't quite seeing the same things Hallie saw. "I think so," she said. "I think it was. I remember Boyd. I mean, I don't remember what he looks like or anything he said or things we did together. But I *remember* him. Right?" She looked at

Hallie as if she had the answers. "That's the thing that counts, isn't it? That I remember him?"

"What do you want, Lily?" Hallie asked. She tried to say it gently—a real question, not a demand.

"I want to remember why I did it."

"Did what?"

"Died."

"Okay," Hallie finally said to that. Because what else could she say?

The house across the road was clearly a farmhouse, but foreign to Hallie—not the right kind of house or barn or even driveway. Too close to the road, though set back some forty yards. Too green. It was a different season here—wherever here actually was—late spring, the grass freshly mowed in slant lines across the big front yard. Three patches of daffodils and tulips lining the drive. It was a white farmhouse, two stories, plain with vinyl siding that looked brand-new.

Hallie looked carefully at the house, the yard, the road in front of it, looked behind her to the trees and the rock hills concealed behind them.

"Where's Hollowell? Is he here somewhere?"

"Reapers never stay," Maker said.

"They *can* stay, though, right? I mean this is . . . Isn't this their place? The under?"

"They never stay," Maker repeated.

"Then who made this?"

"Memory."

"Boyd's memories? You mean it's from his head?"

Maker looked at her but didn't answer.

As they talked, Lily trotted ahead, her movements graceful and ground-eating.

Maker looked at Hallie. "Remember what I told you," it said. "He has to agree to go with you. You can't just make him leave."

"All right," Hallie said. "I heard you the first time."

"The rules—"

"Okay!" Because that was the one thing she wasn't worried about.

Maker was just turning back and Hallie had just stepped from the road into the shallow ditch that marked the transition from road to yard, when Lily stopped abruptly.

She took a step back, looked at the ground, looked left and right, then started forward again, only to stop abruptly once more.

"There's something here," she said. "I can't get through."

When Hallie came level with her, she stopped too. She couldn't see anything, not even a slight variation in the light. She took a step forward. Nothing. Took another one. She could feel a slight pull, like a gossamer web; then it was gone. She turned around. Lily and Maker were standing where she'd left them.

"Try again," she said.

"No," Lily said. "I can't get through." She pressed the flat of her hand against something Hallie couldn't see.

Hallie looked at them. "You either?" she asked Maker.

The dog sniffed at the ground along the invisible barrier, then snorted and shook its head violently, as if it had smelled something bad. The grass was thick and green on both sides, but along what Hallie assumed was the barrier itself was a swath, maybe a foot wide of dead plant material—grass, small branches with dead leaves still clinging to them, goldenrod and Queen Anne's lace and winter wheat. Hallie grabbed a handful; green grass grew undisturbed beneath it all.

"Hollowell," Maker said.

"So things can't get in?"

"So Death can't find him."

Hallie let the handful of dead leaves and branches fall through her fingers. She grabbed a handful of the living grass. Grabbed the dead plant material in her other hand. "This," she said. "This. How are these different?"

"Outside," Maker said. "One is memory. One is from outside."

Outside. In the world. Hollowell had brought grass and twigs in from the world to create his barrier, because the grass and trees here weren't real in the same way.

"He has less power here," she guessed. Because he couldn't pull power from something that had never been alive.

"Less," Maker affirmed. "Not none," he added, cautioning her.

"You should both go," Hallie said, straightening. "I'll get Boyd. We'll get out. I can find the way back. It'll be fine."

"I want to talk to him," Lily said. Her voice was quiet and determined.

"It could be dangerous," Hallie said. "Waiting here."

"All I do is wait," Lily said. "Here or somewhere else, it makes no difference."

She walked back to the road and found a place to sit under a tree along the ditch. There was no shade; everything curiously flattened, almost real, almost Iowa, but not exactly. Lily didn't look back at Hallie or Maker, like she'd already sort of forgotten they were there.

Hallie looked at Maker, who was sitting with its tongue hanging out, panting softly. "Don't worry," Maker said. "Things happen the way they happen."

"Does that mean you'll take care of yourself?" Hallie asked. She didn't trust it, this harbinger of death. She didn't. But she didn't want it unmade. Not while it was with her, at any rate.

It looked amused. "It means things happen," it said.

"All right," Hallie said. There was nothing else to say.

29

Hallie crossed the lawn. When she reached the house, she knocked on the front door, even though it looked like the kind of front door that no one used. When no one answered her knock, she tried the side door, slightly amused that she was bothering to knock at all—they were in hell, not Iowa.

Somewhere a dog barked, though it wasn't Maker, whom she could see sitting just past the barrier. She left the house and started toward the barn. She took a moment to sling her shotgun and checked that her knife in its belt sheath was easy to get to.

As she approached the barn, there was a thump, a long dry rattle, and the big barn door rumbled back.

Boyd stepped out.

He looked—well, he'd been gone less than twelve hours, so in most ways he didn't look all that different. And yet—he was wearing worn jeans, clean but battered workboots, and a green barn coat with a leather collar, faded at the seams. He had on a baseball cap, the kind with an extra curve to the brim, a faded red one with a cardinal picked out in white.

He looked different even though he'd hardly been gone . . . less precise, younger.

He paused in the doorway. Seeing him again, Hallie felt her doubts and fatigue slip away. Not because he could make everything all right, or because he took care of her or made decisions for her, but because things made sense when he was around.

Her steps quickened. "I can't believe I actually found you," she said. "Do you—?"

Boyd frowned. "Do I know you?" he asked.

Between one step and the next, Hallie froze, the heel of her right boot half-lifted. "What?" she said stupidly.

There was a crackling, like small joints breaking. A scattering of thin branches fell to the ground three feet to Hallie's left. She closed her eyes for a brief half second, then looked up. The tree, a giant oak, maybe two hundred years old, was dead. She cast a quick glance around, expecting Hollowell, but there was nothing, nothing but Hallie and Boyd and Iowa.

"You seriously don't know me?" she said. Though she knew the answer. Because that was the look in his eyes. Or the missing look, more accurately. Recognition.

This was what Maker had warned her about, what she hadn't understood, because it hadn't affected her and she'd assumed or wanted to assume that it wouldn't affect Boyd either. Memory. Like his was gone.

He looked calm, but his right hand tapped steadily against his leg, like he was keeping time. "I've never seen you before in my life," he said. He took a couple of steps forward. For a wild moment, Hallie thought if she just touched him, he'd remember. Like magic. Like wanting it and having it would finally be the same thing. But she knew that it wouldn't.

He didn't remember her.

"Maybe if you told me where you think we met," Boyd said. He smiled, not the quick half smile that she remembered so vividly, something less . . . personal, less real.

There was a deadline; bad things were happening. There were

things in this world that could make her disappear forever, but she'd figured she'd have Boyd at least.

"You know," she said. She held up a hand, palm outward. "Maybe I'm just—maybe you remind me of someone." She had to look like this was not that important, like she wasn't a creepy crazy person, like he could at least talk to her. Because she had a shotgun and she'd appeared out of nowhere. And Boyd had to agree to go with her.

She pointed back toward the road. "I'll . . . go now," she said, though she wouldn't. She'd pretend to leave, maybe, but she'd come back. She'd always come back.

"Wait."

Hallie stopped. Was she wrong? Did he know her after all?

Shrubs along the double garage rattled dried leaves, half of them dead or dying, half of them still lush and green. An acrid scent rose off them, like they'd died so quickly, they'd burned.

Boyd closed the distance between them. "I— What's your name?" he asked.

"Why?"

Something like pain flashed across his eyes.

Hallie almost reached out, almost touched him, then remembered she was trying to be nonthreatening. "Are you all right?" she asked.

Before Boyd could answer, the air filled with the sound of something howling, like the soul-shredding scream of a dozen dying mountain lions. In one quick motion, Hallie shed her backpack, grabbed her shotgun, and raised it to her shoulder. The lines of sight weren't as good here as they could be. Trees lined the far side of the yard to the road and the driveway. Across the road was the shallow wooded area she'd come through with Lily and Maker, a few more trees and another cluster just "south." The scream sounded again. Hallie turned to her left, heart thumping against her ribs. It sounded so close. And yet, she could see nothing.

Boyd's voice came from several paces behind her and to her left. "Put the gun down," he said. "If you want to talk, we can talk. Really. It will be all right. But you need to give me the gun."

Hallie let out a breath, almost a sigh. Because that? That had sounded almost exactly like the Boyd she knew, even though it wasn't. Because the Boyd she knew would know her.

She turned slightly so she could see him in her peripheral vision and still scan the open yard, road, woods in front of her. "You didn't hear that?" she asked.

"I don't hear anything," he said. "Give me the gun." His voice was still slow and deliberate, like they couldn't talk about anything else while she was holding it in her hands.

Another scream. Closer this time. Wind, hot and damp, swirled around the corner of the house, like monsters lurked just out of sight, panting. The hairs on the back of Hallie's neck stood up. She wished Maker were with her, not stuck outside the barrier, because maybe he would know what that was. Maybe he would tell her. "We—I," she amended, because Boyd still didn't know there was a "we." "There's something out there. It's not safe here. Okay?" Hallie said.

Boyd shifted maybe two steps to his right. Hallie had to admire the way he did it, easy and smooth, like she might not notice, like she might not realize he was moving a bit out of range and closer to cover. He might not remember things, might not remember her, but his instincts were still fine.

Hallie stepped to her left so the farmhouse was more or less to her back and she could easily see a clear 270 degrees or so. She lowered her shotgun. "What do you remember?" she asked him.

He ran a hand across his forehead, tipping his baseball cap back slightly. He straightened it and said, "What do you mean, what do I remember? I remember—" He stopped. "You and I, we've never met before. Is that what you're asking?"

"South Dakota," Hallie said. "Taylor County. You're a sheriff's deputy in Taylor County, South Dakota. Before that, you were in the Polk County sheriff's department in Iowa. Where do you think this is? Who do you think you are?"

"Where do *you* think this is?" Boyd asked her.

Hallie's arm, the one the unmaker had slashed with its claws, felt like hot needles were pricking her flesh. She shook it, like it was just asleep, like if she ignored it, everything would be okay. She was thirsty, wanted the water in her backpack desperately. And hot. And sweating more than she probably should be. She ignored all that.

"I don't know," she said.

"Maquoketa," Boyd said. "Iowa."

"This is your parents' farm?" Hallie asked him.

"This is my farm," Boyd said. "I bought them out last year."

"No, you didn't."

Boyd's teeth showed in a thin straight line as his jaw muscles worked overtime. "This is my farm," he repeated. "I have a hundred and twenty head of dairy cattle, seventeen replacement heifers, and twelve bull calves to sell at auction. I have seven hundred and twenty acres of arable land and another two hundred and fifty in managed pasture. I've been farming my whole life except when I was at Iowa State University in Ames, Iowa.

"I'm engaged," he added. "To be married."

"To Lily?" Hallie swore under her breath. Only some memories gone, then. That made sense—a certain amount of sense.

Boyd's eyes narrowed. Behind him, Hallie could see the rest of the shrubs along the garage dying, just like that, leaves turned dry and brown, branches brittle. A sound as they went, like shattered icicles dropping from rooftops. But still no Hollowell. Hallie's finger twitched against the barrel of the shotgun.

"How do you know that?" Boyd asked.

Hallie bit the inside of her lip. "Lily's dead," she said flatly.

Boyd rocked back on his heels, like she'd hit him. "Why would you say that?"

Another wild scream like angry monster cats—this one so close, it sent a chill up Hallie's spine. She still saw nothing. "Seriously," she said. "You can't hear that?"

Boyd looked at her for a long time without saying anything, looked at her face and at the shotgun in her hands. Hallie stood as still as she possibly could because she sensed that this was an important moment. Why it was important, she didn't completely understand, but she had a feeling that what Boyd did or did not remember was seriously mixed up with who he actually was and who this place was trying to convince him he was.

After a moment, he nodded once, as if making up his mind. "Come inside," he said. "Let's talk."

Hallie took one last look around, still didn't see anything, and said, "Okay."

Five minutes later, she had washed some of the accumulated grime from her hands and face and was sitting at a gleaming oak kitchen table while Boyd sat across from her, his hands on the table in front of him. The kitchen was neat but not sterile, with bright blue and yellow curtains, a sunflower runner on the round table, and roosters—dozens of roosters—salt and pepper shakers, towels, single tiles on the backsplash, cushions on the chairs. There were red and yellow pots filled with African violets in the windowsill over the sink and at the end of the table.

As if a bell had gone off somewhere, Boyd started asking her questions. "All right," he said. "I've let you into my house, so I think I have a right to know some things. Who are you? Why are you here?

How do you know me? And what do you want?" He'd taken off his coat and hat when they came in the kitchen door and hung them each on separate hooks just past the door, two pairs of work boots neatly lined up underneath.

"Why are *you* here?" she countered.

"I live here," he said.

"No, you don't."

"I—"

"No," she said. "You tell me what you've been doing the last ten years. Tell me."

His expression as he looked at her was a mix of compassion and confusion. In some weird way, she knew that he had to wonder why he was talking to her. Because it didn't make sense—a stranger with a shotgun who heard things he didn't hear. He had to wonder what had made him listen, compelled him to invite her into his house—or what he believed was his house. Somewhere his brain knew the truth of things. She was sure of it. "I know who I am," he finally said. He rubbed a hand across his face. "Look," he said. "I went to college. I graduated. I came home to—to—"

One of the African violets in the window, like time-lapse photography, wilted and died.

"You don't know, do you?"

He blinked. "I know who I am." He sounded angry. The knuckles on his hands turned white from clenching them so hard. "I was born here. I grew up here. I graduated from Maquoketa High. I went to Iowa State. I met Lily. I—" He stood up and crossed to the sink.

"Yeah," Hallie said after a moment. "I bet it all makes sense if you just don't think about it. But, you know what? It's wrong. And somewhere in that head of yours, you know it."

Silence.

Boyd rose from the table, walked to the kitchen sink, and looked out at the barn and near fields. Finally, he turned and leaned against the counter. He looked remote. And confused. Which Hallie figured was progress.

He wore a long-sleeved gray T-shirt with a short-sleeved red T-shirt over the top, both of them old and faded but clean. Weird to see him in T-shirts, though, when she'd only ever seen him in button-down shirts. It made him look even younger, which hardly seemed possible. He rubbed a hand across his chin, and Hallie noticed that he hadn't shaved.

"Who *are* you?" he asked.

And suddenly Hallie didn't know how to answer that. Because it was all tied up with Martin, with Lorie's death, with seeing ghosts, with magic and blood sacrifice. It took her a minute to realize all she had to say was "I'm Hallie Michaels. I'm from South Dakota."

"I—," he began, then stopped, like he had no idea where to go from here.

"You live in South Dakota," Hallie said helpfully. "You're a deputy sheriff there. You've lived there a year and a half. Before that, you lived in Des Moines. You haven't lived on this farm since you graduated from college, except for a week or two at harvest, maybe. You have dreams."

Boyd looked startled. He said. "Everyone has dreams."

"Not like yours."

"I don't—" He shook his head. "Everyone has dreams," he said again, as if repeating it, it would become the truth. But she could tell—because she still knew him no matter what he knew. He had dreams, his kind of dreams, and she was willing to bet that in his head, in what he remembered right now, he didn't think he'd ever told anyone.

"Dreams," she said, almost patient. "About things that haven't happened. About things that will."

Breath whispered out of him like a sigh. "Yeah," he said. Just . . . yeah.

Hallie was hot and tired and really, really thirsty. And she knew that they needed a plan. Thinking about that kind of thing seemed infinitely difficult, like her mind was full of cotton candy and spiderwebs. More than anything right now, maybe more than she'd ever wanted anything in her life, she wanted Boyd back in the game, wanted him to know her, to know what they'd been through together, to know that he was a deputy sheriff and smart and—she wanted help was what she wanted.

30

"I don't know what they mean," Boyd said, "the dreams. But yes," like he was admitting to his deepest secret, "I have them."

A long minute passed; Hallie waited. Right now this was all on him, on what he decided. When he finally spoke, it wasn't about anything she'd said, wasn't about dreams or memory or Hallie. Like he couldn't figure out what to say about it, but hadn't yet worked himself around to dismissing it. And that was her hope, every moment he listened, every bit that he accepted. "I have to do chores," he said, like he could still fit this all into "normal" if he just worked at it a little harder.

Hallie blinked. She wanted to tell him it didn't matter, that this wasn't a real farm, there weren't real cows. But he had to agree to leave with her. She had to convince him. For him, right now, those cows were real.

"I'll help," she said. She was tired and thirsty and the cut on her arm had gone from pinpricks to full-blown throbbing, like it might fall off at any moment, but this was the only game in town, and she was playing it to the end.

"It's fine," Boyd said. "I don't need your help."

"Look," Hallie told him. "I'll milk cows or pitch hay or clean gutters or whatever it is you need to do right now. And while we do that,

I'll tell you who you are. Who I know you are." He was difficult to read at the best of times, but now—she both knew him and didn't know him, could see the guy he'd been yesterday back in South Dakota. And she could see the difference in him too. "If I do that, if I lay it all out, will you listen? Will you hear what I'm saying?"

He didn't answer right away. He crossed the kitchen, grabbed a pair of work gloves from a basket near the door, and retrieved the baseball cap he'd been wearing earlier. He spent what seemed to Hallie a long moment settling the cap on his head. Then he turned away from the door back to her. The brim of the cap curved across his forehead so his eyes were shadowed.

"I got up this morning and I almost knew who I was," he said. "I grew up here. With my parents and my brother. I know this place like the back of my hand. I *know* this stuff. But I don't—" He paused. "—I don't actually remember one specific thing I did three weeks ago. Or last year. And I haven't been worried about that. Which is . . . wrong. It's just wrong.

"So, you have something to tell me? Great. I will listen to every single word you say. Because something's not right. I look at this"—he indicated the room they were standing in—"and it feels solid and real and right. I look at you and even though I know I've never seen you before, I look at you and everything else—this—feels wrong."

Before Hallie could reply to this, there was a low rumble followed by the shriek of wood tearing loose from its moorings. Boyd ran into the hall. Hallie grabbed her backpack and shotgun and followed him. Dust filtered through the gray air, thick and dense near the floor, thinner higher up, casting everything in pervasive gloom. The front wall of the house twisted away from its framing, as if something huge had just wrenched it open like an old-fashioned tin can. Hallie grabbed Boyd's arm. "This place is held together by your memories!" she shouted. "The more you question, the more it comes apart."

Outside, desperate barking pierced the air.

Maker.

Hallie dropped Boyd's arm, turned back to the kitchen, and ran outside and toward the road. She heard Boyd behind her. "Hey. Hey!"

At the edge of the lawn, she saw Maker. Three unmakers chased him. "Here!" Hallie shouted to Maker, who had turned and was backing slowly away, its scruff raised and its tail rigid.

"Can't," it said without looking at her.

Oh. Right. The barrier.

Hallie fired at the lead unmaker, pumped the slide, and fired again. The unmaker disappeared. The two remaining creatures stopped. They turned their heads in perfect unison to look at her with eyeless faces.

Hallie heard pounding footsteps. "What the hell is going on?" Boyd asked as he reached her. "What are you shooting at?"

"Jesus, you seriously can't see that?" Hallie said. Her shotgun was trained steadily on the two remaining unmakers. "I can hold them off," she said to Maker. "Go!"

Boyd started to step in front of Hallie, as if the problem was that she couldn't see *him*. She shifted her foot and blocked him with her body. He grabbed her arm just above the wrist, like he was going to pull her away.

"Whoa," he said.

Hallie took a half step sideways to look at him and still see the unmakers, but he was already gone, running toward the house. She felt like she was falling, like her heart had dropped from her chest. Because Boyd didn't run. Even if he didn't remember her. Even if he thought she was crazy. Even if he had no idea what was going on. He stood. That was what he did. That was who he was.

Right?

Apparently not.

She faced the unmakers squarely. She'd handled lots of other things on her own. If she had to, she'd handle this too.

"Why are you not already gone?" she asked Maker, who appeared to be backed right up against the invisible barrier.

Lily—and Hallie'd been wondering where she was—trotted out of the trees along the driveway and joined Maker on the road. "I've been thinking," she said to Hallie. "I think it would be nicer if he stayed."

Jesus, really? Like another country heard from. And no matter how sorry she felt for Lily, who'd died too young and hadn't asked for any of it, Boyd staying was not an option. "He's not staying," Hallie said. "He's not dead."

Lily watched the unmakers, an edge in her gaze, as if she hadn't planned on them. "He has to want to leave," Lily reminded her.

"He will," Hallie said.

"He doesn't remember you, does he?"

"He will." Hallie repeated the words through gritted teeth.

She heard running footsteps behind her and Boyd was there again, standing beside her with a pistol in his hand. Hallie's breath caught. He'd gone for weapons. To help. Not running from, but toward. Even if he couldn't remember South Dakota or deputy sheriffs or Hallie. He was still Boyd.

And that was something.

He grabbed Hallie's arm. "I can see them when I touch you," he said. "It's crazy, but I see them. What are they?"

"It's . . . difficult to explain," Hallie said—understatement of the decade.

"I called the police," Boyd said. "Or tried to. There was no dial tone."

"Yeah, this isn't actually Iowa," Hallie said. And really, even if they were in Iowa, even if there were police, what would they do against unmakers of the undead?

Boyd took a deep breath, as if he had to remind himself that he, at least, was real. He pulled the clip from his pistol, presumably to load it.

"Regular bullets won't work," Hallie said. "It has to be steel—the bullets—and sacrament and dead man's blood, all three." But she recognized his gun. It was *his* gun, his own gun from back in the world. He'd had it on him when Hollowell pulled him away. "Can I see your bullets?"

He removed his hand from her arm and reached into his pocket.

Oh, yeah. Hallie almost laughed. The bullets she'd given him—steel and dead man's blood and sacrament. "Those will work fine," she said. "Just fine."

She realized that in the few seconds she'd been talking to Boyd, the unmakers had moved—without seeming to move at all—closer to Maker and Lily.

"Look," Hallie said to Boyd, her voice urgent in a way she hoped he would accept without asking questions. "You have to shoot them twice before they disappear. But they will disappear.

Lily had been quiet since Boyd returned, but now she said, "You can shoot them?"

Boyd looked up. "Lily?" He took three quick steps forward and would have gone straight across the barrier into the road if Hallie hadn't grabbed him.

Lily looked at the unmakers with an intent expression. Boyd wrenched out of Hallie's grasp and reached Lily in three quick strides. He grabbed her arm. "Trust me," he said to her, his voice low, like he was trying not to panic her. "We have to get out of here now."

"Give me your gun," she said. "Please?"

Boyd looked at Hallie, like nothing was the way it was supposed to be and he didn't understand how to fix it. Hallie almost laughed a second time, because this was the one thing he was right about—

nothing was the way it was supposed to be and she didn't know how to fix it either. "Here." She handed her shotgun to Lily and pulled the prybar she'd used yesterday on Hollowell from her backpack—had it only been yesterday?

Lily hefted the shotgun in her small hands, lifted it to her shoulder, and fired it at the nearest unmaker. It staggered back and she ratcheted the slide and fired again. It disappeared. "Goddamn!" she said, ratcheted the slide and fired again; then she fired a fourth time and the last unmaker popped out of existence.

"Oh, yeah," she said as Hallie took the shotgun back and proceeded to reload it. "I've wanted to do that for years."

"You can see them?" Boyd said. "Those things? You can see those things?" Hallie could watch him trying to fit this new piece of information with the Lily he knew or thought he knew.

Lily put her hand on his coat sleeve. "You're not in Iowa," she said.

"He doesn't remember anything after college," Hallie said.

"Wow," Lily said.

Hallie handed the prybar to Lily. "This will work too," she said. "Like the bullets."

"Awesome," Lily said. She smacked the prybar into her open hand.

"What the hell is going on?" Boyd asked, like there would be an answer that would satisfy a guy who thought he was a farmer living in eastern Iowa.

31

Hallie was tired—exhausted—not to mention still really, really thirsty. Black flickered at the edges of her vision too, but she ignored that. Her watch didn't work. Time itself didn't actually seem to work here. An hour was meaningless; half a day was meaningless. Except it wasn't. For her, it wasn't. If she didn't get out of here—get herself and Boyd out of here—she'd be gone forever. More dead than Lily. More dead than Dell.

"Will they be back?" Boyd asked.

"What?"

"Those . . . things. Are there more of them? Will they be coming?"

"There are always more," Maker said as it came up beside them. Down the road, Lily stood just this side of the curve. She turned and looked back at them.

Hallie rubbed a hand across her eyes. She didn't want to be in charge of this. Or in charge of anything, for that matter. She was good at getting things done, seeing a goal and accomplishing it. She was good with space and patterns and knowing things by looking that other people would need to measure and tote up with a pencil and paper. She could tell how much wire was needed to mend a fence line, what the enclosed acreage was, how many cattle could be grazed for how long. She could calculate gas mileage in her head, the fuel mix for a small tractor, the number of cattle that could be fed on a stack of big round hay bales, and the distance to target and likelihood of hitting said target with whatever gun was at hand. In Afghanistan, she'd been a good squad leader—get a goal, achieve a goal, bring everyone with you and back.

But that wasn't being in charge. She had no ambition to be a general or president or the ruler of hell, just to get things done. Getting things done was simple.

This was not.

Right then, everything—the front lawn, the trees lining the driveway, the tulips and daffodils in the flower beds beside the front door—died, like a frost had descended while they were standing in the road and killed everything. The house had already collapsed half in on itself. Only the garage and the barn still stood, though they looked older than they had earlier, neglected. "Huh," Hallie said. This place had been built from Boyd's memories. And now it was falling apart.

"We need to go," she said to Boyd. "I need you to come with me."

"Go?" he said, his voice rising. "Go where? How?"

Boyd looked at the pistol in his hands, pulled the clip, looked at that, then shoved it back in the pistol. He watched Lily as she walked back up the road toward them, looked at her hard, like something must be real out of all of this, because there was Lily right there and he knew her, had known her, remembered her. He wiped a hand down his sleeve, like smoothing out the fabric, then turned back to Hallie. After a while, he said, "Who are you?" Like this time when she told him, it would make sense.

Hallie didn't look at him as she said, "I died in Afghanistan and I can see ghosts." She'd said those words to him once before. He was the only person she'd ever said them to. Saying them now felt like a punch to the gut, because this was wrong, all wrong. Wrong for him to stand there and not know her. Wrong for them to be here at all. Just wrong.

She continued. "I can see other things too. Things that people—other people—can't. I'm not sure why, not really, but I see things that are dead or that have never been alive. Black dogs. Those creatures—the unmakers—reapers."

"Am I dead?" Boyd asked her.

"What?" Hallie turned involuntarily and looked at him.

Lily, who had by this time reached them again, said, "No, you're just in hell."

"I think it's more like purgatory," Hallie said. She added, "Travis Hollowell, who you remember, right? Well, he died seven years ago. Lily died with him. Because she was trying to save you. Now he—Hollowell is a reaper. And he's doing the same thing to Lily's sister that he tried to do to Lily." Told too fast and not enough detail, but she didn't have detail in her right now.

"Beth? He's after Beth?" Lily's voice rose and cracked on Beth's name. She grabbed Hallie by the shirtsleeve. "You have to stop him!"

"I'm—we're—working on it," Hallie said. Jesus, that was the whole point of the exercise. "But we need to leave here. We need to leave this whole place."

Boyd shook himself, not like a dog out of water, but like something ice cold had just brushed the back of his neck.

"None of this makes sense," he said.

"Yeah," Hallie said. "What do you want me to do about it?" Maybe they should just forget the past, forget she ever knew him or he knew her or any of that. She took the last bottle of water from her pack and drank half of it, then reluctantly capped the remaining half and put it back in her pack.

"Are you all right?" Boyd asked.

And that? That right there? Sounded so familiar, so much like Boyd that Hallie, completely and totally uncharacteristically, wanted to cry. "No," she said. "I'm not." She wiped a hand across her face.

Her injured arm felt hot and heavy and she felt like she could drink enough water to turn the world to desert.

"There's something else you should know," Lily said. She looked at Boyd, talked directly to him, like Hallie wasn't even there. "There's this guy, right? This guy with a cane? He calls himself Death. Like, *the* Death. The guy who's supposed to be in charge of all this. That guy?

"He's my father."

Hallie shifted her shotgun from one hand to the other. "Wait?" she said. "Did you always know? Did you know when Hollowell was . . . well, when he was alive?"

Boyd and Lily stared at her like she was babbling, and maybe she was, but— "Is that why you're still hanging around?" Hallie asked her. "Because you're waiting for Death to save you?"

Lily flushed. "I didn't know until after," she said. "Until I came here. The dogs told me."

"Huh." Because it was Maker who'd told her. Maybe the dogs had had their own agenda for a while.

"She said he was her dream. He *came* to her in dreams," Hallie said, remembering what Beth had told them.

"To my mother," Lily said, "yeah. But who knew what *that* meant? I'm not even sure my mother did."

"What *does* it mean, though?" Hallie asked. Because Death came to her in dreams too. And he'd better not want to sleep with her.

"You're Death's *daughter*?" Boyd said, like he was working as hard as he could to catch up.

"He won't talk to me," Lily said, not answering either of them directly. "I go where I hear he's been and he's not there. I ask the dogs to take messages, but I don't know if they really do or not. I used to see him in my dreams once in a while before I died, but not anymore. But I remember him. I remember. And I want to know why. I want to know who I am. I mean, I know I'm dead. I know I died. But it doesn't change anything."

She started to cry. Boyd put his arms around her. Hallie closed her eyes. Then, she said, "Maker says that if you marry Death's daughter, you live forever."

"But I died," Lily said.

"So did Hollowell," Hallie pointed out. "I think if he convinces Beth to marry him or maybe just agree to something, because he's trying to convince her to come to purgatory to see you—if he convinces her, he must get—what? A second chance? He told me he gets immortality. The other reaper said that he wants to be a real live boy. So, maybe he gets to live again and live forever?"

Lily just looked at her, like, Yeah, I don't remember. So frustrating, because no one seemed to remember anything, and Hallie plain didn't know.

Maker had said Boyd wouldn't live forever—because Lily had died, she assumed. Killing Beth to stop Hollowell wasn't going to be an option. But there had to be an option. There had to—

A loud explosion rent the still, close air, like too-close thunder. The ground shook.

"They're coming," Maker said.

"Lily, do you know the way out?" Hallie asked.

"I didn't even know there was a way out," Lily said. "And believe me, I've looked." Her voice sounded to Hallie like a combination of resentment and fear. Because there were unmakers right the hell out there. And because Hallie and Boyd were leaving. And Lily was not.

Was probably not. Because at this point, who knew what was possible.

32

We'll need a diversion," Hallie said. "Something to draw them off so we can get out."

"Why can't we drive?" Boyd said.

"How would we drive?" Hallie asked. Because they were in hell, right? Not Detroit.

"My Jeep's in the garage," he said.

Hallie took a half step backwards. "Does it run?" she asked cautiously. Because there was no reason it would. But then again, judging by what she'd seen, there was also no reason it wouldn't. Except, she thought, as three windows shattered on what remained of the second floor of the house, for the part where it was all falling apart. As Boyd questioned, as he remembered, at some point the Jeep was going to fall apart too.

Boyd shrugged, just one shoulder, somehow managing to be both tense and irritated.

"Yeah, okay," Hallie said. "Let's try it." She didn't expect the Jeep to operate beyond the boundaries of the under, but if it got them to the exit . . . well, that would be something. Right now, she really wanted Boyd to save them. Wanted him to remember who he was, realize that she was rapidly losing her shit—and not because she couldn't handle this. She could handle this. She could handle whatever she had to handle. She always had—western South Dakota in winter, Afghanistan in war, her mother dying, Dell dying. But time was running out for her, like her bones were hollowing out, like her breath was too thin.

Well, suck it up, she told herself, because Boyd wasn't going to rescue her—or even himself. Not this time. She was the one who knew there was a way out, even if she didn't know exactly where it was. She was the one who would have to get them there.

She backed up a step to cover Boyd while he headed toward the garage.

"Things falling apart," Maker observed.

"Yeah." Hallie scanned the area. "Where the hell is Hollowell? Shouldn't he be here?"

"Reapers come, but they don't stay," Maker said. "Not in this level."

"Because they don't have power here," Hallie said, remembering the live grass and branches brought in to make the barrier.

"Don't have much power," Maker agreed.

"But when we leave—he'll know Boyd's leaving?"

"He'll know."

"And he has no power."

"Not *much* power."

And Hallie wasn't sure exactly what that meant. She hoped it meant she could kill him. She hoped she'd have the chance to find out.

She heard the garage door rattle open.

She asked Maker the question that had been lurking in the back of her mind, asked it quick, like she didn't want Lily or Boyd to hear. "Stopping Hollowell won't repair the walls between here and the world, will it?"

Maker tilted its head, neither a yes or a no. "No one knows," it said.

"Not even Death?"

"Death is not—" Maker stopped. "Not really here."

Because the lines were too thin.

"Are people still disappearing?"

"Still dropping through? Yes."

"Damnit."

Boyd's Jeep pulled up in front of them. Hallie was surprised at the relief she felt seeing that Jeep, like there was one normal thing, like if there could be something normal—even if it wasn't really normal, even if it was just as uncanny as everything else in this place—then maybe they really would get out of here.

Maybe.

Boyd got out and went around the front of the Jeep. It was dark enough now that he'd turned on the high beams, lighting his face so it hollowed out his cheekbones and cast his eyes in shadow.

"How much time do I have?" Hallie asked Maker, knew it would understand what she was asking, glad that someone—something—knew at least.

"Two hours," Maker said as it passed her, meaning two hours left before she needed to be out of here, before she would be unmade. Which didn't seem possible, so little time left, but she wasn't going to argue. Because everything worked differently here, time probably did too.

She reached the Jeep, unslung her backpack, took out the last bottle of water, and drank the remaining half in one last glorious rush of cool clean liquid. It was like a cold blast to her system.

"You told me not to leave South Dakota," she said to Boyd, who had reached through the open front passenger window to unlock the back door.

"I did?"

"When I wanted to go to Iowa with you," Hallie said, like it was important, like everything hinged on what she told him right now, standing under the fake yard light in his fake front yard in fake Iowa.

"You told me something was going to happen when I left South Dakota. Told me you saw it in your dreams. And you were right, I guess. Though it doesn't really matter. Even if I knew one hundred percent, even if there was nothing I could do to change it—your dream. I'd still come.

"You should know that," she said. She didn't say it because she thought she was going to die, because she didn't think she was going to die, despite where things were at right now, but because it was true, whether Boyd ever remembered her again, whether they both made it out or not, whether everything had been predetermined a million years before either of them was born. She'd still have come.

That was the important thing.

Boyd frowned. "Are you trying to tell me something?" he asked.

"If I don't make it out of here," she said, "remember that I knew exactly what I was doing."

She had her backpack by one strap in her left hand, her shotgun still held in her right. And she still felt as if she couldn't figure out what to do with her hands, as if she should kiss him or hug him or punch him in the shoulder. Something. Like they weren't just strangers.

Because they weren't just strangers.

"We'd better—," she began, but before she could get more than those two words out, there was a loud crack.

Boyd shouted, "Look out!" even as he was grabbing her by the waist and pulling her sideways. She had to drop her backpack so she could hang on to her shotgun. She hit the ground hard, rolled quickly, and was back on her feet in time to see half the oak tree by the farmhouse collapsing to the ground with a hard thump that raised rough clods of dirt and snapped twigs.

Hallie coughed. Boyd climbed to his feet, all right, just slower than she'd been, a tear in his jeans across one knee. Lily walked out of a cloud of dust. "That was—"

A wrenching shriek like wounded animals, and the axles on the Jeep disintegrated. The windows collapsed inward. And the handle fell off the front passenger door, landing on the gravel driveway with a single sharp ring of metal against stone.

"Run!" Hallie shouted. "We'll have to run for it." She herded them, like sheep or soldiers, her hand light on their arms, turning them, pointing the way. She grabbed her backpack from the ground as she passed. "Go!" She urged them forward. "Keep going!"

They ran.

Boyd might not remember her. Lily might not remember anything. But they knew trouble and they knew when to move.

They got as far as the corner of the yard when they saw the unmakers.

And Travis Hollowell.

Hollowell in front and the unmakers behind him. Seven of them now, big hulking shapes that seemed to fill all available space.

Hallie dropped her backpack, raised the shotgun, and fired, hitting Hollowell square in the chest. She ejected the shell and fired again. He staggered and faded. Hallie drew in her breath.

A flicker, like an old movie reel, and he was back.

Goddamnit.

33

Hallie staggered. The pain from the unmaker's claw had moved along her arm to her shoulder and down into her chest, spidering out like a slowly expanding web of heavy black emptiness.

But that was all right. That was the kind of thing that didn't matter. She pushed it aside. Or down. Somewhere outside what mattered. Because she couldn't change it. And the unmakers were moving forward.

The sky was a uniform gray, not like it was cloudy, but like there was nothing but gray, like blue or clouds or sun or night had never existed, not in this place. The grass was gone from the front yard. As far as Hallie could see, the ground around, in front, beyond them was flat and featureless. A cold wind blew across the back of Hallie's neck. A lifetime of living on a ranch in the West River, and she wanted to give it a direction—the wind out of the west or the north or the south. But there was no direction here, no down to or over from or into or out of. There was only here. Only now.

She heard a sound, the scrape of a boot, and turned her head to her right to see Boyd coming up beside her.

"I remember this," Boyd said. The unmakers were even with

Hollowell now, who seemed to be waiting for something. Hallie shot the nearest unmaker twice. It flickered and disappeared. It didn't return. She had five shells left.

"You remember me?" And was sorry she said it. Because that didn't matter either. That she would do this for him had nothing to do with whether he knew her or cared about her back. Except it did. It did matter. If this was the last thing, their last stand, then it would just be nice if he remembered her.

"This place. Standing here."

"Oh."

"You shouldn't have come," he said to Hallie.

"I would always have come," she replied.

"Hey!" Lily shoved between Hallie and Boyd, would have gone straight past and bang up to Hollowell if Hallie hadn't grabbed her by the arm. She shouted across the space between them. "I remember you, you son of a bitch!" she said.

Hollwell grinned. "It's not too late for you," he said. "We should talk."

"Leave my sister alone," Lily said. She slapped the prybar in her hand. "I think we can take them," she said to Hallie and Boyd.

Hallie didn't roll her eyes.

"You can't stay here for long," she said to Hollowell, because wasn't that what Maker had told her? That reapers could come to this place, to the under, but they couldn't stay.

Hollowell's grin didn't change. "Neither can you."

He dropped his hand. The unmakers surged forward. Hallie raised her shotgun, saw Boyd move closer to her, draw Lily a bit behind him, all of them doing the right thing, working together. Not enough, though. It wouldn't be enough. Right now, her only hope was that it would matter.

She had time to fire three times before one of the unmakers reached her and hit her a glancing blow that knocked her six feet through the air. She was already rolling when she landed hard on her left shoulder, scrambling to her feet and reaching for her last two shotgun shells.

Then the universe split open.

The ground underneath Hallie's feet rose like the deck of a ship on hundred-foot seas. Hallie stumbled sideways and almost fell. One of the unmakers tripped on a steep uprising of earth and tumbled back the way it had come. A deep crack opened in the ground, another in the fake sky above them, a low rumble like the grinding of a thousand heavy millstones. The cracks appeared to exist in all dimensions at once. Light spilled through—down, up, sideways. It reflected off particles of purgatory dirt, the widening gash in the ground sending more dirt into the surrounding air.

Boyd reached out quick, grabbed Lily by the back of her shirt, and hauled her away from a splintering crack.

"What's happening?" Lily asked. "This is— I've never seen anything like this."

The fissures widened.

"Jesus." And Hallie could see it—in the growing cracks—the world outside. Brown prairie grass and low gray skies, a long horizon, a sparse line of trees in the middle distance. She smelled rain and dry grass like straw and something burning.

All of it thrusting forward into purgatory, past the unmakers, like a river from its source, a glow like the rising sun behind.

"What is this?" Boyd asked. He sounded angry and scared and fed up with the whole thing, which might have struck Hallie as funny at any other time, the fed-up part, because he didn't know the half of it, not even close.

"The walls," she said. "The walls are coming down." Surprised that it was something that could even be said, because it was the same as saying the end of the world, the end of time, the end.

The gap widened, more fissures spreading out like crackling ice. Hallie could see birds, a circling hawk veer suddenly in flight and then recover.

34

Hallie grabbed Boyd's arm. "We have to get out. Now."

He looked at her like she was speaking a foreign language.

She pointed toward the widening fissures. "Out."

Boyd indicated the unmakers, who were standing at the edge of a fissure that had just opened, already working out a way across. "What about—?"

"If there are no more walls, there's no world and if there's no world, then Travis Hollowell doesn't matter."

It had started in the world, had started with Martin and Uku-Weber. So she figured—hoped—it could be fixed there. And that would take care of Hollowell, right? She wasn't certain she actually believed that, but there was at least one way to find out.

And she had to get out—get out now before she was unmade. Though she didn't say that. Blackness crept in at the edges of her vision and she figured she didn't have much time left.

They just had to get past—

"I'll take care of Hollowell," Lily said, looking across the cracked ground at Hollowell and the unmakers; the fissures that had just ripped open were already trying to reseal themselves. "I want to take care of him," she repeated. "And I can't." She looked at the sky where slanting afternoon sun poured through, at the promise of South Dakota prairie visible along the horizon. "I can't leave here anyway."

"You don't know that," Boyd said. "You don't—"

One of the unmakers took a running start and lunged across the closing fissure. Hallie and Boyd fired simultaneously. The unmaker dropped into the gap, clawing at the broken surface and then, just disappearing. Across the gap, Hollowell had stepped back, seemed almost to be fading. Maybe his time was almost up. Or maybe it was just beginning.

Hallie had one shell left. "Come on!" she shouted. They could sort the metaphysics out later, when they were out.

A roar like a thousand thousand thunderclaps filled the air—so loud, it felt like the air itself was vibrating. The light, the glow Hallie'd seen earlier and thought was winter prairie sunlight leaking through, grew brighter and brighter until it became an orange county truck with a snow blade on the front bursting through the widening gap between the outside world and the under. Its entrance caused another rolling shudder across the half-shattered ground beneath their feet, closing one wide fissure and a deep crack in the sky and opening three more. Hallie had time to notice torches burning on the corners of the blade, the truck cab, and the dump bed before she was diving frantically out of the way even as the truck was braking and trying to stop. It pulled up, the snow blade less than a foot from her nose.

Pabby leaned out the driver's window. "Need some help?" She grinned.

The passenger door opened and the white reaper was there, saying, "Get in!"

Hallie struggled to her feet, realized she'd dropped her shotgun, and scrambled to pick it up. Her head felt like it was stuffed with iron filings and wire.

Boyd grabbed Hallie's arm and it startled her, like she was

zoning out. "Come on," he said. "Come on!" She stumbled toward the truck.

Lily looked from the truck to Hollowell to Boyd.

"Come on!" Boyd grabbed her arm.

"I can't," she said.

"Try," he told her.

She came, both of them past Hallie, who didn't feel like she was slow, but she was, had to be because they were already past her and at the truck.

The white reaper was swinging down, Lily had grabbed the door handle, and Boyd had his hand on her back to boost her up.

Then between one step and the next, between Lily grabbing the door handle and her foot leaving the ground, between existence and extinction, the under disappeared and they were—all of them—in the Uku-Weber parking lot.

Hallie knew it by the scrape of the north wind on her face, knew it before she saw the storm-dark sky, the building, or even the cracked concrete under her boots.

The unmakers and Hollowell had crossed over too, were standing across the parking lot less than thirty yards away.

Three unmakers and Hollowell.

Hallie had one iron-loaded shotgun shell left.

She stepped in front of the truck.

"Hallie!" Boyd shouted from somewhere behind her, and she wondered briefly if he remembered her, Because they were out, right? Though there was still black creeping around the edges of her vision and she still felt like her bones were hollowing out. There wasn't time for that, though, or to worry about Boyd.

A shaft of sunlight broke through the thick gray blanket of clouds, and the unmakers, like the opposite of lights, winked out.

Hallie blinked.

Hollowell looked around like he couldn't believe it either. Were they permanently back? Had the walls fixed themselves? Redrawn the lines?

But no, because already Hallie could see bands across the parking lot, light then dark then light again. No wonder she still felt like she was fading, because she was still there—in the under—and here—in the world—at the same time. Too late. Maybe it was too late.

No. It wasn't too late; she wouldn't let it be too late.

She was facing the Uku-Weber building, and behind Hollowell she could see the fountain, black still pouring from it—billowing, smoky blackness boiling out, and where it touched—the clouds, a light pole, prairie grass—it changed. Like a photographic negative, like the light-dark-light across the parking lot, like the lines between the world and the underworld.

The fountain.

Hallie struggled to make the connections, felt stupid for not making them sooner or faster.

"Get down!" Someone ran into her and knocked her to the ground. Her shotgun skittered across the parking lot. Something exploded. She felt heat and concussion. Something stung the back of the neck. She rolled over. Boyd hauled her to her feet and she almost blacked out. She could see Hollowell, could see that he was drawing power from the prairie, prairie grass dying in a long brown arc to the north. Could see the blackened crater where whatever he'd thrown at them landed.

"We have to stop him!" Boyd shouted at her, though Hallie could hear him perfectly clearly.

"No, we—" She stopped. Because they did have to stop him. They did. But the fountain. They had to.

But . . . "No."

And it wasn't just that she was having trouble seeing straight, or that she felt hollow inside, like emptiness consumed her. She was actually seeing some things a lot more clearly, like how it worked, like what they needed to do. "It's not Hollowell. Or not all Hollowell, it's the—" And it was obvious, what they needed to destroy. All back to Martin, to Uku-Weber, to the fountain in the courtyard spewing black into the sky—letting out the under. "You know what, Boyd." She turned to him, put her hand on his arm. She looked straight at him and still couldn't tell if he remembered her or not. "You need to hold him off for me. I need—I think I can stop this. Yeah. Stop it. I think." Then, she stopped talking because she was repeating herself, sounding like, well, sounding like Death, which she didn't want to—wasn't going to—think about.

Boyd frowned, not as if he didn't like what she was saying, not afraid or doubting, more like he was taking what she'd just said in and trying to figure out how to make it work.

"How many bullets do you have?" she asked him.

"Five." Then he turned and fired twice at Hollowell, who was forming another fireball to throw at them. Though Boyd hit him solidly in the chest, he flickered but didn't disappear.

Perfect.

Hallie rubbed a hand across her face. What would destroy that fountain?

Blood and steel and sacrament.

Like a voice in her head, but not a random voice. Just hers.

They needed more than a prybar, though. They needed big. They needed massive.

"We need an explosion," Hallie said.

"Funny you should say that." Pabby had left the truck and approached them. "Look in the back."

Hallie jumped up on the wheel well, almost stumbled, but grabbed the side of the truck, hauled herself up the rest of the way, and looked in the back of the truck. She grinned. Fertilizer. "Yeah," she said. "That'll do."

"We thought we might need it to get in," Pabby said. She grinned back, like she hadn't had this much fun in years. "I guess anybody can get in these days, though."

There was no time for finesse, no time even to consider if it would work. Because the light-dark-light across the parking lot was spreading to the prairie, was growing every minute, every second that they stood there. And there was Hollowell who had stepped back toward the prairie fields to the north, the ones he hadn't reaped for power yet. If Hollowell knew what she had in mind, he'd do anything to stop her.

"Where's Lily?" Hallie asked.

"She's—" Boyd hesitated. He seemed uncertain what to say. "She comes and goes," he finally said. Hallie looked to her left. Lily was flickering—light/dark/light. When she moved, it looked like an old movie reel, slow enough to see the individual frames.

Hallie reached over and grabbed her. It made her look a little more substantial, a little more there. "I need help," Hallie said. "I'm going to—" She hesitated, which wasn't like her, but then, this wasn't like anything she'd ever done before. "I'm going to try to fix things. Or destroy us." Because either seemed likely.

Lily looked at her for a long, discerning moment, then nodded, like she'd been waiting seven years for something, to do something that mattered.

"That fountain," Hallie said. "We're going to blow it up. Not just blow it up—steel and blood and sacrament."

"Dead man's blood," Lily said, like she knew, maybe hadn't always known, but knew now, now that she was here.

"Mine," Hallie said.

"Mine too," said Lily.

It took Hallie a minute. "Okay," she said. "Yes. Yours too.

"Give Boyd the prybar," Hallie said. "He has to hold off Hollowell."

Lily handed the prybar to Boyd. Before he turned away, Lily grabbed him, pulled him toward her, and kissed him hard. He looked startled, but she'd already turned away and he gave Hallie one wide glance before he moved past them both and past the truck toward Hollowell on the near side of the parking lot.

The world began to blur. Time had run out for Hallie, and she knew it.

She pulled off her flannel shirt, soaked it in the blood from her arm, the arm bleeding freely now, dripping onto the ground. She hadn't had time to ask why Pabby was here or the white reaper or where Beth was. There wasn't time now to say good-bye to Boyd or I'm sorry I wasn't or didn't or hadn't or couldn't—

She streaked blood along both sides of the truck, along the tailgate and the front grille and the big plow blade, then threw the shirt into the back to land on top of the bags of fertilizer. Lily borrowed Hallie's knife, sliced across her left forearm, and gave it back with a grim smile. She painted small bloody *X*'s on each window, on the door handles, and great swooping gestures across each tire.

They pulled the torches from the corners of the truck's front blade and threw them in the dump bed. Lily threw the two torches from the back of the truck in as well. Then she climbed in the cab and started to reverse the truck before she'd even shut the door.

Hallie grabbed the door handle and jumped up on the running board. "Wait!" She was afraid her words would be lost in the loud rumble of the truck and the overhead noise, like something was shattering—like everything was. Lily eased up on the gas and looked at her.

And Hallie didn't know what to say. Thought *she* should be driving the truck—she should. But it was—

"Go," she finally said. "Just go!"

She jumped up on the runner, elbow through the mirror arm. Lily revved the engine and rumbled forward, gaining speed as she moved.

There was a jolt as the truck jumped the curb. Hallie loosened her grip, grabbed the door handle. "Jump!" she said.

Lily looked at her but didn't take her hand off the wheel.

"Jump!" They both said it, Lily not even looking at Hallie, her eyes fixed on the fountain and the blackness pouring out of it.

Hallie waited until the last minute, then dived for the ground, didn't even know if she was in the world or the under. Felt the rumble of the big truck in her bones as it sped past her. Then a shattering loud explosion followed by a wash of heat that felt as if it scalded her back. And screams. The screaming went on and on and on.

Hallie tried to rise, got halfway to her knees, and almost fell back over. The fountain was burning, the blackness running along the ground now, flames pursuing it, turning the black red-hot, then solid, like hardened lava flows.

Hallie heard a roar, like someone gone mad, saw Hollowell—Jesus, Hollowell—saw him hit Boyd hard, palms outthrust, and knock him backwards half a dozen feet. Boyd on his knees, Hollowell's hands around his neck. Boyd struggling to reach the prybar, inches from his grasp. Losing. He was losing. Because Hollowell was stronger. And not human.

Hallie was on her feet, stumbling into a run, reaching for her knife in its belt sheath.

Hollowell would not kill Boyd. Hallie wouldn't let him. Not after all this. Not after everything.

The moment of death.

The thought brought her up short. Reapers were vulnerable in that one brief instant, in their victim's moment of death. That was what Laddie had told her, what the dead had told him.

Jesus.

It hadn't worked, though. Not when Hollowell had tried to kill her. Because she was already dead? Had died? But it could work. Might work. What had Prue said? When it mattered. If she just—she stopped three feet away. Watched Hollowell squeeze Boyd's throat, her jaw so tight, she could barely breathe. Hollowell didn't even have to squeeze, because he was a reaper. He could kill with a touch.

She waited.

The light began to fade from Boyd's eyes.

She stopped breathing.

And waited.

Watched Boyd beg her, then not. Because she wasn't saving him—and he knew. He knew *her,* knew it was wrong, knew she would always save him—wanted him to know but there wasn't time and—

Now.

Hallie leaped, closed the gap between them, and slid the knife between Hollowell's ribs with a thrust so hard, it almost broke her hand. His hands dropped instantly from Boyd's throat. He looked at Hallie with a mix of surprise and confusion. Because it wasn't supposed to work. Because no one had ever told him. Because he'd never believed in his own death, that he deserved to be a reaper, that he could die.

He could.

Hallie dropped to her knees. Cold ran up her arm as she held the knife hard into Hollowell's chest. She looked up to see Boyd's face—dispassionate and cold, one hand touching his throat. Did he think she hadn't saved him? She'd done it to save him, to save everyone.

The cold worked up her spine. Was this what it felt like to be unmade? She didn't let go of the knife. Didn't even know how to let go anymore. Someone yelled from a long way away. A buzzing in her ears grew so loud, it drowned out the world.

She fell and she didn't hear anything for a long time.

35

Full moon. Half moon. Quarter moon. New moon. Thin clouds in a black sky. Black water. White moon. White birch trees in winter. Hollow hills collapsed to dust. Empty gravel roads. Fog. Half-drowned mausoleum. Gargoyles. Dry river beds. Snow. Ice. Sunrise. 1963 blue Ford tractor. Footprints in snow. Smoke from a stone chimney. Pine boughs. Home.

Hallie woke, but knew almost immediately that she wasn't really awake. She'd been here before, at least one too many times. It felt almost real here, maybe it had fooled her the first time, back in Afghanistan. But it was too dark; the edges of things were too sharp and they changed too quickly.

Besides, Death was here.

He looked the way he did the first time she'd seen him. No longer young, white hair cut close to his head, thin face, pale eyes—two of them—long and lean, dressed in black. His gold-knobbed cane looked sturdy, though he used it lightly.

"You look good," Hallie said as she rose to her feet. "Am I dead?" She hadn't asked that question the first time she saw him, way back. She hadn't even known it was a question you asked. Even as a soldier, even in Afghanistan, she actually hadn't thought that much about death. She'd thought about paying attention, about doing her job, about being ready. But not about dying. If she'd thought too much about dying, if she'd thought at all about dying, she wouldn't have been able to do the rest.

Death smiled, which wasn't exactly comforting. "I want to tell you a story," he said. "And then, I want to thank you."

Hallie didn't say anything. She didn't want to hear a story from him. She wanted to go home, wanted to know that she could go home, wanted to be done with this.

"I was human once," Death said, taking her silence for assent. "It was a long, long time ago now."

"The beginning of time?" Hallie asked, because there'd always been Death, right?

Death smiled again. "No," he said. He didn't seem to do anything, but suddenly there were chairs, comfortable leather chairs. And a fireplace. The kaleidoscoping images that were always in the background when Hallie talked to Death faded, as if they were just in his library, chatting over brandy. Hallie wasn't much for sitting or chatting or brandy, but she wanted to hear this. It had better be good. "I wasn't the first. And I won't be the last. But I have been Death for a long time." He paused. "Some of it is routine. Much of it is boring. But it's all . . . necessary."

"Okay?" Hallie said. She had no idea where this was going.

"At first I was delighted. I had power. Death often just happens, but sometimes there are decisions to be made. Balances to be regained or upset. And it was fascinating. Like an eternal study of humanity and its nature. But—" He stretched one long leg in front of him, his right hand resting on the knob of his cane. "—inevitably, I suspect, I wanted to feel human again, to feel again. So I went off for a short while to experience life. Never completely human, of course. Never *in* the world. But near enough. I met a lovely woman."

"Lily and Beth's mother," Hallie said.

"Yes. A lovely woman," he repeated. "Smart, well read, and so pleased to have someone who saw that in her. I truly thought I loved her. Especially after Lily was born. To see a child born. It's a marvelous thing, you know."

Hallie stood and started pacing because she was sitting here—wherever "here" was—sitting here with Death. She didn't want to be here. She didn't want to be sitting. But, answers? She'd like to have them.

"I thought I loved her," he said. "But I couldn't stay. And she couldn't leave." He plucked at a nonexistent piece of fluff on his jacket's sleeve. "In the end, I think we can be clear that while I thought I loved her, I didn't. I'm fairly certain, however, that she loved me. And I ruined her. She never left. She never reached her potential. She never found anyone who really did love her."

"Maybe that's just the way it was," Hallie said. "Maybe she was never going to leave or reach her potential—whatever that means—or be loved."

"Maybe," Death conceded. "Still, I left and I barely looked back. I paid a bit of attention to Lily and Beth, but I didn't prepare them for who they were or for the danger of someone as smart and desperate as Travis Hollowell."

"So, he really would have lived forever if he'd married Lily?"

"That's the way it works. If you marry Death's children, then death doesn't touch you. Aging doesn't touch you," he amended.

"But your own children die."

"They can die."

"Seems pretty fucked up to me."

"It's complicated," Death admitted.

"Yeah," Hallie said. She looked at him hard. "Boyd was married to Lily," she said. "Is that—is he going to live forever?"

"She died," he told her. He looked up at her, his pale eyes reflecting light from the fire. "After that, things become less . . . certain. And then—Hollowell killed him, you know."

Hallie felt something colder than a ghost's touch run raw down her spine. "I stopped him," she said. The words choked in her throat. "I stopped Hollowell. Boyd was fine. Right? He was fine."

Death looked at her. "Perhaps you did." He smiled.

Goddamnit.

"He's not dead. Right? He's not dead." She started across the room that wasn't a room. He would answer her. Or send her back so she could find out for herself.

"He's alive," Death conceded.

"But—?"

"He's alive."

"But—?" she repeated, insistent. Because she'd had to do it and she'd live with it, but she wanted to know what it meant.

"It's complicated," Death said.

"Yeah." Hallie sat back down. Goddamnit. "Yeah."

After a moment, she said, "Why are you telling me this?"

"Two reasons," he said. "A warning and an offer."

Hallie waited.

After a moment, he said, "If you're going to leave, you should leave."

Hallie's anger flared. "How is that any of your business? I mean, who the hell asked you? Did I ask you to bring me here, wherever here is? Did I ask to sit in your chairs and talk about, well, whatever it is we're talking about?"

"What I'm saying," Death went on as if Hallie hadn't spoken, "is that if you don't leave Boyd alone, you'll ruin him, as I ruined Lily and Beth's mother."

Hallie didn't respond immediately. She hadn't expected the conversation to end up here, with Boyd. "I won't ruin him," she said. "He won't—he's not destructive. Not self-destructive. Not even . . . not violent or . . . he's just . . . I won't ruin him," she said, as if saying it firmly would make it a fact—and she couldn't imagine ruining him, couldn't imagine being that person or Boyd being the person that happened to. "He won't care that much."

"Yes," Death said. "He will."

"Is that the warning or the offer?" Hallie asked, like, We're not discussing this.

"I want to be human again. Really human," he said. "I want to retire."

"Why are you telling me?" Her hands gripped the back of the chair hard enough to leave marks.

"I want you to take my place."

The second time Hallie woke, she was back in the world. She was in a hospital bed, which she should have expected, but she hadn't. There was no transition between waking and sleeping, just—blink—and her eyes were open. Boyd stood by the window all trim and precise in his uniform, looking at something Hallie couldn't see. She wondered immediately if he remembered her now, followed by the thought that she didn't want to know. Because if he didn't remember her, she wouldn't be able to stand it.

"Boyd."

He turned away from the window, and Hallie was sure she was right, was sure he didn't remember her. She felt a sense of loss so stark and deep that it made her sit straight up in the bed, like an uncoiling spring. Because movement was better. Anything was better. If she kept moving, then it couldn't matter if he didn't remember. If she moved forward fast enough, the past would drop away.

"Hallie," he said. His expression relaxed. He looked familiar again, though there was still something, some distance that hadn't been there before. "They told me you were sleeping," he said. "That you were just . . . sleeping. But it's been so long."

"How—?" Hallie had to stop and clear her throat. When she'd woken, in that one minute to the next, she took in—hospital, bed, Boyd. Now she could see three vases of flowers and half a dozen cards on a small table. The nearest vase of flowers, mostly daisies and miniature carnations, was already fading, petals dropped off like the end of a season. "How long," Hallie tried again, "have I been here?"

"Almost a week."

He stepped away from the window and sat in the chair next to her bed. Hallie put out a hand and touched his face. "I'm okay," she said.

Boyd reached up and put his hand over hers. "You almost died," he said.

Hallie leaned back. She pulled her hand away and he let her but kept hold of it, though lightly. "So did you," she pointed out.

His radio crackled quietly, like it was talking to itself. She wondered if he was on duty—but she thought, despite the uniform, probably not, because surely this was the Rapid City hospital. So probably he'd driven over after signing out. "We can't keep doing this, Hallie," he said.

"But it worked," she said. Because it must have worked because she was here and he was here.

"What did we do?" he asked. "Exactly?"

I stood by and watched you die. But she wasn't going to say that. Though she should. Though it was probably an important thing to talk about. She couldn't do it yet. "We destroyed the fountain, right?"

"Yeah." His voice was dry. "Ole's been explaining to anyone who will listen that it was a gas leak that destroyed the fountain, most of the courtyard, and several of the two-story glass panes at Uku-Weber."

"Ole?" Because that didn't sound like him.

"I think Ole knows more than he says," Boyd told her.

Hallie was learning that most people knew more than they said, that that was how the world worked, how secrets were kept, how things moved on.

"Are they back?" she asked.

"The people who disappeared? No. They're back. They don't remember anything." He paused. "I don't remember much. Just dark and fire and—Iowa?"

Hallie smiled. "Yeah, that's about what there is to remember." Except Lily. And the end. When Hollowell killed him. When she killed Hollowell. And if he remembered that, remembered her waiting, he would say something, wouldn't he? He'd be different.

She pulled her hand from his and got out of the bed. He reached a hand out—to steady her? To stop her? But then withdrew it. She looked through the single cupboard in the room until she found a bag containing her clothes. They were wrinkled and dirty and smelled like smoke and nitrogen fertilizer.

"I can call your father," Boyd said. "He can bring clothes over when he comes tonight."

"I want to get out of here," Hallie said.

"They won't just release you."

"Yes, they will."

He laughed, and the flat seriousness that had characterized his expression since Hallie awakened fled. "They probably will," he acknowledged. He rose, crossed to her, and put his arms around her even though she was holding her dirty, smoky shirt and jeans. His grip tightened. "Remember when I said I would never tell you to stay?" he said.

"I remember," she told him.

"Please stay."

He kissed her.

She dropped her clothes.

* * *

Later, driving back to Taylor County, he told her that Beth had disappeared.

"And Lily?" Because the last thing Hallie remembered was Lily in the big truck heading for the fountain.

"Lily? She's—"

"Yeah." Lily was dead. Had been dead since long before this whole thing began. But where was she?

"She was there, you know," Hallie said.

Boyd let out a breath. "I thought she was. I thought—but it didn't seem possible."

"Beth really disappeared?" Hallie said, still catching up. "You can't call? She's not back home?"

Boyd shook his head. She could see that it bothered him. Beth had asked for his protection, and where was she now? "I dreamt about her, the first night back. Beth and Lily, both. Or," he amended, "the first night I got any sleep after we got back. They told me not to worry. That it was fine. But, well, I was tired and I was worried—"

"And you don't believe it was really them."

"I don't," he said.

"Yeah." Death had offered Hallie his place, offered to make her Death. And she wanted to believe that wasn't really him, that it wasn't really an offer, that she, like Boyd, had been tired and worried and—well, it hadn't been wishful thinking, because she didn't wish to be Death—but she wanted it to be a dream. Though she was pretty certain that it wasn't.

Hallie told him about the end—about Lily, the county truck, and the fountain.

"But she was out, right?" he asked, painfully wanting it to be true.

She didn't jump. Hallie didn't say it, but not saying it didn't make it untrue.

Boyd said he had put out a "Be on the Lookout" alert on Beth.

And maybe now he'd put one out on Lily. Which made sense to Hallie, though Boyd said if anyone ever connected the two, Boyd's BOLO and a description of his wife, they'd probably send him for a psych eval.

"Well, nobody's going to do that," Hallie said. Then, "Oh wait." Because all the most unlikely things seemed to happen lately.

"There's something else," Boyd said. His tone serious, official, like, Ma'am, I'm your local deputy sheriff and I'm come to give you some bad news.

"Is it Pabby?" Hallie asked.

Boyd's head jerked slightly, like he thought she'd surprised him and then realized she hadn't. "Yes," he said.

"She's dead, isn't she?" Hallie said. And if Boyd had failed Beth, well, she had failed Pabby. "She left the circle. To help us. I hoped it wouldn't—she helped us, Boyd, and she must have known she was going to die doing it."

Boyd reached into his shirt pocket and pulled out an envelope. He handed it to her. It was a cheap envelope, the kind you could see through. Inside was a folded square of notepaper and something else. "She left this. For you," he said.

Hallie turned the envelope over and over in her hands. She wanted to rip it to shreds or crush it in her hands and toss it out the window. She'd briefly—for about half a second—thought it might be the date of her own death. Or Boyd's.

No.

She wasn't going to be afraid of that. Not after everything. She tore open the envelope like ripping a bandage off a wound. Inside was an old color photograph curling at the edges and a brief note.

She lied to me, the note said. *Because she was my mother.*

"What?" Hallie said.

"What?" Boyd echoed.

"I don't know." Hallie picked up the photograph. It depicted a young woman who Hallie guessed might have been Pabby. She had Pabby's nose and red gold hair that shone even in the photograph. She was standing in front of what looked like Pabby's horse barn, only new or at least newly painted with another woman and a man. The man had the same nose as Pabby, and the woman—

"Whoa," Hallie said.

"What?"

"The white reaper," Hallie said. "I think it was Pabby's mother."

Hallie figured that would be the last thing, but it wasn't. Because there was never a last thing. She needed to stop expecting it.

Her father was outside walking up the lane from the horse barn when they arrived at the ranch. He didn't seem to hurry, but he was right there when they stopped. Without saying a word, he wrapped her in a hug so tight, it almost took Hallie's breath. Then he stepped back, like he'd said everything that needed saying, more maybe than he'd meant to say—like, You scared the hell out of me and I'm glad you're home and Jesus, Hallie, you're all I got left.

Things you never said out loud, or at least Vance Michaels never did, not out here, but Hallie knew them all the same.

He coughed. "They say you were okay or did you just leave?" he asked.

"I said I was going to leave and they said okay."

"Hmmph."

He didn't ask her what had happened or how or why. Hallie didn't know if it was because he believed what Ole had said about the gas leaks or if this was one of those things he'd decided not to know. Someday he'd ask, out of the blue—when no one, least of all himself, was expecting it, in the middle of a snowstorm herding cattle or standing in the barn watching rain pour down. At this point, with everything more or less over, it could wait.

Two weeks later, Norman Henspaw, lawyer for half the ranchers in Taylor County including her father, called and asked her to come over to his office in Rapid City. "Why?" she asked him.

"If you come over, let's say ten o'clock tomorrow," he replied, "I'll tell you."

At which meeting, he told her that Pabby had left the ranch to her.

"No, she didn't," Hallie said, caught between panic and wanting it so desperately, it surprised her.

He showed her the will.

"But when?" she asked.

"She called the day—actually, the day she died. Told me I had to come out there and there wasn't any time to fool around. It's legal. There are witnesses and it's been notarized. Maybe she just knew it was her time," he said.

"Well, goddamn," Hallie said.

He told her it might be several months before she actually got possession, but he was the executor and he'd arrange things so she could take care of the animals.

After that, she called Kate Matousek three weeks later than she'd promised. "No shit," Kate said.

"Stuff happens how it happens," Hallie told her, not entirely sure what she meant herself. She wouldn't say there weren't regrets, that she didn't think how things would be if she hadn't died, if she hadn't come back, if she weren't staying. But this would be all right. She could commit to this. And one thing Hallie was good at was committing to the path.

She was at the ranch on a wintry day the first week in December, unloading hay off the back of her pickup for the horses. It was already snowing steadily and she wanted to get things done and get back down the drive before it became impassable. She'd tossed the last bale into the rack when she saw him, like a shadow sliding through the snow-covered stalks of grass. Hallie jumped out the back of the pickup and walked to the edge of the hex ring.

"Maker," she said, happy to see it and realizing how crazy that was—who would be happy to see a harbinger? "Don't you have things to do? People to . . . uh, harbinge?"

Maker laughed that silent dog laugh. "I have you," it said.